## "Did you want me to propose properly? On my knee?" Noah glanced around awkwardly.

Clare shook her head. "No! No, thank you. It's all right. It's not like we're…in love."

She cleared her throat and straightened further. "I'm not some silly woman who needs all that foolish romance and fuss. Our marriage is just an agreement to assist me at a difficult financial time. As much as I am grateful to you for it, Mr. Livingstone, I just need to say that I value my freedom. If college has taught me one thing, it's that I should be deciding my own life."

"Of course." The soft words were slow. It was clear he had no idea what she was talking about.

"So if you think you will be making every decision for me," Clare continued to explain, "I'm here to tell you that that won't be happening." There, she'd said her piece.

She looked up at him. Good grief, was that a sparkle in his eye?

One corner of his mouth twitched ever so slightly. "You're welcome?"

**Barbara Phinney** was born in England and raised in Canada. After she retired from the Canadian Armed Forces, Barbara turned her hand to romance writing. The thrill of adventure and her love of happy endings, coupled with a too-active imagination, have merged to help her create this and other wonderful stories. Barbara spends her days writing, building her dream home with her husband and enjoying their fast-growing children.

### Books by Barbara Phinney

### Love Inspired Historical

*Bound to the Warrior*
*Protected by the Warrior*
*Sheltered by the Warrior*
*The Nanny Solution*
*Undercover Sheriff*
*Rancher to the Rescue*

### Love Inspired Suspense

*Desperate Rescue*
*Keeping Her Safe*
*Deadly Homecoming*
*Fatal Secrets*
*Silent Protector*

Visit the Author Profile page
at Harlequin.com for more titles.

# BARBARA PHINNEY

## Rancher to the Rescue

HARLEQUIN® LOVE INSPIRED® HISTORICAL

Recycling programs
for this product may
not exist in your area.

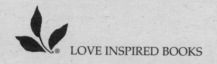 LOVE INSPIRED BOOKS

ISBN-13: 978-1-335-47144-4

Rancher to the Rescue

Copyright © 2017 by Barbara Phinney

www.Harlequin.com

**Printed in U.S.A.**

Who can discern his errors?
Forgive my hidden faults.
—*Psalms* 19:12

Dedicated to my loved ones. My patient husband and children and such local friends as Barbie, Joan, Eva, Karen and Sally. Thank you for all your support. I couldn't have my writing without you. God bless.

# Chapter One

*Proud Bend, Colorado, April, 1883*

"Did I read that right?" Clare Walsh peered up from her chair at the Recording Office in Proud Bend, Colorado. She blinked rapidly. "My parents are gone?"

Standing over her with a deep frown, Noah Livingstone lifted the telegram again. A moment ago, Clare had thrust it at her supervisor, hoping and praying she'd misunderstood the shocking words. She now watched him scan the paper yet again, her breath held so tight that her lungs hurt.

*Please, Lord, let it not be so.*

"I wouldn't put it quite like that, Miss Walsh," Noah hedged.

She rolled her eyes. "They're on a ship that's now missing! How else am I going to put it?" She didn't care that her tone was sharp. The telegram that had arrived less than fifteen minutes ago held nothing that warranted polite hedging, even from the calm and reserved Mr. Noah Livingstone.

She swallowed and bit her lip. Her parents' steamship had been lost at sea.

Noah pulled up a chair and sat close to her. The Recording Officer scanned the telegram one more time, as if, like her, he might hope to read something different in it. When his gaze lifted to hers, his intense blue eyes softened.

Her heart flipped.

"The telegram says that their steamship is overdue at Liverpool, England," he said in a gentle tone that rolled over Clare in the soft, soothing way she so appreciated. "It says it *may* have been lost at sea."

The office around them was small, already crowded with two desks, numerous filing cabinets and a small glassed-in private office for Noah. With the other clerk, Mr. Pooley, hovering close by, the whole interior felt suddenly claustrophobic. Noah carefully folded the telegram and set it down on Clare's desk, before taking her cold hands into his.

His fingers were warm and the grip, while not hard, was firm enough to offer a welcome sense of security. When she sniffed, his fingers tightened around hers.

She could also smell the scent of his soap, faint and slightly stringent, as he leaned closer to her. She wanted to inhale deeply, it was so pleasing, but fought back the urge. This was hardly the time.

It had been six weeks since her parents left rather hastily for the *Kurhaus* in Baden-Baden, Germany. They were to be gone for six months in an attempt to bring relief to her mother's crippling arthritis. A cure, touted by the new doctor who'd moved to Proud Bend last summer, offered hope where there hadn't been any before.

She and her superior sat and did nothing for the longest minute of her life. Noah stared at their interlocking hands. Clare's gaze wandered from his ruggedly handsome face to fall upon an open letter on her desk, another portent of bad news that had arrived by an errand boy mere minutes before the telegram. In it, the bank manager had firmly requested a meeting to discuss her parents' overdue mortgage payment.

Her whole body then seemed to coil and tighten. She wanted to push everyone away, to shout and deny both sets of terrible news.

But then she shut her eyes again, took several deep breaths and fought the impulse. She was stronger than this. She could handle any situation.

She also wanted to stop herself from gripping Noah's warm hands even tighter. In all the months she'd worked here, he had been nothing but professional with her. To have this—this sudden familiarity—was quite frankly too much of a comfort for the modern woman that she was.

Still, Clare took it just the same, as she recalled the last day before her parents left.

Six weeks ago, while Mother had ushered Clare's much younger brothers into her bedroom with her so they could help her pack up the last few items, Clare's father had divulged that he'd emptied his bank account, paying only March's mortgage payment. He had been concerned that they might need extra funds for the long journey and promised to return whatever money he had left once they arrived in Germany. Clare had expected the money any day now.

With an inward cringe, she stole a furtive look at the letter she'd left open on her desk a few minutes ago. Her father had knowingly left her broke. He knew the next payment would be overdue. Why had he done that?

"When exactly did their ship leave?" Noah asked quietly.

Clare looked at him through blurring tears as she reluctantly untangled their fingers. She fumbled for the small calendar on her desk, all the while staring at the bank's letter.

"They left for New York six weeks ago, and arrived there a week later. Father had wired me the name of the steamship they'd booked passage on." She flipped to the previous month on which she'd written the name. Her voice quivered. "The SS *Governor* was to leave three days after they arrived. Crossing the Atlantic is supposed to take two weeks. The ship was due to arrive at Liverpool two weeks ago, and then depart immediately for Rotterdam, where they were to take a river barge to Baden-Baden. If all had gone well, they would have arrived at the *Kurhaus* by now and the money would be en route back to me."

Clare cleared her throat. "According to the telegram, the ship is two weeks overdue. When was the telegram sent?"

Noah picked it up again. He consulted the clock on the wall. "Early last night. The ship's company office in New York sent it."

Clare nodded glumly, hating how little the telegram told her. What had been done to find the steamship?

Had other ships been told to look out for *Governor* on their journeys across the Atlantic? Maybe the ship had been found, and another telegram with good news was on its way to her.

"Anything could have happened," Noah told her softly. "We don't know for sure that they're gone. Don't think the worst yet."

Clare pulled back her shoulders. Those kind words were meant to be a comfort, but they felt like a smothering cloud of smoke. She opened her desk's bottom drawer, exposing her purse. "I need to tell the boys," she muttered as she stood.

Her little brothers, Tim and Leo, were in school right now, but Clare could remove them for the day. Miss Thompson, their schoolteacher, would understand.

Noah jumped to his feet, stepping quickly sideways to block her exit from the back area of the Recording Office. Mr. Pooley, the other clerk who had been hovering close by, threw a fast look at him. "Don't tell them yet," Noah said.

Clare stopped, rolling her own gaze up to his handsome face. Tall and slim, yet as strong as braided wire, Noah Livingstone had a rancher's frame with tanned features and clear blue eyes. In his day suit, he was a fine figure of a man. If it were any other circumstance, she'd revel in the thought of how close he stood to her. It would warm her the way a stovetop warmed milk pudding. He was everything she could admire in a man.

Clare blinked away the thought. She should be ashamed of herself for that disrespectful notion at such a time as this. Thankfully, Noah had been nothing but professional with her. Still, he was a man she could relish watching anytime, if she was given to such folly.

She gave herself a firm mental shake. Yes, it was a good thing that college had schooled such romance out of her. College, and her mentor, Miss Worth, had taught her that women needed to be strong at all times and independent to the core. There will come a day, Miss Worth often predicted, when women will have as many rights as men. It was time women earned those rights by setting aside simpering affections for the less fair sex.

Men. Boys. Her brothers. Clare's heart sank. She had to tell them something. Every day, Leo asked about their mother.

Tears pricked her eyes as a difficult realization dawned on her. She was to be their mother *and* father now.

She'd always been honest with her brothers. Even when she was a mere teenager and was impatient with them, she'd never been anything but truthful toward them. Keeping this terrible news from them felt like a lie to her. No doubt, they would ask again about Mother and Father. It seemed pointless to avoid the inevitable.

They'd always challenged authority, more out of curiosity and love of life than impudence. She would have to tailor that trait now, tell them they were strong enough to handle the loss.

"Don't tell your brothers anything yet," Noah repeated quietly, leaning down and tipping his head to interrupt her thoughts. "Let this news sink in first."

She shot him a fast look. "Wrong choice of words."

A wry but sad smile tugged at one corner of his mouth. He nodded. "You're right. I apologize. But think about it first. Their ship is only two weeks late. Anything could have happened."

Her shoulders ached they were so tight. "My brothers deserve to know."

"Yes, but not necessarily today," he answered with a shake of his head. "Give yourself time to think about what you're going to say. In fact, go on home."

Clare took the moment to study him. Crystal blue eyes, framed by tanned skin and the tiniest of smile lines, more likely from the sun than any jocularity. Despite the reason for his proximity to her, she wanted that moment to last.

"Why should I go home?" she asked softly.

"You should take whatever time you need to get strong enough to tell them."

Immediately, she bristled. Wasn't she strong enough now? Again, her gaze fell on the bank's letter on her desk. It lay there, wide-open for any and all to read, asking her to make an appointment to discuss the overdue payment.

Something clutched at her. Maybe she *wasn't* strong enough. Maybe being a guardian to her brothers these past few weeks had drained her of the strength she would need to take on the role of parent. Tim and Leo were active and needed strong supervision and she would need to be at her best to handle them after they learned about their parents. What if Noah had seen that need where she hadn't?

She snapped her eyes from the bank's letter, hating how it reminded her of her troubles. But to lean forward and rip it from the desk as though it was a burning pot on a hot stove would call attention to the fact that the bank needed to see her, that its errand boy had hand-delivered the letter. No doubt, those around her would realize that her father had left her nothing with which to pay his bills.

And yet, Clare thought with a sigh, that news certainly didn't surprise her. Her mother had often mentioned how her father tended to be flippant about money. Yes, he'd been busy with his work until Mother's illness worsened so badly that he'd fussed over her incessantly. Her father had been more focused on her health than earning enough to cover their expenses. Late last year, he'd even let it slip that he'd started dipping into their savings.

Clare rubbed her forehead.

"Go home," Noah told her, the words themselves firm though his tone stayed soft and gentle. "Do you need someone to go with you? I can send for the pastor's wife. Or would you prefer I walk you home?"

Head still down, Clare stared at Noah's boots. As usual, they shone. She knew he'd ridden in on his horse and had changed from his cowboy boots to these fine shiny ones. He had such attention to detail. His house was probably immaculate, too.

"Thank you, but no," Clare answered with a brisk shake of her head. This morning, in her haste to round up her unruly brothers and send them off to school, she'd left their house looking as though a windstorm had barreled through it.

College hadn't fully prepared her for the life she now faced. She'd taken good housekeeping courses, as all women at that college were required to take, but her studies had mostly focused on moral philosophy, English and geography, and as such, her marks reflected her interests. Good housekeeping hadn't been her best subject.

Clare lifted her chin and leveled a stare at Noah Livingstone. If he felt she shouldn't tell her brothers about their parents yet, then she certainly didn't need to go home to wallow in the terrible news, either. "Nothing can be achieved at home." *Except cleaning it.* "I wish to stay here and work." She paused. "I need my salary."

With a single long-legged stride, Noah reached the small swinging gate and opened it. His face was a mask of concern. "No, Miss Walsh. *Clare.* This has been a shock to you. Take the rest of the day off. In fact, if you need another, or even the whole week, it's all right. We'll manage."

Clare swallowed. Today was Monday. What would she possibly do for an entire week? Brood and worry?

Still, the offer tempted her. No! If her parents were not coming home and the bank needed its mortgage payment, then taking time off work would be the worst decision. Again, she looked down at the letter on her desk. She should have tucked it away immediately after reading it. How could she be so foolish as to leave it open for all to glance upon?

The bank deserved its payments, though. They also deserved to know what had happened to her parents. She could stop by on the way home, perhaps make that appointment the manager had strongly suggested.

All right, she finally acquiesced. A few hours off but not the whole week. She could ill-afford that. But Noah was right to say that she needed time alone right now. Her gaze bounced from Noah back to the letter. She'd wanted so badly to be that model employee every office had. A tall order for a woman some might say, but she'd wanted only to prove it was time for everyone to see that women could do so much more than stay at home and have babies, or work the land until their fingers bled and their backs ached, while men took the jobs that required an education. She wanted to say honestly to Miss Worth the next time she wrote her that she was indeed the strong woman her mentor had demanded of her.

After digging her purse out of the bottom drawer, Clare grabbed the letter that lay open on her desk. She shoved it so hard into her purse, she was afraid she'd poked a hole in the bottom. Then she marched past Noah, careful to ensure that she appeared as strong and resolute as any man might.

"I'll be back this afternoon." Holding her breath lest she release a quivery sigh, she strode out of the office.

As Noah stood at the front door of Clare's family home, he could hear the grandfather clock deep within the Walsh house ring quarter after two. Not fifteen minutes ago, he'd closed the office for the day, sending Mr. Pooley home. It hadn't been busy and Noah had a decent justification if anyone should complain or if Clare wanted to keep her somber news private for the time being. He'd reassured himself with the internal promise that he would check on her and that was exactly what he was doing.

Her bad news had cut into him nearly as much as it had her. Nobody had expected this and to see her hover on the verge of tears drew a lump into his throat and his own tears to spring into his eyes.

But what could he have done to comfort her? Helplessness weighed on him and he prayed hastily for some guiding words.

Anything that would help her.

He shivered. Initially, the day had promised a bit of warmth, but the sky had clouded and the wind had turned, now bearing down from the north and chilling Proud Bend.

He knocked, grimacing at the harsh sound. Then he waited. And waited. Finally, Clare opened the door.

She was wearing a frilly, spotless apron over her work clothes and had pushed up her long sleeves almost to her elbows. Whatever she was doing, she'd either just started it, or it was a clean task. He noticed, however, that her eyes were red-rimmed and puffy and a crumpled handkerchief bulged out the apron's dainty pocket. Her task had been punctuated with tears.

All he wanted at that moment was to draw her into his arms and hold her there, to somehow transfer his own strength to her, the strength he'd learned—

Noah cleared his throat. This wasn't about him, nor was it the time to think about his own situation. Clare needed him. "I'm sorry for dropping by unannounced. I closed the office early because I wanted to check on you."

She looked dismayed and quickly wiped her eyes. "I'd fully planned to return after lunch, but by the time I'd left the bank, I knew I couldn't go back to work." She glanced over her shoulder. "I needed to tidy up anyway. I expect I'll have visitors as soon as word gets out, and I didn't want them to faint at the mess."

It was a small attempt at humor, and Noah offered

her an equally small smile for her effort. "Where I come from, they put a black wreath on the front door. It stops people from visiting."

Clare looked thoughtful. "I haven't heard of that custom before. Where do you come from?"

"A small town west of New York City. It was always easy to get a hold of a black wreath. I don't think we can say the same here in Proud Bend."

"It wouldn't matter. People would only stop by and ask why I have a black wreath hanging on my door." Clare stepped back. "Come in."

Noah crossed the threshold, all the while removing his Stetson. The inside was cool and dark, appropriate for a house of mourning.

Unexpected indignation rose in him. There couldn't be any mourning yet. No one knew where her parents were. So there shouldn't be a need for an unheated house. Clare was being forced into accepting a fate that might not exist.

Noah dug out the telegram, as Clare had not taken it when she'd walked out. All she'd taken was that letter that the bank's errand boy had delivered. "I thought you would want this."

She accepted it slowly. "Thank you." But instead of reading it again, she set it on the small table near the front door. "I should keep it, but frankly, I want to burn it."

"Understandable." Noah cleared his throat as he removed his coat. "Is there anything more I can do, Clare?" Her Christian name slipped from his lips without forethought and he glanced away.

She shut the door and hung his coat on a half-filled tree beside her. "Come into the parlor."

If Noah expected an answer to his question, he needed to follow her there. Like the rest of the house, this room was chilly. It didn't help that the front window offered only the dullest of daylight. Today, there was no warm April sunshine to heat the room. Clare dropped with precious little grace into one of those fussy, high-backed chairs every parlor seemed to have. They were often too short for Noah's long legs, so he remained standing.

"My mother's arthritis worsened the month before they left," she began, as if expecting him to understand wherever she was starting her story. "She doesn't travel well by train, or else my father would have made arrangements to take it all the way to the port of Halifax in Nova Scotia." She looked up at him. "Or to travel to St. John's in Newfoundland. But that would require a sea crossing to the island, also."

Noah listened patiently. Clare was good at reading maps, he'd learned since she'd started working for him six months ago. She must have excelled at geography in college to know the port city of St John's in England's Newfoundland was the closest North American port to Europe. Some of the steamships must stop there before beginning their transatlantic voyages.

"The doctor said that breathing the sea air would do her good, so they wanted to leave from New York City, but I wonder if it might have made a difference if they'd left by one of those other ports."

"What do you mean?"

She rose and walked to the long table against a far

wall. There, she picked up several pamphlets. "I was tidying up today and found these. They have information on the different steamships and their ports of call. Perhaps if they'd taken one of the other lines, they might have arrived safely. These ships are newer."

"Why didn't they take one of them?"

"Mother gets nauseated on trains, so they went only as far as New York City and took *Governor*. It has the longest sea voyage. Honestly, I cannot see how breathing damp sea air is supposed to help arthritis, but I'm not a doctor." Sighing, she set down the pamphlets again. "*Governor* is the oldest ship and also the most expensive, which I realize now was not good for the family finances. Although Father didn't mind spending money." She looked up at him, her expression resigned. "He could be a bit cavalier about that, I'm afraid."

Noah cleared his throat. "Speaking of finances... today, you received a letter from the bank." He'd seen the bank's errand boy deliver it. He'd caught Clare's sinking expression as she read the single page. But shortly after, that awful telegram had arrived, and he'd forgotten all about the letter.

Clare looked away. "I'm sure you can guess what the bank said. Father paid all the bills for March, but that's it. His payments were always due the first banking day of the month." She rubbed her forehead and groaned. "Let me think. Father paid March's mortgage before they left six weeks ago. So April's payment is now two weeks overdue."

"Did he leave you access to his accounts?"

With lifted brows, Clare shook her head. "There was no need. They're empty."

Noah cocked his head, a frown deepening. "I don't understand. Your father paid March's mortgage at the beginning of the month, but didn't expect to be in Europe until the end of the month. Surely, he would have realized that it would take a month to get the money back to you? That would automatically leave you a month behind in your payments, and yet he emptied his account, anyway?"

Clare looked like she was getting a headache. "He was afraid Mother would need extra time to recuperate from either the train ride or the sea voyage. He wasn't sure she'd be able to travel to Baden-Baden—that's where the *Kurhaus* is—right away. The transatlantic trip is said to be awful, and once in Liverpool, they'd need another short steamship voyage to Rotterdam before going upriver to the Rhine. He said he planned to send back enough money to pay the bills. I had assumed he'd paid at least two months, but I hadn't asked."

Clare flicked up her hands. "My father didn't always consider the finances first. He often said that there would always be bills."

*Except it was irresponsible to make those bills worse*, Noah grumbled internally. It might be wrong to condemn Clare's father, and Noah did know of Mrs. Walsh's ill health, but he didn't feel like crushing the uncharitable thoughts rising unbidden in him. "There are more in his family than his wife."

His clipped words cut crisply through the cool air. *Yes, that was true*, he decided firmly. And yes, there was more to life than earning money.

Noah tightened his jaw. People needed to look past their own needs to the needs of others. People needed—

He shut his eyes and stopped his thoughts. This wasn't about *his* family. This was about Clare Walsh, the lovely, vibrant, independent woman in front of him. It was about what was probably the worst day of her life.

Would it be inappropriate to draw her into his arms? Surely if anyone needed to be comforted right now, it was her.

Yes, it was inappropriate, and a woman like Clare would resent the belief that she needed a good, strong hug right now.

"The plan had been to return whatever money they didn't need," Clare was saying. "They had expected to stay for the summer in Germany, but hoped her treatment would take less time. I don't think he even cared that the mortgage would be a month late. My father often thought that there was no point in worrying about money." She sank into her chair again. "I guess he didn't worry about not surviving the first leg of the voyage, either." An angry glance up at Noah told him that tears glistened again in Clare's eyes.

Immediately, Noah dragged a chair closer to her. He perched on the edge of the rounded and uncomfortable seat, his knees poking up into the air. He really hated these fussy, overstuffed things. "Clare, we don't know what has happened yet." He rubbed her upper arm, then dropped it quickly, afraid the touch was too personal. "Did you explain that to the bank manager?"

Looking resigned, she shook her head. "All I did was make an appointment. I can hardly ask them to wait until proof comes of my parents' deaths. That may never happen. The manager may give me an extension, but that will come with a penalty. My wages won't cover even the basic mortgage payment, let alone one with a late fee attached. And what about the other bills, such as food and coal? Where would the money come for them?" She sighed in exasperation. "You see, I can't afford to take time off to sort out my parents' affairs. That would leave us with no money."

Outrage bubbled through him and he struggled to quell it. Her shortsighted father had left her in a bind that no woman should be in. "When is your appointment?"

"Tomorrow. I'll be speaking with the manager. Maybe before I go there, I'll have some better answers."

To what questions? Noah doubted proof of her parents' condition one way or the other would come in the next twenty-four hours. Or the money she needed, for that matter. Again, resentment bit at him with a ferocity that had up to now been reserved for his own parents' manipulation.

*No, this isn't about them. You've left them behind, them and that lie you've agreed to be a part of.*

*Focus on Clare.*

"Clare, let—" He had just begun to speak when the front door opened and juvenile screams tore through the house.

Clare's brothers were home.

Noah felt his eyes widen as they barreled into the parlor. The boys were in a terrible state, their clothes muddied and ripped, their faces smeared with dirt. They skidded to a stop when they spied him rising to his feet.

Clare also stood, although her movements were slower, far more careful. She blinked and swallowed and Noah wondered if she was going to blurt out what she'd learned about their parents. Surely, Tim and Leo, suddenly looking younger than their nine and seven years respectively, could not fully understand what had happened. Yes, they'd understand if their parents had died, but not something as tenuous as being overdue at their first port of call. That they *could* be lost at sea. Children tended to see in more clear-cut ways than adults did.

Noah held his breath, all the while watching Clare, praying she'd say nothing. At least for now.

Eyebrows raised, her eyes shutting for a long moment, Clare sat down again before asking quietly, "Why are you two home early?"

The older boy, Tim, stared at his scuffed and muddied shoes. "At lunch, we went outside and down to the river. There's a part where a spring comes right through the bank. It's all muddy."

"And why did you go there?"

"So we could smear mud on our faces to scare Mary Pemberton. She sits by the window 'cuz she isn't allowed to go outside and get her dress dirty."

"She's a scaredy-cat and told Miss Thompson on us," Leo added.

"Enough of that," Clare scolded. "She reported only the truth and should not be criticized for doing the right thing."

Tim shrugged. "We weren't allowed back in school unless we came home and changed."

The younger boy hastily wiped mud off his cheeks with his sleeve. It had dried and now fell in flakes to the carpet. He then wiped his hand on his torn pants and more mud fluttered down.

From some distant recess of the house, the clock

struck the half hour. "It's two thirty," Noah commented. "How long is your lunch break, boys?"

"And how did your clothes get ripped?" Clare asked quietly.

Tim's gaze dropped to his filthy shoes. "We climbed a tree down at the river. One of the branches goes right out over the water without touching the mud."

"So we could clean ourselves off without coming home." Leo finished his brother's explanation, as if their unorthodox ablutions were perfectly normal. "But Miss Thompson told us to!"

Tim nodded. "We thought it would be better that way."

"In case someone saw you and reported it to me, you mean?"

The boys looked confused. Noah wondered if they were even capable of such subterfuge, or they actually thought it would be easier that way.

"But we fell into the mud," Tim answered. Being the older brother, he knew that they'd done wrong, whereas Leo didn't. Or else Leo was ignoring the obvious.

"I'm hungry," Leo announced, oblivious of his brother's contrition. "You didn't give us enough food for lunch. And it's cold in here."

Noah glanced at Clare in time to see her shut her eyes again. A crimson stain crept up her neck. What was she going to do? They needed discipline. Guidance. They also needed to learn there were consequences to their actions.

"Go upstairs and change," Clare said wearily. After a slight hesitation, she added, "Supper will be a bit late, but I want you to clean yourselves up first, anyway.

Just don't make a mess upstairs, but bring down those filthy clothes when you're done. I'll have to mend and wash them before school tomorrow. Let's hope they dry in time."

For a long moment, the boys merely stared at her, as if sensing something was off. Then, after a nudge from the older brother as he turned to leave the parlor, the younger one followed.

When Leo had closed the door behind him, Clare sagged.

Noah laid his hand on her shoulder. "Don't tell them yet."

"I can't, not without crying my eyes out. They won't understand what it means to be lost at sea, anyway. They don't realize how big the Atlantic is." She sank back into the chair again. "Look at them." She threw up her hand before smacking it against her chest. "Look at me! I can't even discipline my own brothers."

"They're not dogs that need immediate correction. You can do it later tonight. They'll know why."

Clare shook her head. "It won't be fair. I learned in college that children's misbehaviour is simply an expression of another emotion, in this case, missing our parents. Tim and Leo need time to fully work out how they're feeling about Mother and Father being gone."

Lifting his eyebrows, Noah tightened his jaw to stop from contradicting her. He'd seen those boys around town even before their parents left. He'd *heard* Tim and Leo from within the confines of the Recording Office, too, before the school bell rang. He shouldn't ask, but the question slipped from his mouth. "How is missing your parents getting converted into obvious mischief?"

She pulled from her apron pocket that crumpled handkerchief and dabbed the corners of her eyes. "They began to act up when our parents started to prepare to go to Europe. I think they were scared. Misbehaving would bring our parents' attention back to them, and thus reassure them that they're still loved. In their minds, if Mother and Father left, it would be because they didn't love us anymore. It's all quite understandable when you consider how we treat our children in today's world."

Noah had no desire to be drawn into something he knew nothing about, but he couldn't help pointing out, "They misbehaved long before your parents left. Plus, it's been weeks since they left and children adapt easily. What explains their disobedience today?"

"Me. I'm the one whose love they're afraid to lose now. They think I'll leave next." She looked up at Noah with another bleak expression. "It's all well-documented psychology. But that doesn't matter right now. Think about today. How can I tell them that our mother and father aren't *ever* coming home again when they're grieving their *temporary* absence?"

Noah didn't know if he agreed with this modern parenting nonsense. It sounded more like lack of discipline and flimsy excuses. But he wasn't there to argue with her. He needed to tread carefully. Clare deserved that much. "A little bit of understanding is always a good thing."

He felt his mouth tighten. Understanding. He'd had little of that from *his* parents.

Stiff-necked, his parents, mostly his father, had watched Noah leave them, not the other way around. They had gladly opened the door for him, too. Did they ever grieve for him? He'd certainly grieved that they'd refused to accept any wishes apart from their own. They'd refused to accept that Noah had his own dreams that didn't fit into their plans for his life. His father's plans, supported by his mother, who wanted only to maintain peace in her family.

They'd forced him into a situation that became a secret no one should have to keep, he added to himself bitterly.

*Forget it. It was two years ago. Concentrate on the here and now. Clare needs help.* She couldn't yet deal with telling her brothers about their parents, not while she was reeling from the shock and certainly not while trying to figure out how she was going to keep their home.

Noah's jaw clenched. He wanted nothing more than to help her. But how? Offer advice? She deserved her dignity, and wouldn't appreciate him telling her what to do.

*Clare, you need to let go of that pride.*

He straightened. She also needed help and he wanted to be the one who offered it first. "Can you rent out part of your home?"

"To whom? Women usually stay with families. That would leave only men. Would you like me to board single men to earn extra money?" She rolled her eyes as she brushed an unruly tendril of hair from her forehead. It fell back into its vacated place once again, determined to misbehave. "Can you imagine my reputation then? Would that do the Recording Office any good? Or my job, for that matter? If the people of Proud Bend believed I was acting immorally, they'd demand you fire me immediately."

The idea of Clare opening her home to single men sparked a stinging moment in him. A jealous moment that had nothing to do with their office's reputation. "Surely some women need a place to stay?"

"The only single women of any decent reputation live at home or with a selected family."

A thump from upstairs drew his attention to the ceiling. He could hear the boys banging around and wondered what possible mischief they were getting into.

He looked back at her as she wrung her handkerchief. "And if you can't pay the mortgage?" he asked.

Another bang from upstairs. Clare shot her gaze upward as her mouth tightened. "We both know what's going to happen. I'll lose this house. It's the only home I've ever known. I could find a room somewhere, yes, but no one will take me with those rambunctious boys." She sighed. "I appreciate your concern, Noah, but you needn't worry. This is my problem and I will solve it."

With a heavy heart, Noah knew right then what Tim and Leo's lives would be. They'd be sent to different ranches or hired by some unscrupulous mine owner to work underground. Orphanages were rare in the West because there was always menial work for the few boys out here, be it on ranches, in mines or on the railroad. If that happened, they'd grow up seeing neither Clare nor the other brother. And with their record of mischief, their discipline would be harsh. The bleak look on Clare's face told him she already knew that fact and it cut her to the quick.

Noah shut his eyes, hating to look at her expression.

A surge of anger rose within him at the notion of this family being ripped apart.

Compassion flooded in, wringing out the ire and banding his chest. He wanted to grab her, hold her tight to fend off the bleakness of her situation.

Instead, though, he opened his eyes again and the most unexpected words tumbled from his mouth.

"Marry me, Clare."

## Chapter Two

Noah stifled a gasp. Thankfully, he had enough fore-thought not to race from the house and thus insult the woman he'd just proposed to. But that didn't stop him from clamping shut his mouth as he stared, aghast, at Clare.

It wasn't as though he was opposed to marriage. No, he simply hated the idea of marrying to appease a situation of someone else's making. To subjugate a person so as to benefit another, as his father had tried to subjugate him.

But he wasn't naive. He realized that for centuries marriages had been proposed with financial gain in mind. He just didn't want to be a party to one, especially the one he'd flatly refused two years ago. Greed, his father's mainly, had birthed the idea that Noah, as his eldest son, should marry a woman whose family business could be merged with the Livingstone's. The other family involved would get a secure future for their only child, a young woman whose sole purpose in life appeared to be to remain in the lifestyle to which she'd become accustomed.

And, of course, Noah's father would continue to rule all their lives how he saw fit, all the while expanding his wealth and power.

No. Marriage for someone else's convenience was more than distasteful to him.

Resentment tightened Noah's chest as he stared at Clare. He'd told himself years ago that he would not bow to his father's wishes. He would marry only because he loved the woman and thanks to the scarcity of decent women in Colorado, marriage was unlikely to happen.

Noah paused. Had that been an unconscious reason for choosing to go west?

No. For as long as he could remember, he'd nursed a dream of building a special type of ranch in Colorado, one fed by the offer of free land if he worked it and filled it with livestock. In his case, horses and pack animals. They were as necessary as the railroad, yet many had been discarded, especially after the war, or left to turn feral and compete with cattle for water and food. As a result, ranchers who wanted no animals, save their own valuable cattle, to use their precious grass and water supplies rounded them up to sell or sometimes, if the horses got too close, they would shoot them. Abandoned horses and ponies didn't provide the income that cattle could.

He had often thought of creating a program to relocate these magnificent beasts, away from the competition for food and water.

But for others that were caught, Noah knew he could rehabilitate them and other abandoned equine. The offer of free land given him would help. His job at the Recording Office would provide the funds to grow that dream. He'd even saved enough to hire a part-time ranch hand.

His father had been furious that Noah had considered pursuing this dream, even if it offered a chance to become a Recording Officer, the youngest in the state. Eventually the promise of the job had been fulfilled and he had his dream ranch as well as a prestigious position.

But in his father's mind, if Noah wasn't going to do his bidding, the fool son could leave and never return.

That had been two years ago, and the angry, unfair threat still stung, just as the Walshes' choice now stung Clare.

Was that why he'd blurted out that idiot proposal?

No. The idea of defying his father, even if the man wasn't around, wasn't his main reason to propose. He'd realized Clare was in very real danger of losing her family. And the boys, having just lost their parents, were in danger of being torn from everything they had ever known. Noah had proposed to help her fix her situation.

But it had been a foolish offer and Clare's expression right now proved she agreed with that assessment. She knew nothing of his reasons, nor was he going to explain it to her. It was just that she hadn't considered seeking a husband, either.

From upstairs, another series of bangs and thumps drew Noah back to the present. Clare's brothers were definitely up to no good. Oh, yes, she needed a fast solution to her very serious problem.

His answer had been to offer her marriage. And he—

"No."

He frowned at Clare. "What did you say?"

Her shoulders were pushed back, her jaw firmed and she snapped yet again, "I said no. No, I won't marry you."

Clare hadn't expected to blurt out the first answer in her mind, at least not with such force. But it reflected how she felt.

"Did you just turn me down?" His brows knitted together, as if he'd misunderstood her. "Why?"

She bristled. Did he not know anything about her by now? They'd been working together for six months. During that time, he'd heard her say *more than once* that she was *never* going to marry, but rather work hard and prove that women could be a valuable asset to any organization. They might even run that organization someday. If that had to come at the cost of staying single, so be it, for marriage was a prison sentence to a woman. It had turned out that way for far too many of her friends. Hadn't Noah also heard her announce *that* fact on more than one occasion?

Irritation continued to bubble through her. He apparently hadn't listened to her at all. And what's more, he looked genuinely surprised that she wasn't groveling with gratitude. She lifted her brows and shut her eyes in one long, slow blink. "You heard me correctly. I don't know how to say it any more clearly."

Silence fell like a stone between them. Noah finally shut his gaping mouth, only to open it and speak again, this time slowly and calmly. "Your brothers need stability right now. They need a father figure."

"They have a father. Even you thought it was premature to assume he's lost at sea. Any number of things could have happened. My brothers and I have a father and he will be returning. Isn't that the attitude you wanted me to adopt?"

Despite her haughty logic, she swallowed. Her answer wasn't the main reason for her refusal. She was certainly not denying the obvious, that her parents could be gone, but with the irritation still simmering within, she couldn't help but contradict him with his own words. No, the point was that he hadn't bothered to listen to her. Over these past few months, he hadn't paid her words the slightest attention. She didn't go to college and return to her hometown to give up all her dreams at the first faltering. Clare Walsh had a sterner constitution than that.

Noah's jaw tightened and his brows pressed together. "And if your parents don't come home?"

Clare flinched but refused to waver. "I'll deal with that when the time comes." She cleared her throat, knowing it sounded like she was denying the obvious possibility, but she wasn't. She was simply being strong when she needed to be. "I don't need anyone, thank you very much. I can handle this situation as well as any man."

"We're not discussing the virtues of your gender, Clare, just your ability to keep going in your current state. You're not going to make it."

She flared up. "I can and I will. I've already told you I can solve my own problems."

A deep crease forming between his brows—those perfectly shaped ones, Clare noted—Noah leaned forward, closer to her. "You don't need to do this alone, Clare," he said softly.

Temptation tugged at her, and she battled it back with tight words. "Are you just saying that to ensure you have a good employee who's ready to work?"

Clare watched as hurt flickered over his features. It was quick, and disappeared as quickly as it appeared. But in its wake was a tight jaw with narrowing eyes. They were also brief as he schooled his expression. "Clare, I have only your best interests at heart here. Nothing more."

Did he? Clare was hardly a master at reading people, for her life here had been sheltered and college had seen more of the same. But for a few moments after his words, she wondered about their veracity.

She should stop the suspicion. Of course, he would not want her to lose her brothers, or end up in the poorhouse. But still, was there something more behind his words? Clare wasn't sure.

One thing she was sure of was how his soft words and strong expression drew her closer to him. If she just leaned forward a mite and reached out her hand, she could brush his cheek, feel his warm breath on her face and revel in the deep attraction she was feeling right now.

Pulling herself together against the nonsense, she stood abruptly. How dare he assume she'd fail and need his help! Then she marched into the hall, returning to the parlor doorway with Noah's Stetson and coat. "I think you should leave. Thank you for stopping by. I will be at work as expected tomorrow."

Noah sighed and his tone softened further. "You don't have to come in if you don't want to."

"I do. I need the money, and I obviously need to prove to you that I am going to persevere." She would. She had no idea how, but she would. "Good day, Mr. Livingstone."

His mouth set grimly, Noah donned his coat and took his Stetson and his leave. Clare kept her gaze steady on the interior of her family's parlor. Only when she heard the front door open and shut, did she cross over to her chair and sink into it with eyes closed against the tears that were already forming there.

*Lord, what am I going to do?*

Only silence answered. Stiffly, she rose and plodded into the kitchen. She bent to stir the cool embers in the firebox of the stove, knowing hot water would be needed to clean her brothers' clothes. Not to mention needed for supper. She could hear the boys upstairs, the renewed bangs and thumps telling her that they were doing more than cleaning up. She'd get their evening meal started and then investigate the situation up there.

In the pantry, she glanced around. For the last few weeks, she hadn't had much time to shop for staples, leaving their meals sparse and lean. Today, as suppertime approached, she lifted the lid on the corned beef barrel.

Empty save for one small scrap of fat. Supper would be biscuits and milk with the few winter vegetables she had left. She could braise them in that bit of fat. Then she would boil some eggs for the boys' lunches, reminding herself not to eat any biscuits so they could take the remainder in the morning. Squaring her shoulders,

Clare walked over to the small tea canister on the shelf at the entrance to the pantry. Mother always kept grocery money in it, in a small pouch under the leaves. She hadn't had time to check how much was there.

Her heart sank as the realization hit her.

The pouch was missing. Father had taken it.

A loud crash followed by a *whomp* and a riotous screech startled her. "Clare!"

She raced upstairs, growing ever more horrified as the smell of burning kerosene met her nostrils halfway up. Tearing into the boys' room, she gasped. Their small rug was on fire, the overturned kerosene lamp nearby fueling it!

Yanking the half-dressed boys out of the room, Clare lunged for the lamp to right it, snapping back her hand before she burned it. She then grabbed the water basin, dumping it onto the fire. It sprayed burning droplets of fuel in every direction.

She let out her own scream.

She grabbed the boys' bedspread and smothered the fire, falling on her knees to smack the last few errant flames beyond one corner of the spread.

Reaching behind her, she poured the rest of the water from the jug onto the floor, the bedspread and the rug that peeked out beyond another corner. Then she scoured the whole room to ensure no wayward embers smoldered, crawling on her hands and knees the entire way. Satisfied there was no more danger, she rolled up the rug and bedspread to take them outside.

Still on her knees, all she could manage was to drop her head. *Thank You, Lord. Thank You for not allow-*

*ing this to become worse. Thank You for keeping Tim and Leo safe.*

Only after repeating her prayer several times, in utter gratitude, did Clare look up toward the door.

Tim and Leo were peeking into the room. Their faces were *still* smeared with dried mud. Filthy and anxious, they looked like they'd fallen out of their favorite Henry Castlemon book, the one where the boys chased a raccoon through a swamp.

"You didn't need to light the lamp!" she told them harshly.

"I'm sorry. It was cold in here and we're not allowed to start a fire in the stove." It was the older brother, Tim, who spoke as he pointed to the small potbellied stove nearby. "Don't get mad at us. Please?"

Fighting tears, she struggled to stand, but sagged again when she saw the section of her skirt below her apron was smeared with wet ashes from the burned rug. Her only work skirt was ruined. In fact, her entire outfit was soaked and rumpled, save the section protected by her apron. Clare whimpered when she noticed a burn hole at the sleeve of her blouse. She sank down farther.

And looked at the floor. Although the damage was minimal, the black, scorched area would need to be repaired. How did one fix such a large scorch mark? Not to mention how much water had seeped down through the plaster ceiling below.

Helplessness washed through her. How was she supposed to mind her two brothers when they couldn't even be trusted with the simple task of cleaning themselves up?

Clare dropped her head into her hands and shut her

eyes. As she knelt there, she could feel her brothers creep in and sit down on the floor near her.

One boy laid his head along her left side and gripped her arm. The other shifted in front and hugged her knees, dropping his head into her wet lap. Automatically, Clare reached out with her right hand and stroked his hair. The straight, silky strands told her without looking that it was Tim. Leo had the curly hair.

"I miss them," Tim whispered, knowing she would understand who he was talking about.

"I know. I miss them, too." When Clare heard one of them sniff, she fought to stop her own tears. She wrapped her left arm around Leo and drew him close.

She'd told Noah that she couldn't punish these boys. And still she couldn't. She loved them. She understood them. She missed their mother and father right along with them.

Sitting there until the damp seeped through to her stockings, feeling her hunger gnaw at her stomach and knowing she didn't have enough food for a decent meal, she finally admitted to herself that one awful detail.

She couldn't do this. She couldn't do any of what she'd boasted to Noah a few minutes ago. Not by herself. How had her mother managed a house, battled crippling arthritis and controlled two unruly boys?

Clare swallowed. Father had been there to help, taking time off work. He'd seen the boys off to school, given them strict orders to return home immediately after and had set out chores for them to do, all to help ease his wife's burden. Clare had been away at college during most of that time, money no doubt spent on her when it should have been saved. When she had returned home last fall, she'd pitched in, even after taking a job as clerk at the Recording Office.

Yet, in the last six weeks since their parents had left, Tim and Leo had grown wilder, and Clare had struggled to keep their family home life stable.

She needed to get up. There was simply too much to do tonight to sit there feeling sorry for herself. Laundry, supper, cleaning up this mess, and the one below in the dining room—it all had to be finished before she could crawl into bed. Before tomorrow.

*Before tomorrow, when she would ask Noah if his offer still stood.*

With a gasp, she lifted her head. Was she really considering his proposal? When she heard Leo sniff, she bit her bottom lip, and cold, hard reality gripped her. She could no longer keep going the way she had been. They'd either have a house to turn over to the bank or, if Tim and Leo weren't watched more carefully, no house at all. Either way, they would lose it. No doubt after that, her brothers would be taken from her. She couldn't afford a solicitor to fight for her family, either.

Moving them aside, Clare rose wearily, cringing at her soiled skirt. Perhaps mindless work would help her form the words she needed to say to Noah Livingstone in the morning.

She should start with an apology.

Noah was always the first one in the Recording Office, an admirable work ethic. Through the window, Clare could see him poring over some paperwork in his small, glassed-in office.

Normally, she would've plastered on a bright smile,

for a good attitude was as important as good training. But as she pushed open the door, her heavy heart wasn't allowing any of that.

Noah looked up from his desk as she walked in. Eyes wary, expression guarded, he said nothing as he watched her. Her heart sank further. Oh, what damage had she inflicted in turning him down? Had it really been that personal?

This morning, she'd been churning possible words around in her head. But seeing Noah now, all thought escaped her. Could she really expect him to gather the pieces of his pride and propose to her again? Did she really want him to?

Tears stung her eyes. Yes, she did. She had two little ruffian brothers, and they were a family, and families shouldn't be separated. But no man would want to take on the responsibility of parenting those boys, and surely her employer realized that. If she asked Noah to propose again, would he? Was that what she needed?

Yes, unfortunately. He'd only proposed to repair her financial situation and the look of consternation on his face immediately after proved he regretted his impromptu suggestion.

But did she really *want* to get married? Who would take her career seriously then? Married ladies didn't work, didn't aspire to be successful businesswomen. They allowed their husbands to control their lives. She'd seen it with all of her college friends who'd abruptly cut short their education in order to wed.

She remembered seeing the disappointment in their eyes when she asked if they were still pursuing the dreams they'd shared while at college.

No, she couldn't bear for that to be her.

Noah Livingstone would surely sense the resentment she would no doubt harbor. It was only his nobility that had done the talking yesterday.

*Forget it.* She would not ruin his life to ease her own financial burden. Miss Worth had said more than once that strength came from discipline.

Clare stiffened, all the while fighting both tears and her indecision. She'd finished her crying. Miss Worth had a valuable saying about women's tears. They were a weak woman's weapon. A strong woman used her head.

No, Clare would not cry anymore.

Having listened to Clare quote her mentor on more than one occasion since returning from college, her father had disagreed with most of the woman's opinions. They were too general, he'd scoffed, though he offered no other explanation, nor practical advice.

At the memory, resentment rose unexpectedly within Clare. She hesitated as she quietly closed the office's main door. Resentment? At her father? She shouldn't be feeling that at all. That emotion wasn't the most important thing right now. She would deal with it later. First, she needed to be sensible, not flopping back and forth like the long ears on Leo's favorite stuffed toy.

Gathering her courage, she pushed through the small swinging gate at the end of the counter and came to a stop in the threshold leading to Noah's private office.

She could hear the clock on the wall behind her ticking, as if marking time, impatiently waiting for her to follow through with the important decision she'd made last night.

Testing her, like a professor waiting for the correct answer to a timed question that would determine whether or not she passed life or failed it.

Except that Clare was no longer confident that her next move was the right one.

Or even if Noah was still willing to help her.

There was only one way to find out. She drew in a deep breath and began to speak.

## Chapter Three

"Good morning." Clare groaned inwardly. Her words sounded so stilted.

"Good morning." His attention returned to his work. Clare could practically feel the temperature drop in the room.

She threw back her shoulders. This was far too serious a situation for her to be intimidated by him. Noah had proposed to her. And as much as she hated what it really meant to her freedom, she knew she needed to accept it. If the offer still stood, that is.

"Yesterday, you proposed to me."

"Yes, I did." He then paused without looking up. "If I remember correctly, you turned me down."

Oh, how she wished he would just look at her. She crushed the urge to snatch away the paper he was pretending to read. "About that. I think we need to—"

The door behind her flew open until it banged against the wall. In lumbered Walter Burrows. Having lived in Proud Bend all her life, Clare knew both his name and his reputation.

The tough, mean rancher seemed to have a perpetual chip on his shoulder. Clare knew he had a wife, but in all her years of living here, she had yet to meet the poor woman. But Clare had seen Burrows often enough. He'd come into the Recording Office several months back, and in the course of his business, he'd claimed he'd caught a feral pony a number of years ago. After having no success at breaking it—Clare was hardly surprised as the man was rough and cruel—Burrows had wanted to put it down. He'd heard that Noah had a "foolish notion of rescuing stupid animals," as he'd put it. Maybe Noah could buy it from him.

That day, Clare had watched Noah take the pony off his hands for the cost of a sack of barley. It was the first time Clare had heard of Noah's dream of saving horses.

Today, he rose and squeezed past Clare as if she carried a plague. He strode to the counter. "Mr. Burrows, what can I do for you?"

"I bought me another stretch of land. I need to register it. I watched Miz Walsh come in just now and figured you were already open. You know how late women can be when it comes to work."

Biting back a snappy retort, Clare glanced at the large clock on the wall. There was still a good thirty minutes before opening and Mr. Pooley wasn't even in yet. She was not late, thank you very much.

After a fast glance at Noah, Clare quickly removed her jacket and hung it up. She heard him clear his throat before pulling out the appropriate ledger and approaching the counter. He usually asked her to assist the customers. Was he saving her from having to deal with the rude man?

"How are you going to work the land, Mr. Burrows?" Noah asked conversationally. "Have you hired some extra help?"

"Not yet." The man's voice was gravelly, a perpetual grumble. "But there are always plenty of young 'uns needin' a roof over their heads. I hear an orphan train is coming west in a few weeks' time. In fact, I read in the newspaper that there Children's Aid Society will be picking up a few brats along the way. I can get me a few tough little guys and train 'em up properly."

Clare couldn't stop the gasp. Both men glanced her way, and she tried her best to hide the sudden fear leaping in her chest. She doubted she was successful, for all she ended up doing was slapping her hand over her mouth and looking like a fool.

Noah frowned as she forced herself to walk to her desk, where she fell into her chair with very little grace. Her vision swam in sudden tears.

When people got wind of her situation, someone would inform the authorities. No one would expect Clare to be able to raise her hooligan brothers by herself. The Children's Aid Society would then make a point to stop by.

Clare swallowed. She needed to speak with a lawyer. Even if Noah repeated his proposal, both of them would need to adopt her brothers formally. Yes, some states were less stringent in their enforcement, but both Clare and Noah worked at the Recording Office. How would it look if they were to ignore the laws?

One step at a time, she reminded herself. If Noah's offer no longer stood, would she be forced to surrender the boys? Not necessarily to Mr. Burrows, of course, but perhaps to someone equally disagreeable, and maybe farther away?

She shut her eyes. *Lord, please guide me.*

When she opened them again, Mr. Burrows was shutting the door behind him, and Noah was darting a cautious glance her way as he returned to his desk.

*He has proposed to you. Do you really want to risk losing Tim and Leo?*

*If he won't propose again, you must!*

She swallowed around the gravel in her throat.

Clare shut her eyes again. In the distance, muted by the exterior walls, came the sound of the school bell reminding her that she must consider Tim and Leo first. Screwing up her courage, she rose and walked into his office.

Noah looked up from his paperwork, his blue-eyed gaze still wary, a slight frown marring his ruggedly handsome features. Before this nightmare had begun, when she'd just started to work here, she'd found his attention to her pleasing, warming her cheeks and making her feel as gooey as pudding inside. She'd loved it, even though he'd never been anything but professional with her.

Now her heart constricted unexpectedly. His proposal had been just him offering a solution to a bad situation. There was no affection involved. Nothing but his good character showing and even then he'd regretted blurting out his offer. She was sure of that much.

What had she expected? A confession of love? She would have still said no, because marriage was what weaker women searched out. She was made of sterner stuff.

Until she realized she could lose her brothers. Now, knowing her options, her hopes plummeted.

Noah's brows lifted in expectation, as if waiting for her to explain why she'd barged in here as she had. Why she now lingered beside his desk. Clare fought to hold on to the courage that could waver at a moment's notice.

"You proposed to me yesterday," she practically barked.

Leaning back, Noah folded his arms. "We've already discussed this. You turned me down."

"I…I was premature." She swallowed the hard lump in her throat. "Is the offer still available?"

Yesterday, Noah had let his mouth decide his fate. The last time he had done that, he'd walked out of his home without so much as a backward glance. There had been no second chances then, even if he'd wanted one, which he didn't, he told himself fiercely. There had been no way to take back what he'd said to his father. There had been no chance to rescind the promise to his ex-fiancée of keeping an ugly secret that still tormented him today.

But now? Here was an opportunity to correct the mistake caused by his impulsive mouth. With one simple no, he could show exactly how Clare's refusal had bit into his pride.

When Noah's father had told him that he was to marry Elizabeth Townsend because her father's business, not to mention his own, would benefit from merging, there had been an expectation that Noah would roll over like a submissive mongrel and do exactly as his father had deemed appropriate.

No. He had his own dreams to pursue, and marriage was far too sacred an institution to be based on financial gain, especially his greedy father's.

Besides, he'd realized in retrospect, he could never shake the feeling that he couldn't trust either Elizabeth or her cagey father. No, marrying Elizabeth had never felt right.

But now, he'd offered it to Clare and only to solve a financial problem in *her* life. To solve something *her own* selfish father had created. The proposal was an insane idea, one that should never have been offered. His gaze drifted down her frame.

Then he noticed the stain on her skirt. Or should he say where a stain might have been? It looked like she'd scrubbed the material right at its middle, so much so the dye at that one spot had faded. Clare was always a sensible dresser, a woman who looked professional and modern. She'd always been neat although he'd noticed she had only one suitable skirt.

It was no longer suitable.

His train of thought turned to her brothers. Their clothes would have been washed last night, also, and most likely repaired. Like Clare with her work skirt, the boys' clothes they'd sullied were the only ones they owned that were suitable for school. Yes, children arrived wearing whatever they had, but only farm boys wore overalls. It was a point of pride to wear a nice jacket and knickerbockers. Clare would do her best to ensure her brothers weren't dressed like ragamuffins.

Then he remembered her gasp a few minutes ago when Mr. Burrows had announced he would take a couple of boys from the Orphan Train.

That institution had been created to foster out children to good homes, to be loved and cared for. While it worked as such sometimes, there were protests out East by people who felt it was nothing but farming out indentured servants, or worse, a different kind of slavery. Noah couldn't say one way or the other. He did agree that it wasn't an ideal solution, but with thousands of orphaned and abandoned children in cities, what else could be done?

He groaned softly and berated himself for his stupidity. *Of course.* Clare's gasp should have told him immediately what she was thinking.

His breath stalled in his throat. Had his own defensiveness overshadowed Clare's fear? Mr. Burrows's crass remarks just now had proven that the Orphan Train was the worst fate for her and her brothers.

*Lord, I don't know what to do. It's wrong to marry for financial gain. It's wrong to take sacred vows simply to correct other people's selfish errors.*

There had to be some affection, surely?

"Is the offer still available?" Clare asked again, this time softly, a melodic question that rolled through him like a tune on a delicate flute.

He forced his attention back to the conversation at hand. Clare looked tired this morning and he felt his brows press together at the sight of the violet shadows under her eyes. "Did you tell your brothers about your parents?"

Her expression clouded. She offered him a single, slow sigh and he knew her answer before she spoke it. "I couldn't. Not yet." She wet her lips. "I'll think about what to say but I need answers to some of my questions, first. Hopefully, they will come today at lunchtime."

"What questions? Besides you seeing the bank manager, what else do you need to do?"

"Well, I need to find a carpenter—"

"A carpenter?"

She hesitated before clearing her throat. "There was a small incident last night."

"What happened?"

"Just after you left, the boys tipped over their lamp and the rug caught fire."

His heart stumbled and he gasped. "Is everyone all right?"

"Yes," she added hastily. "We're fine."

"Why did you light the lamp, anyway? It wasn't dark out when I left."

"I didn't. One of the boys did. I don't know which one, and frankly, I think both were involved. They said they were cold and they aren't allowed to put on a fire. They don't always think first."

"You need to start disciplining them."

Her chin wrinkled and for a few long moments, she didn't speak. "I can't," she whispered. "They miss our parents. They're grieving because they think Mother and Father will be gone for what seems to them to be forever. I don't have the heart to start punishing them, and then, a short time later, tell them our parents are never coming back! It's cruel and unfair. So, please don't ask me to punish them. I can't! I miss our parents, too. I know how they feel."

Another pause followed. "And frankly, well, I feel betrayed, too," she added.

She dragged forward the chair that sat against the glass wall and collapsed into it. Her hand covered her nose and mouth, but Noah could see tears welling up in her soft brown eyes before she laid her arm across his desk and dropped her forehead onto it.

Disconcerted, he glanced around. Was there something he was supposed to do? "Your parents—"

Her head snapped up, her eyes, although watery, flashed pure anger. "Don't tell me they'll be coming home, because we both know that is very unlikely!" The anger dissolved immediately. "This is insane. I'm not mad at you. I'm furious at them for leaving us in the lurch."

Noah guessed he must have looked a little confused, because she threw up her hands. "I don't care if it doesn't make any sense! That's the way I feel, if you really want to know."

If truth be told, Noah *didn't* want to know. Still, something gripped him deep inside at the sight of Clare's anguish. Life was far more unfair to her than it had been to him. He'd walked out of his home because his parents had tried to force him to do something he didn't want to do.

It was a choice. If he'd chosen the opposite, he'd have lived an opulent life, married and had children, and not wanted for anything.

Except his freedom.

But because of their poor planning, Clare's parents had forced her into a far more hopeless situation. And all choice had been ripped from her. Suddenly, Noah could fully understand the resentment rising in her. It was rising in him, too.

Which meant only one thing, he realized with a sudden chill. His offer of marriage could not be rescinded.

His jaw tightened and he tried his best to relax it. "Yes. The offer still stands," he muttered, cautiously meeting Clare's soulful gaze.

"Thank you," she said in a soft voice. "I'll marry you."

She blinked. If he'd expected a look of relief, he was to be disappointed, for right then, Clare burst into tears again.

## Chapter Four

Even through her tears, Clare could see Noah's sinking expression. He really hadn't wanted to marry her, she told herself. And it didn't help that she'd dissolved into tears. She shouldn't be crying, not right after a marriage proposal.

Friends of hers from college had been giddy and blushing, enjoying the excitement and romance of that special moment when their beaux had sunk to one knee and proposed.

Clare felt herself stiffen, which was probably a good thing considering the unladylike draping across his desk had resulted in her corset digging into her flesh.

Yes, but those women who'd married beaux while at college soon learned what marriage really meant to women. Clare wanted the narrow wooden chair she'd dragged forward to swallow her up. She was joining their ranks.

Noah rose and walked around his desk, all the time pulling his neatly folded handkerchief from his breast pocket. He dangled it in front of her, and she snatched it. Drawing it up to her face, Clare caught the scent of his light cologne, a woodsy smell that was slightly stringent and cedar-like in quality and totally suited to him. She couldn't help but draw it in with a silly, noisy sniff. After dabbing her eyes and nose, she stood and offered it back to him.

He held up his hand. "Keep it. If we are to be married, you'll probably be washing it sooner or later."

*Truer words were never spoken*, Clare thought with dismay. Oh, she didn't mind doing laundry, all the sorting and siphoning off the soft rainwater, not to mention the boiling and wringing, were necessary and mindless tasks, done all day once a month if everyone stayed clean. But it was what all that represented. All of her principles, her beliefs that women should be treated as more than indentured servants, would be washed away like the mud on Leo's pants. She was a person, and should have the same rights as men, and at that moment, the laundry chore Noah had just mentioned in passing was proof she would never see that dream in her own life.

She balled the handkerchief up in her palm. With a swallow, she said, "I won't cry on our wedding day. I promise you that much."

"Thank you. In the meantime, Mr. Pooley will be here soon, so I suggest you dry your eyes. Of course, he already knows of your loss, so tears are bound to be expected."

She pulled herself together. Tears might be expected, and yes, she'd done her share of crying yesterday, but she wouldn't give anyone here in this Recording Office reason to think she was a wilting woman unsuitable for the workplace.

They stared at each other, Clare hardening herself and Noah looking like a lead actor who'd forgotten his lines at the climax of a play. After glancing awkwardly around, he asked almost vaguely, "Did you want me to propose properly? On my knee?"

Clare shook her head violently. "No! No, thank you. It's all right. It's not like we're…in love."

She cleared her throat and straightened further. "I'm not some silly woman who needs all that foolish romance and fuss. Our marriage is just an agreement to assist me at a difficult financial time." Her tone became frostier. "As much as I am grateful to you for it, Mr. Livingstone, I just need to say that I value my freedom. Don't get me wrong. I won't sully your reputation or that of this office, but if college has taught me one thing, it's that I should be deciding my own life."

"Of course." The soft words were slow. It was clear he had no idea what she was talking about.

"So if you think you will be making every decision for me," Clare continued to explain, "I'm here to tell you that that won't be happening." There, she'd said her piece.

For now.

The one corner of his mouth twitched ever so slightly. Good grief, was that a sparkle in his eye? "You're welcome."

Flushing, Clare stood and brushed past him to exit his office, her skirt swishing with disapproval as she walked. Why on earth had she blurted out that awful diatribe? Noah had done nothing to warrant her icy speech. She stopped and returned to his office, where he still stood watching her march around the desks like a tin soldier.

"I'm sorry. That was rude of me."

Oh, dear. She didn't sound very regretful, either. What a way to start an engagement. Sure that she would be apologizing her entire married life, she straightened her shoulders. "I truly appreciate all you're doing for the boys and me. I won't make you ashamed of me or regret this decision, but you'll have to be patient, Mr. Livingstone."

She paused. The whole time she'd been working at the Recording Office, she'd been focused on land deeds, first transcribing damaged ones then recording new information as it came forth. "I mean, I have to admit I'm not sure what paperwork needs to be completed."

"I'll take care of the license. They expect me to do it anyway."

Clare fought another bubble of irritation. Applying for a marriage license shouldn't be confined to the man. Still, Noah was hardly lording it over her. "Thank you, Mr. Livingstone."

"Perhaps we can start by calling each other by our Christian names?"

Clare blinked at him. "Of course. But what about here?" As if to add to the question, the door opened and in walked Joe Pooley, the young clerk Noah had hired just before he'd taken the chance with her last fall. They both nodded stiffly to him.

Noah glanced around the office. "We should maintain a certain formality here, I think. I know some people keep that formality even at home, but do you think that's necessary?"

"No, but I hadn't thought I would ever marry, either."

Quirking a brow, he asked with a hint of surprise,

"You never harbored those girlish dreams of finding true love?"

She sniffed. "I did when I was much younger, yes, but college taught me otherwise. My mentor, Miss Worth, often said it did women the world over a disservice simply to hand over our freedom to our husbands, and I witnessed it firsthand with several of my friends. They were the perfect blushing brides, but then I saw them a few months later, asking their husbands for advice, for money, or to be taken places. Those women had reveled in their freedom at college. We answered to no man. My married friends lost all of that elemental freedom."

"Surely they realized that beforehand. I mean, if you wish to call marriage a loss of basic freedom."

"Most realized it was gone. And they missed it. They aren't even allowed to get a job anymore, something my mentor thought was important. That's what chasing true love has done for them. All I wanted was to decide my own life."

She stopped it there, expecting amusement at the notion, or a blunt contradiction. Instead, Noah merely stared at her. Gone from his blue eyes was the wariness, now replaced by something she couldn't explain. Was it sympathy? She hated that she couldn't identify it. "I was going to own my own business someday, and not just some small enterprise like a sewing room or laundry service or an extension of my husband's business like the general store here. My career was going to be big, like owning a warehouse that brought goods from overseas, or a string of haberdasheries up and down the Rockies with my name on each of the marquees."

Noah looked perplexed. "Then why come back to Proud Bend and take a minor job here?"

"Mother needed my help." She felt a pang of hurt deep inside. "There were days she could barely get out of bed. I knew I needed to learn administration beyond what I took in college, and there aren't too many places where I could learn it while still helping to care for my mother. I came home on faith that I would find something that could start me on a career path. My father got me this job."

"Your training got you your job. Your father just arranged for it," Noah reminded her. "He said something about putting your education to good use." After a short pause, when Clare said nothing, he added with a shrug, "Allow me to sort out what's needed for our, um, wedding. Is there a preferred date? Pastor Wyseman will want a few days to publish bans. He is a bit old-fashioned that way."

Noah's crisp tone sounded like he was arranging for a tailoring session, or a bank appointment, Clare thought with a sinking heart. His self-sacrificing proposal was a noble gesture, but she felt, well, begrudging. She hated that his stellar behavior made her feel petty and ungracious.

She cleared her throat. "Anytime is fine. It's just a business arrangement, anyway." Then, head held high, she strode from the office.

Noah watched her leave. He'd had a way out of the situation that had been similar to the one that had forced his hand back home. But what had he done? He'd offered the proposal again. He was truly a fool. Clare Walsh had told him, not in so many words, that her ideals from college were so important to her that only the direst of circumstances would cause her to deviate from them.

Yes, her circumstances were indeed that. As a result, their marriage would only be a business arrangement. She'd said that last part quite bluntly. It was going to be a frosty life together.

Heat burned up his neck and into his cheeks. His noble act now slapped him in the face. *Remember what you told your father a few years ago? You're hypocritical, Livingstone. You'd said you would only marry for love.*

His parents and Elizabeth's parents had wanted a marriage of both families and fortunes. It was strictly for their benefit, with Noah's father thinking he was getting the monetary advantage.

But here, Clare was at risk of losing everything she held dear. Even her freedom, which now must be sacrificed in order to save other things, like family unity and her home.

Her house. It would soon be hers, if her parents really were lost at sea. Clare had wanted to own her own business, and probably her own home. She was getting one of those dreams, but might soon have to rent it out just to pay its mortgage.

At that thought, Noah walked out of his office. He stopped in front of Clare's desk. Beyond, Pooley was helping a young couple at the counter, leaving him a modicum of privacy.

Clare was in the midst of copying the last of the land deed ledgers. Last year, when Noah had hired her, it was to fill the temporary position of copier, transcribing thick ledgers that had been damaged when the roof had leaked. Now that she was full-time, she continued that work at her desk, all the while helping at the front counter if the need arose, which it rarely did. Noah watched her for a moment as she carefully transcribed a line, taking pains to be neat and accurate.

She looked up, a question on her face. Those big, soft, sad eyes made her complexion seem paler today. Her pert little nose was slightly red. Today, she'd neglected to apply the powder most women preferred. A telltale sign that she was out of sorts.

Noah scrubbed a hand across his jaw, knowing he should do more for her. She was grieving and yet kept insisting on going about her regular business as if nothing was amiss. He cleared his throat. "You returned to work because you felt you needed the money. You have bills to pay and a mortgage to sort out."

"Yes."

"Since we're engaged, that's not the case anymore, so you don't need to be here." When she opened her mouth to argue, he hurried on, "You can be at home taking care of other things. As soon as I get the necessary paperwork in order and at Pastor Wyseman's convenience, we can get married. It could take a few weeks, though, so keep that in mind when you meet with the bank."

He watched her throat bob slowly, hating how he sounded as though they were discussing a small task here at work. "Here's a thought to present to the bank. Why don't you rent out your house? Many families who want to move West will often want temporary lodging while they're building a home for themselves. If you rent yours, it can pay your mortgage. There may be enough left over for other expenses like taxes."

Clare blinked those long black lashes at him. Did she not understand him? Had he not made himself clear enough?

He explained further, "However, you'll first need to gain some legal control over your parents' estate. You won't be allowed to rent out the house until you have care and control of it. Did your parents arrange for that?"

Those soft lips pursed and she shook her head. "Not that I'm aware," she finally said. Her expression might give the impression of innocence more often than not, but today, it showed only hurt. Then, abruptly, her jaw tightened and she set down her pen. Her hands dropped to her lap and she shut her eyes.

She was angry. Noah folded his arms. "What arrangements did your parents make? Surely they knew that crossing the Atlantic wasn't without risk?"

She shrugged, but from the color rising in her cheeks, he knew the action was anything but casual.

"How quickly did your mother decline before they left?"

"Quickly enough to make my father forget."

"So he probably forgot to make any legal arrangements or update his will, if he had one," Noah said, keeping his tone reasonable. He pulled out his pocket watch to consult the time. "You'll need to see a lawyer, then. You said you were going to the bank at lunch. It's too early for that, but you should consult a lawyer first, anyway. Go do that now. And ask him how long your parents need to be missing before they are presumed dead and death certificates are issued. I haven't yet had to deal with that situation here."

How crisp and businesslike he sounded, Clare decided, fighting back a sudden surge of irritation. Seeing a lawyer first *was* good idea. Something she should have already thought of.

Was that why she was upset? That she should have considered it before he did?

Resentment rose above the anger and she hated it. A few minutes ago, she'd practically asked Noah if he would solve her problems for her. Now she was upset when he was trying to! When did she become so fickle?

Her cheeks burned. She shouldn't have had to take her problems to a man. To anyone, for that matter. She was college educated, someone her parents had entrusted with their youngest children. She'd taken a semester of family law, albeit one tailored for ladies only, but one nonetheless. She should have had these answers already.

"Is there something the matter?" Noah asked again.

*Not something. Everything.* She tried not to look miffed, instead, leaning forward and plastering on her face the calmest expression she could manage. If she was going to be married to this man, she should at least be honest with him. "I can't help but feel as though the idea of renting my house should have been…well, mine! Frankly, I don't think I should be turning to you for the solutions to all my problems."

Clare felt her heart plummet. Oh, how petty she sounded!

To add to that, grief draped over her.

Noah looked surprised. "You would have thought of it eventually. You have a lot on your mind right now."

"That's very gracious of you, Noah," she said, only remembering after speaking that he'd suggested more formality in the workplace. "I mean, Mr. Livingstone. But I don't agree. It's not just having a lot on my mind. I have to give up my home, the only one I've ever had. It's, well, sad."

"It's for the best. I own a ranch. I can't leave it."

"I don't know how you manage both a job here *and* a ranch. Animals need care all the time."

"The ranch is small, and I have a hand come in twice a week to help."

"But it's still a ranch!"

Noah cleared his throat. "I only have one animal right now."

"Really?" She could feel her expression go slack. "That one you bought from Mr. Burrows?"

"Yes. As I mentioned before, I want to run a ranch for rescued equine. All kinds. Pit ponies, feral horses, abandoned mules."

"I know that." She frowned. "But why? Old horses and such can only be put out to pasture."

"Because they're not just put out to pasture! Grazing land here is valuable and given only to cattle. Feral horses and retired mine ponies are seen as stealing grass and water. I want to start a program of saving them. Some I will be able to rehabilitate."

"What good will that do? Most will be too old or cantankerous to have any value."

"But not all. Some will be useful, pulling carts, teaching children. There is a new society that cares for animals that relies on donations, so perhaps my ranch will, also." His voice rose. "After the war, many horses were put down, and I feel that was such a waste. We can't be cruel to animals. That's not what God wants of us. We're caretakers of this earth. It's time we started acting like it."

She arched a brow. "Even wild or feral ones and their offspring?"

"Yes! Can't anyone see that horses, mules and ponies built this nation? But they're treated well only as long as they serve men." His tone had a fierce edge to it.

"So you care for this pony each day before you come in?"

"Yes. I can even show your brothers how to care for him. They'll need to learn to do chores anyway."

She bristled. "They have always had chores. This morning I had them sweeping and bringing in wood."

"I can teach them how to work around horses. My father might have owned a large manufacturing company, but we also had a dozen draft horses doing much of the work, like hauling goods and all the heavy lifting in the factory. Father hired men to care for them, and I learned stable duties and care from them."

Clare frowned. "You didn't learn how to run his business?"

Noah shifted back from her desk. "Yes, but every spare moment I had I was in the stables. Horses fascinated me. I learned how to coax the best work out of them. It's not by the end of the whip, either. I can teach Tim and Leo the same thing. It'll do them good to work in a stable."

She jumped to her feet. "Why? So you can '*train 'em up good*,' like Mr. Burrows wants to do? I've lived here all my life and I know what he's like!"

At her loud words, Pooley turned around. Noah held up his hand. "I'm not Mr. Burrows. He just wants free labor. I want Tim and Leo to have a chance to learn some valuable skills. Learning how to control a big animal through love and care can help with their unruly natures. They'll learn patience and personal discipline. I've seen the stablemen who worked for my father coax Percherons to do almost anything with just a soft, patient word."

With a remorseful expression, she sat down again. "I'm sorry. I just don't want to lose my brothers, that's all."

Noah pressed his palms onto her desk and leaned forward. He was so close, she could smell the faint cologne she'd noticed on his handkerchief. "I'm sure someone at Anderson and Haley law firm will be able to help you keep custody of them. Go see them this morning. Then go to your bank appointment."

"And pile up more bills," she muttered.

"It can't be helped. I expect you back to work at one. After work, you can fill me in on what happened, all right?"

With a short, tight nod, she stood. As she walked past him, she stopped, her voice dropping to a mere whisper. "After we're married, will I still get to work here?"

She rolled her gaze upward until it bumped into his. She could hear the naysayers now. Taking a job from a man, taking food from some family's mouths. Was she expected to stop work just because of a marital status?

Noah looked grim. "This is not the time for that discussion. You have more urgent issues."

Clare sagged. "I'll do my best to get this sorted out as quickly as possible." She waited a moment, before adding, "I'm grateful I've been able to share this with you. Regardless of why any, um—" she glanced over at Mr. Pooley as her voice dropped "—marriage is formed, honesty is still paramount in it, don't you think?" She offered a small, hopeful smile. "We're off to a good start, and you've been noble to a fault. I appreciate that." Before he could protest, she hastily shook her head and quickly retrieved her coat and hat before leaving.

Noah felt a chill race through him. Noble? Honest? He was neither, and neither virtue had prompted his proposal. Thinking of Elizabeth and of her humiliation, *the humiliation he'd caused her*, he recalled again how he'd agreed never to reveal the true circumstances surrounding their broken engagement.

At the time, he'd believed it was the least he could have done for her. But back then, his faith in God had been weakened by an unchristian father who cared little for religion and who wanted only to line his pockets. Being in Proud Bend, listening to Pastor Wyseman's excellent sermons and seeing the man's resounding faith, Noah's own faith had been bolstered.

But now it faltered, tripping over the lie he'd allowed to stand for two years. And had yet to reveal to Clare.

He could fix her situation with a proposal, but he wasn't completely noble in his motivation, or in his inaction these past two years.

The honesty upon which Clare thought their marriage was going to be based was nothing but a sham.

And like Clare with her own situation, he had no idea how to fix it.

## Chapter Five

It was at work, in the late afternoon of the next day, when the whole situation seemed to weigh the most heavily upon Clare. She'd thought she'd known all about getting married. After all, she'd helped several of her college friends prepare for their weddings, and she'd been a bridesmaid just a few weeks ago when her friend, Victoria, had married Mitch MacLeod.

Victoria had asked both Clare and her cousin, Rachel Smith, to attend her. But since Rachel had married the sheriff's brother just before last Christmas and moved to some town in Illinois, returning only for the wedding, the bulk of the preparations had been on Victoria and her aunt Louise.

Clare had underestimated the number of forms to fill out. They should have been second nature to her, what with her job at the Recording Office, but she had found her hands shaking as she'd written her own name on several sheets attesting that she was indeed Clare Margaret Walsh, a spinster.

Also, her heart had pounded like she'd run a mile

when Pastor Wyseman met with her and Noah, and even more so when he'd met with her privately in his tiny office at the parsonage.

"Are you being coerced into this marriage?"

She gaped at the pastor. "I beg your pardon?"

It was a question that Pastor Wyseman had felt morally obligated to ask, he explained.

All Clare could do was shake her head mutely until he'd asked her to speak out her answer. Her voice cracked with nerves. "No, I'm not being coerced."

She was merely saving her family, she added only to herself.

"And your parents, Clare?" the pastor asked. "Are they coming back for the wedding? I would have thought they'd be in Europe by now, but Noah has asked for the ceremony to happen as soon as possible. Why is that?"

Clare swallowed. With eyes wide and body as still as stone, she found she couldn't answer.

Then, suddenly, she blurted the whole story. The events, including what Noah had said, that her parents might still be found alive—everything poured out from her like a torrent. She couldn't stop a single word, even if she tried.

Pastor Wyseman listened, his attention riveted to her. Then, after some quiet words of comfort, and one short reprimand admonishing her for not asking for his help earlier, he prayed.

"It sounds to me like you're still unsure of what to do," Wyseman said after ending his prayer. "I won't issue the bans, as is my custom, until you're ready, Clare. Let me know before the service on Sunday."

Relief swept through her. Just giving voice to all the anguish made her feel better.

Still, it would be best to have the ceremony as soon as possible. She wasn't the sort of person to put off a task based solely on its level of unsavoriness. "The end of next week is fine."

He consulted the small calendar on his desk. "Friday, April 21?"

She nodded. The truth settled into her. She would be married that day. Less than two weeks and she hadn't told a soul. Precious few knew about her parents.

Clare bit her lip. She didn't really want anyone to learn her parents' fate yet. She wanted to tell her brothers first, and she needed time to figure out what she would say.

Besides, plenty of people in town would criticize her father for leaving his children in such a bind. She didn't want to deal with them yet.

Sitting in the pastor's office, Clare had felt her stomach tighten and had wanted to cry all over again.

Yesterday, Thursday, she'd finally had a sit-down appointment with the bank manager. Thankfully, he'd shown compassion and understanding, willing to wait another month to allow Clare to sort out her situation. Despite the relief she felt, she'd left the bank with a heavy heart. Even with a month's grace, she had yet to solve her financial woes. Surely Noah could not afford to pay her mortgage, even if she was given to asking him.

That same day, she'd spoken to the lawyer, told him of the events surrounding her parents' disappearance. Although he could only meet with her briefly, he'd assured her he would file the appropriate documents to allow Clare to get full control of both the house and her brothers. He also agreed that being married would certainly help her case of keeping guardianship of her brothers should it come before a judge.

That evening, after supper, Mrs. Wyseman had dropped by her home to offer both her congratulations and condolences, in the same breath and sentence. A mixed blessing, she had added. Clare's marriage, her upcoming wedding, were apparently the blessings.

And later that evening, after tucking the boys into their big bed, and after she had made sure they were clean, and had said their prayers, she leaned forward to kiss Tim on the forehead.

"Why are you so sad, Clare?" he asked. "Do you miss Ma and Pa, too?"

A lump threatened to choke her. She shut her eyes a moment, wondering if this was the time to tell them.

No. They needed their rest. She still needed to figure out the right words, to soften the blow they would receive.

"Yes," she admitted honestly. "I miss them, too. Now, no talking or playing. We all need sleep, you know."

Tim frowned, then with a glance at his sleepy brother, he dropped the subject, nodded and rolled over. Clare sagged with gratitude.

Now, this Friday afternoon, watching Mr. Pooley depart early for the day to look after his sick wife, Clare looked hollowly over to Noah. "Mrs. Wyseman dropped by after supper. How am I supposed to respond to both a congratulations and a condolence?"

Noah shrugged. "With a thank-you. Say you wished

your parents could be here for the wedding. It can't be easy for anyone to offer both at the same time. I wouldn't know which to say first."

"Condolences are never easy. I remember dropping by Rachel Smith's house after we heard about her father. I was surprised to learn she and her mother had been ill. I was horrified to learn that Mr. Abernathy had tried to poison them. But still, Rachel had been strong and gracious enough to come down to the parlor to accept my condolences."

Rachel was about ten years older than Clare, and had been thought of as a dedicated spinster, devoting her time to her ministry of caring for the soiled doves in town. Her father had tried to acquire full ownership of the bank, at the same time his partner tried to do the same. Both men had ended up dead.

Shortly after that, the sheriff had gone missing in what turned out to be an unrelated case. Not long after that, Rachel had met the sheriff's twin. He'd come looking for his brother, and with Rachel's help, had found him. And before long, Rachel had married the twin.

Clare had noted that Rachel, although wealthy enough to not have to work, had continued her ministry after marrying.

"If she can do that, so can you."

She looked at Noah. He was talking about how emotionally strong Rachel had been in the face of losing her father. But his words took on extra meaning. Rachel was strong enough to push for her independence. Clare could only hope she was, also.

At that moment, the boys spilled into the office. Clare peered over the counter at them, thankful she was ending that conversation with Noah. He was right in the suggestion of just a simple thank-you, but did he really believe she was as strong as Rachel was?

Brushing aside her questions, for she had no time for speculation, Clare smiled tightly at her brothers. They were here, and since word was sure to spread through town about her parents, she needed to tell them the truth, whether or not she was ready for it.

Noah had glanced their way, then eyed her closely. "You're going to tell them, aren't you?" he asked quietly.

Clare nodded. "Will you stay?"

"Would you like me to tell them instead?"

A knot tightened in her throat. Another noble act. As much as the offer was genuine and kind, she couldn't accept it.

"No, thank you. It needs to come from me." She stood, smoothed down her skirt, cringing slightly at the faded part where she'd had to scrub away the ashes from the fire upstairs. A replacement skirt would have to wait, though. "Come here, boys. I need to talk to you."

His heart pounding, Noah listened to Clare's gentle words. Sunlight streamed in through the small window beside the door, catching tiny bits of dust as they danced in the rays. They looked almost jovial. Over the scents of the woodstove in the corner were the traditional smells of paper and ink, comforting odors to him usually. Clare sat the boys down on one of the wider chairs, both sharing it. She pulled another chair closer to them.

She had asked him to stay as if he was some chivalrous guard who could protect her.

He wasn't. Yet, somehow, the idea of Clare doing

something that would surely hurt her, gripped him. It wasn't right for her to bear this burden alone. He should help.

Before he could offer again, she took her brothers' hands in hers. "You two know I love you very much, right?"

They nodded mutely, with Leo turning his head up toward Noah as if to gauge his reaction. Then he looked back at Clare.

"I will never leave you," she continued. "I'll always take care of you."

Again, they said nothing.

"But Mother and Father aren't coming back."

Her words had dropped to such a whisper, Noah strained to hear them. He wondered yet again if this was premature, but when would be the right time to announce such sad news? Would Tim and Leo understand there weren't going to be any caskets? Would they understand what *lost at sea* meant?

"Why aren't they coming home?" Leo asked.

"Their ship has gone missing. We don't know where it is, but out there on the ocean is dangerous. It's likely that the ship has sunk." Her voice cracked. "I'm afraid that Mother and Father have died."

With that, she pulled them into a hard hug and they clung to each other for a long time. Noah watched helplessly, wondering if he should allow them some privacy. He could see Clare's expression harden as she stared past her brothers' heads.

He knew her thoughts, how angry she was at her mother and father. He could feel his own resentment rising toward them once again. How could her father not have thought that they might not return? Noah knew that her father was always chasing the next dream, be it another job, or lately, a new cure. He loved to spend money, Noah had heard.

And in doing so, he'd left his children to fend for themselves.

Clare set her brothers back, but immediately, they reached for her again. This time, her embrace was a tender one; the younger one, Leo, climbed up onto her lap and clung to her.

They cried. She cried. Noah felt tears sting his own eyes.

"What are we going to do?" Tim asked.

"We're going to take care of each other. And Mr. Livingstone is going to help us."

Both boys peered up at him. "How?" Leo asked.

Noah saw Clare swallow. "He's going to marry me."

His eyebrows shot up. She hadn't yet told them that they were getting married?

"Why?" Leo asked.

Clare stroked her youngest brother's hair, trying unsuccessfully to tame the errant curls. "We're going to live with him because we can't afford to live in the house anymore."

"Why not?" Leo's tearstained face pinched into a frown.

"Because Father can't pay the bills anymore."

"But you can," Tim reasoned. "You work here."

"I don't make enough money to pay the bank for the house."

"Why does the bank want money for our house?" Leo asked in confusion.

"They lent Father the money to buy it. One must always pay one's debts. But my wages here aren't enough."

After stealing a glance at Noah, Tim tilted his head to one side. "So why doesn't Mr. Livingstone just give you more money?"

The boy's childish logic made for a good question, Noah thought. He did have some savings, maybe not enough to pay the rest of Clare's mortgage, but enough to allow her to stay in her home with her brothers. Those savings, however, were earmarked for his ranch, to buy and care for rescued horses until the ranch could sustain itself. He couldn't do that without his savings to start it all.

Clare would not take a handout, anyway. If she only considered marriage as the final option, accepting cash from her supervisor wouldn't even make it to the table.

Meanwhile, Clare flushed. "He can't. It's not his job to decide how much money I get. Mr. Livingstone only runs the office. It's the state of Colorado that decides my wages." She shook her head. "That's not for you two to worry about, anyway."

"Where are we going to live, then?" Tim asked, suspicion marring his features as he set himself away from her.

"We're going to live with Mr. Livingstone, at his ranch."

"Why can't he move into our house?"

"Because he has a ranch and it will soon have lots of animals," Clare answered calmly. "He'll need to take care of them."

"Like Mr. MacLeod's cattle? Matthew MacLeod says his pa has hundreds of cattle."

Noah listened. The boys would know Matthew and his brothers, for they went to school with them. No doubt the boys were swapping stories.

His ranch would never be like Mitch MacLeod's. Moreover, with the ready-made family Noah was inheriting, he knew he wouldn't have the funds to buy many animals, even if they were rescues. "No. Right now, besides my horse, I have only one pony," he told the boys. "But I plan to get more horses. A ranch can have horses or sheep as well as cattle."

Neither boy said anything. They just stared at him, as if sizing him up. Finally, Leo turned back to his sister. "Clare, I don't want to leave our house. I like it. I like our room, even with the burned floor."

Burned floor? He'd forgotten about that.

"Will Mr. Livingstone feed us?" Tim asked.

"Of course," Clare answered.

"More than you? I'm hungry and we didn't get much for lunch. Father always gave us more than you give us."

Noah's arms fell to his sides as cold washed through him. He cleared his throat, pulled up a chair and sat facing the boys. "It's Friday. Why don't we have supper at my house? We can see where you'll sleep and you can meet Turnip."

"Who's Turnip?" Tim tipped his head to one side, and his eyes narrowed.

"That's the pony I have. He was feral once."

"What's that mean?" Leo asked.

"He used to run free wherever he wanted. His parents were wild, but they may have been tame at one time."

The boys' faces lit up. "Can we ride him?"

Noah hesitated. "Not yet. I still need to train him.

But someday I'm sure he'll be broken. He's smart. I've seen him figure out how to open his stall door with just his mouth."

The boys were suitably impressed.

"So don't worry," Noah finished. "We'll get him trained."

His promise seemed to satisfy them, although, Noah noticed, they still clung to their sister, the only one left from their family. Clare, he noted as well, wasn't ready to release them from her embrace. She was right when she said they were missing their parents.

"Well, then," he said, smacking his knees gently as he rose. "Let's finish up here." He had enough food at home, thankfully, to give everyone a decent meal. And thanks to the few chickens he had, there were eggs. He also had several loaves of bread, plenty of carrots, and onions to go with a steak big enough to share. He helped Clare into her jacket and gave her an encouraging smile.

She returned it hesitantly. "Did you bring your cart in this morning?"

He shook his head. "No, but I've arranged for some staples to be delivered at lunch. We have plenty of food."

Clare flushed. "Do you cook all your own meals?"

"I have to. My ranch hand can't cook worth beans. It's not fine restaurant fare, but it's good. I hope you like steak."

She rolled her eyes. "I grew up in Proud Bend. Of course I love steak. As for fine restaurant fare, Proud Bend is sorely lacking in that department. I don't go into the saloon for their noon meal, nor would I visit that place down by the train depot."

"I'd question your ability to taste if you did eat at the depot."

Clare pulled a face. "No, thank you. I've heard they serve the same coffee, day in and day out, but just boil it again with a few extra grounds. I'm sure it would peel the skin off one's tongue."

Something warm washed through him. This was the Clare he'd hired full-time six months ago. Bright and outgoing, with a lively sense of humor. Noah couldn't help but welcome her back. "What did you eat when you were out East at college?"

"There was a dining hall, and it had standard fare, but beside our dormitory was this little English inn that sold meat pies—"

"You were allowed to go unescorted into an inn?" His brows lifted. "I question your college's leadership."

She laughed, albeit softly. "No, we weren't, but a few brave ladies sneaked in. Of course, I was not one of them," she added hastily.

"Of course."

"Anyway, they had English pasties and these things called scones."

"I've heard of them. Aren't they just biscuits?"

"Oh, no! They're drier, and served with jam and clotted cream, which sounds horrible, I know, but it's really delicious. They sweeten it with honey. It's thick and a little bit tangy and they serve it at 'teatime,' which is an afternoon meal made only of scones and spreads." She looked down at her brothers, smiling. "The boys would love that."

"Sounds fussy. I don't think I could live on that."

"It's only a snack." Clare laughed again, the sound

tinkling through the quiet office like a wind chime in a gentle breeze. It had been days since he'd heard the sound and after the tearful moment earlier, Clare's soft laugh was welcomed. It did much to lift the mood around them.

Before long, they had locked up the Recording Office and were on their way to Clare's house for her wagon. Noah walked his horse. After changing their clothes, the boys helped Noah hitch the family wagon to their horse, but needed no help to scramble up into the box. Clare also changed into a more suitable outfit, and now sat on the bench beside him. Noah took up the reins and they settled in for the short, fifteen-minute ride to his ranch. He'd tied his own horse to the back of the cart and, looking over his shoulder once, he noticed that Leo was stretching out over the tailgate to try to pet the animal. Tim yanked his brother back and both dropped to the floor of the box.

"We're almost there," Noah reassured them as he turned onto a short trail.

"Do you have a name for your ranch?" Clare asked.

He shook his head. "At one time, I thought I would name it after its first equine resident."

"Some people name their ranches after a special pet," she offered.

"Well, my dog's name is Nero, which is all right for a dog but not for a ranch."

Clare's eyes twinkled. "So that leaves Turnip Ranch."

"Which doesn't appeal to me."

"I don't know why." She smothered a giggle.

"I do." By now, they'd reached his home, a modest ranch house compared to Clare's fine two-story clapboard home. It was made mostly of logs, but more sprawling than most. Along the south side, the promised green of summer had started. He pulled to a stop beside the garden he'd planned to plow and cultivate this week. Nero bounded over. Ahead was the stable and beyond, in the small fenced-in paddock behind it, the pony, Turnip. The animal lifted its head and stared at them, his ears pricked forward. He stopped chewing and snorted, but did not move.

"Can we see the wild pony?" Leo asked Noah as he helped Clare from the cart.

"Let me change out of my suit first."

Once on the ground, Clare smoothed her skirt. "Why don't I start supper and you three can unhook the horses." She looked gently at her brothers. "Only after those things are done can you see Turnip."

Noah watched her enter his house. Was she going to poke around, clean and fuss and make herself at home? He'd always prided himself on being neat and clean, but surely, a woman would rearrange things to suit herself.

He swallowed. This was the home he'd made for himself after leaving New York State. It had been his escape, a place he didn't have to share, and now a woman, the fiancée he didn't even love, was striding toward it with the speed of a lit fuse cord toward dynamite.

He shook off the unflattering comparison. Clare wasn't as bad as that. She was merely full of life, open and honest with her feelings.

Honest to a fault.

*You should tell Clare about Elizabeth.*

As swiftly as the internal prompt appeared, he shoved it away.

Once in the stable, after being allowed to help him release the horses into the paddock with the pony, the boys received their first lesson on taking care of the tack. Noah took down a bottle from the shelf. "Tack should be cleaned every day, but sometimes we can't do that. If you don't have time, at least clean the noseband of the bridle. It's the part that catches the most sweat."

He showed the boys how to wash the tack and scrub the noseband. "You should always oil the leather, but not too much because it may make it stretch. You can shake out the blanket or beat it if you like. But don't wash it with soap. The most it needs is a good beating."

Noah threw the blanket over one of the stall doors and handed one boy a rug beater and the other a small broom. They began to beat the saddle blanket with great enthusiasm.

Satisfied he would get a clean blanket, Noah walked out into the paddock where Turnip was grazing. "It's okay, boy," he crooned softly as he approached the skittish stallion. "I'm home."

Noah had been working with Turnip for months now, and the animal had shown some signs of acceptance. He could lead the pony out in the mornings, and oftentimes, lead him back in, as long as his movements weren't too sudden.

Today, thankfully, Turnip allowed Noah to take hold of the bridle, hooking it to a short, braided lead. They walked together into the stable.

A shriek ripped through the building, with Leo swinging his beater around in a wide, dangerous circle, while Tim ducked each time to arc the broom about a foot above the straw-strewn floor. Leo jumped over it, taking that time to flail the carpet beater about.

Turnip bolted away from Noah, who still gripped the short rein. With the pony's sudden movement, Noah felt his arm wrench backward as Turnip twisted away from the wild scene. In the turn he made, his haunches knocked Noah down to the dirt floor.

Knowing immediately what would come next, Noah leaped to his feet and shoved both boys out of the stable, before slamming himself to the floor.

# *Chapter Six*

The pony kicked, thankfully bucking only into the dusty air. Then, with a sharp scream of its own, the pony raced out the back stable door and into the paddock.

Noah scrambled up, and, gripping his painful arm, he managed to slide the back door to the paddock tightly closed. He doubted Turnip would return to wreak more havoc, but refused to risk it. When he turned and fell against the door, he spied Leo scurrying into the house. The small boy stumbled on the doorstep, but finding his footing again, he rushed inside. Cradling his sore shoulder, Noah sagged with relief. He was okay, but where was Tim?

As if to answer him, the other brother peeked around the front stable door before stepping over the threshold. In front of him lay both the broom and the rug beater, each dropped in the terror of the moment.

"Are you okay?" Noah asked the boy.

Tim nodded, his youthful eyes wide with horror. The saddle blanket slipped from where it hung over the stall door. It fell with a thud. Tim jumped back in fear. Beyond, the back door banged open and out hurried Clare. She was followed more slowly by Leo.

She skidded to a stop at the open stable door, pulling Tim close to her. Thanks to the closed one behind Noah, she eclipsed the daylight. "Noah? What happened?"

He walked up to her. "The boys spooked Turnip."

"Where is he?"

"He raced out into the paddock. I just closed that door."

"What were they doing?"

Noah walked outside to sit on the narrow bench beside the door. He hugged his arm close to his chest. "They were fooling around with the rug beater and the broom. I should have realized that when I brought in Turnip that their wild swings would startle him, but he'd been calm up to that point."

Swiftly, Clare patted Tim down, turning him around for an inspection until she, with her hands, captured his pale face to peer hard into his shocked expression. Then she inspected Leo, who kept his distance from the stable.

Satisfied that both brothers were okay, she straightened. "Go into the house, both of you. Sit in the kitchen until I come inside. And don't touch a single thing. Do you hear me? Not one thing!"

Noah watched the pair trudge slowly toward his home, not fully convinced that Clare's simple instructions would be obeyed. With a groan, he stood and walked up beside her. "The last time you ordered them to do something, an 'incident' occurred that included you needing to find a carpenter."

Her answer was only a gaping look of realization, followed by a sinking expression. "True, but this time,

I think they're really scared. Usually they question everything. Look at them now, though. Scared silent." She paused and thought a moment. "I should be taking advantage of this."

Not yet able to smile, Noah watched Tim's and Leo's slow, wary steps, with Tim's backward glance toward the adults as they disappeared into the house.

Clare turned to him, her sharp stare inspecting the length of his frame. "Are you all right?"

He grimaced and letting out a short, breathy noise, he returned to the nearby bench. "Turnip wrenched my shoulder. I wasn't expecting him to move so suddenly. Then he knocked me over as he spun around. I landed wrong, but it was a good thing."

"How so?"

"I landed close to the boys and was able to jump up and shove them outside. By that time, Turnip had turned and started to kick, but thankfully, he only caught the air."

With a gasp, Clare paled.

"It's all right," he said with a grimace. "I'd figured out pretty quickly what he'd planned to do, so no one got hurt. Turnip then raced out into the paddock. I closed the door, but I might have wrenched my shoulder more doing that."

"I can see you're hurt, and badly, too."

"I'll heal." He watched Clare's growing concern. She sank down on the bench beside him, her face etched with worry. Blinking rapidly, she reached for him, but he shifted away. It wasn't just his tender shoulder he didn't want her to touch. If she started to fawn all over him, it would do their business arrangement no good.

She'd already stated in no uncertain terms that marriage was a last resort, so he'd be crazy to start thinking theirs might grow into something more intimate.

No. He'd been injured before. He'd heal. But the heart was a different matter. He'd been hurt by his family and wouldn't subject himself to being hurt by Clare, for surely, an independent woman like her wouldn't go for the foolishness of love.

"Go into the house, Clare," he told her quietly, trying to keep the pain from his voice. "See to your brothers. They need you more than I do."

Clare glanced over at the door, unsure of what to do. She needed to get back into the house. As neat as it was inside, it wouldn't remain that way for long with her brothers in there, regardless of her orders to them.

But they *were* scared, so maybe that fear would curb their mischief.

She glanced back at Noah, in time to catch his cringe as he tested out his aches and pains. Her heart lurched and she felt a chill wash through her. He was in pain. Surely, he needed help, didn't he?

He didn't want her to help him.

*Should I stay, Lord?*

She threw back her shoulders. Noah needed help. *Her* help. The boys were fine for now.

She reached forward and touched his hand gently, the one that cradled his shoulder. When he looked up at her, she leaned toward him. "Let's get you into the house," she said softly. "Maybe I can get you a cold cloth? Do you have any liniment we can put on your shoulder?"

Clare ran her hand over his, allowing it to trail down

his arm, hoping she might gauge his reaction and get a better sense of whether or not to take him in to see the doctor.

Noah grabbed her wrist and pushed it down to her side. "Don't."

"Why? Does it hurt?"

His answering look seemed odd. It wasn't one of pain, but determination, as if fighting some battle within. Why didn't he want her to touch him?

Then, as he released her, his gaze dropped to her lips. She felt it more than saw it. He swallowed and suddenly her own mouth became as dry as dust. Finally, she swallowed, also. He looked, well, hungry, like the boys always did when supper was delayed as Mother struggled with her pain.

Clare bit her lip. Why was he looking at her mouth as though he wanted to kiss her?

Her heart leaped in her chest. *Oh.* Could it be because…

"Go into the house," Noah told her again, his voice firmer. "In the cupboard above the stove is a small, clear bottle."

"What is it?" She gasped. "It's not liquor, is it?"

"No!" He shook his head, stopping suddenly as he cringed. "It's Mexican Mustang Liniment. I use it on my horse sometimes, but I think it warrants testing on me today."

As he tried to stand, she leaned toward him. "Let me help you up."

"No. Go inside. Put on a fire. It would be nice if the liniment was warmed a bit. I'll be in shortly."

She rose, hesitantly. "All right. I'll warm it. Then I'll rub it on your shoulder." She reached for him again.

"No! Just go inside!"

Stepping back, Clare swallowed, then nodded. She hurried toward the house. At the door, she turned, but Noah hadn't moved.

She should go back to him, insist on helping him and refuse to take no for an answer. Whatever foolish pride was stopping him from accepting help needed to be ignored.

But what if he *was* attracted to her and didn't like that idea? It certainly would do nothing but complicate the simple arrangement they had, and frankly, Clare told herself fiercely, she shouldn't even be thinking about such an improper thing. She'd just lost her parents, despite the hope that maybe their ship, *Governor*, was only overdue.

Noah had looked like he'd wanted to steal a kiss. At the same time, if he could have pushed her right off the bench, she was sure he would have. Maybe his injury stopped him. Or had he realized before she had that such a bold move must not happen?

Clare bit her lip. This marriage was only a formal arrangement to help her financially. Noah's sudden attraction, no doubt a product of his vulnerability, should be curbed. Indeed, Noah was wise to stop it before it got out of hand.

Sudden regret twisted her heart, and she found her breath catching in her throat. Regret? Had she actually wanted him to kiss her?

Yes, she admitted to herself. She'd admired Noah

since she first met him, regardless of the fact that she had not wanted a beau, or a marriage.

It shouldn't be pursued, anyway. There was to be no love between them. This was a marriage only to keep her family together. She'd seen her friends turn from independent women to simpering fools because of love. And Noah needed to keep his focus on his budding ranch. That was his love.

For a moment, Clare felt her heart flip in warning. Yes, one moment of weakness could lead to a lifetime of regret.

Oh, how she'd seen that in some of her college friends. They'd given in to the weakness of a soft moment, carried along by the romance of courting and the promises made by the men who'd set about wooing them. Those men had filled their silly heads with nonsense, and before long, her friends were married, plucked from college and placed in homes like indentured servants.

Clare closed the back door slowly. One friend of hers had tried to return to college and her husband had pulled her registration and refused to pay the tuition. Then, in front of the staff, he'd dressed her down.

She shut her eyes. That friend had allowed herself to be trapped and become a device used only to produce heirs and run a household.

Clare stepped into the kitchen, feeling both regret and gratefulness churn like oil and water. Just now, Noah had wisely curtailed any folly. He'd remembered how their marriage was different, not subject to foolhardy affections that trapped womankind.

A swell of resentment rose unbidden in Clare as she shook off the unsettling feelings. She should have had enough sense to nip that moment of intimacy in the bud. Instead, as he had before, Noah was the one showing wisdom.

She glanced at the back door. Yes, she was resentful that Noah had been the wiser of the two of them, but at the same time, the notion of one tiny moment of intimacy would have been welcomed. A small bit of proof to show her she could care again after the loss of her parents.

Never mind. She'd only be showing a dangerous vulnerability.

In the center of the kitchen, Clare straightened her clothes firmly, the action designed to seal out any foolish attraction. But for one moment, she pressed her fingers against her forehead and shut her eyes. When she turned, her expression would be a mask of reserve and competence, she hoped.

Tim and Leo were sitting in two of the four kitchen chairs, their expressions hollow and lost and incredibly sad. She steeled her calm expression further. Yes, she was here for them and only them.

"What were you two supposed to do?"

Leo looked down, and it was Tim who answered. "We were supposed to beat the horse blanket."

"And what were you doing?"

"We were playing instead."

"Was that the right thing to do?"

Tim looked down. Leo peeked up. "No."

"Why was it not the right thing to do?" she asked them.

"Because we would be punished?" Leo suggested.

Suppressing a smile, Clare answered, "No, because

it's dangerous to swing things around, especially inside. You scared Turnip, and he could have hurt you two, and Noah, very badly."

As she spoke, a shiver rippled through her. Things could have turned out far worse. "This is a lesson you two need to learn. I'm going to think about a proper punishment for your behavior. In the meantime, you two will help me make supper."

The brothers nodded, and in a moment of compassion borne of thankfulness to Noah for his swift action, she gave the boys a fast hug before dishing out instructions on what they could do to help her.

The boys hugged her back.

Alone in the yard, Noah blew out a heavy, relieved sigh. The pain snaking through him was only a portion of the problem.

Clare was by far the bigger issue. She had wanted the situation they were in, this engagement of theirs, even less than he had. Hadn't she initially turned him down? And then, when she'd set aside her pride and finally asked if his offer still stood, *and* after he'd said yes, hadn't she promptly burst into tears?

The facts were irrefutable. She didn't want to be married to him. He couldn't blame her. He was too focused on his ranch, and to that end, his work as Recording Officer.

He had earned that position fairly, through hard work, aiming for the job when the previous Recording Officer retired. It came with a decent enough salary to start his ranch. Being Recording Officer also put him in contact with a variety of folks who would have old horses and mules to give away, no longer wanting to care for them.

He just wanted to save those poor animals' lives. That was all, and enough to make him a poor companion for a vibrant woman like Clare.

Noah rose, finding he ached more than he expected. He'd better get that liniment on him as soon as possible if he didn't want to stiffen up like a dried leather strap.

Standing at the open door of the stable, he glanced into it at the back door, the one that led into the paddock. It remained firmly closed. Being in the company of the two geldings out there, his and the Walshes', should help calm Turnip down. Noah had hoped that bringing Tim and Leo out here would show the boys that living on a ranch wasn't so bad.

Would he be able to convince them now? Probably not. What just happened would make their moving out here in a week all the more difficult.

Maybe he should just keep them here until the wedding. He needed to show them they had to get back up on the proverbial horse, so to speak. If Clare were to rent out her home, she'd need to pack up their belongings and prepare the house for tenants. She couldn't do that with Tim and Leo underfoot and she refused to take time from work in order to do it while the boys were in school. That would leave only her evenings.

He grimaced. Clare was so determined to be strong she wasn't even giving herself time to grieve. He doubted she would welcome any suggestion to that effect.

He opened the door and stepped into the kitchen. Tim stood on a stool at the dry sink, washing a few of the wrinkled potatoes Noah had set out on the counter this morning in order to use up. With sleeves shoved up, Clare had already started a fire and was now scraping carrots, while Leo collected the scrapings to toss into the garden.

Everyone froze and stared at him. Clare set down her knife to pick up the liniment bottle she'd set on the warming plate of the large stove. Wordlessly, she handed it to him, and wordlessly he took it before walking into his bedroom. There, he pulled a face as he tested his shoulder.

"They didn't mean to scare Turnip," a soft voice from his doorway said a few minutes later. "They feel bad for it, too."

Noah turned, cringing at the pain. Clare stood in his bedroom's open doorway, her arms folded. "Of course," he muttered, gingerly peeling off his jacket.

Clare stepped over the threshold, arms extending, obviously ready to assist him. He held up his hand. "I can manage just fine, thank you."

She stopped. He noticed how she bit her bottom lip. He looked quickly away. "The boys were fooling around," he added. "Don't forget, Turnip was born feral and has had to deal with Burrows since he was captured. He's not some mild-mannered dobbin. He's also a stallion, and thankfully, my horse and yours have been gelded, so there's no competition."

"Do you know how old he is? Will he grow anymore?"

"I don't think he'll get any bigger. He had too harsh a life during his growing years. Or else his parents were small. We don't really know."

"I don't think any of us realized that. You have your hands full."

"I can train him," he ground out. Once trained, Turnip could be sold and the profits returned to the ranch.

Clare's expression doubtful, she asked, "Are you sure?"

"Yes." Even to his own ears, the word sounded harsh.

She lifted her brows. "What kind of experience do you have training horses?"

"Remember how I said that my father employs plenty of draft horses for transporting his shipments?"

"Yes." Clare glanced to her right, to something out of his line of sight. There were no sounds of mischief, but that meant nothing, he was realizing. She looked back at him, her gaze still assessing him. "You said something about how they do heavy lifting in your father's factories. Why doesn't he have machines to do things? I hear there are some good steam engines that move things around now."

"My father felt it was too expensive to convert the factory. Regardless, we still need the draft horses to move the shipments to market, and they need care. After my studies each day, and during every bit of free time I had, I was in the stables."

"Your father approved?"

"My father didn't know."

From the look on her face, that surprised her, and Noah felt irritation rise within him. "I wasn't always the staid and boring person I am now."

She reddened. "I have never called you that!"

"I'm focused, Clare. I want my ranch to succeed more than anything else." Noah continued, "My father's head groom was excellent with horses. He could get even the most cantankerous ones to mind him. He taught me how to handle them. I loved it in the stable. I felt...calmer there."

He undid the top button of his shirt. "Turnip just needs time."

Clare stepped closer, but remained at the threshold. "What if he can't be tamed? I mean, if we bring Tim and Leo here, and that pony stays skittish—"

"He won't. As I mentioned, I can train him. Until then, Tim and Leo will have to stay out of the stable."

"Easier said than done," Clare scoffed. "And the other horses and mules and ponies you hope to get? You want to run a rescue ranch. I don't expect these animals to be pleasant and grateful."

"We will sort it out as we go."

Clare didn't seem convinced. "Turnip has hurt you. You won't be able to take care of him for a while."

"I have a part-time ranch hand. Turnip's been on his own most of his life, so don't worry about him." Noah pulled a face. "It's my own fault. I should have released him as soon as he turned. I just didn't think he was going to turn that fast." He grimaced, not liking that he'd admitted this fault.

About to remove his shirt, he stopped and looked pointedly at her, expecting her to give him the privacy he needed to rub the liniment on his shoulder.

She didn't budge. "I came to tell you that Tim and Leo are upset. Can you talk to them?"

"And say what? They shouldn't have been fooling around, Clare. They need to learn to do as they're told."

She blinked. Then, after she glanced back down the

short hallway toward the kitchen, she whispered, "You know it's hard."

Sighing, he came close to her. "No, it's not. You're the adult. You have a strong personality. You're the one they must learn to obey, so you have to put aside your own feelings and be their parent now."

His shoulder ached, stung and throbbed, all at the same time. Right now, he didn't feel like showing Clare how to be a parent, certainly not to those two ruffians who'd scared his only rescue animal and probably set back months of hard work he'd put into training it.

He didn't want to have to tell Clare how to step up and be the kind of parent those boys needed right now. But when he glanced at her, he saw her eyes welling up with tears and her chin wobbling.

His shoulders sagging, he wanted to kick himself. Clare was as much an orphan as her brothers and here he was telling her to stop grieving and pull up her stockings. What kind of heartless fool was he? His injury was temporary. In a day or two, with the help of the liniment, he'd be as right as rain. Clare, however, would never be the same.

"You said they might not be lost at sea," she whispered. "You were the one who encouraged me not to give up hope. Now you are telling me that I may as well get used to the fact they're dead and start being a mother to my brothers!"

"You know I meant only until they return." He watched her for a moment, then added gently, "Let me take Tim and Leo for a few days. They need to get used to this place, anyway, and you need time to pack up your things."

"Clare!" Tim's voice rang down the hallway. "Leo just ate a raw potato!"

Leo's voice followed. "Tim says I'm gonna die!"

Clare shut her eyes. With a sigh, she retreated from the threshold, and Noah hurriedly shut the door. His hand still on the brass knob, he blew out a long breath. The only answer was for him to take control and help Clare with the boys.

But he knew perfectly well what would happen if he did. Clare was going to resent him. Hadn't she already admitted that she resented her parents for abandoning them, even though she knew it hadn't been their intention? And hadn't she said that she didn't like that he was the one showing wisdom with his suggestions? That resentment she was sure to feel would fester, until that one day she fought back and hurt those around her.

Resentment was never a good way to start a marriage, not even one in name only.

# *Chapter Seven*

By the time supper was over, Clare knew she needed to face the facts. If she were to rent out their home, she needed to pack up all her parents' belongings. She couldn't take time off work for it, nor could she get much of it done if she was to plan her wedding *and* watch her brothers. Yes, even children as young as Tim and Leo could help, but if she was facing harsh facts, she may as well admit that they'd be more a hindrance than a help.

Noah was right when they'd spoken in his bedroom doorway. They were all going to move into Noah's home, so the boys may as well do so now.

She set down her knife and fork on the sturdy porcelain plate. Their supper was finished, and Clare knew now that the boys' bellies were full they'd be more conducive to change. "You boys are going to move in here before I do."

Leo looked up, alarmed. "Why can't you come?"

"Because I'm not married to Mr. Livingstone yet."

"I'm not, either, and you're making *me* move."

Clare suppressed a smile. She heard Noah snicker

behind his coffee mug. He'd been silent throughout their meal, and she could only hope the liniment, which added a pungent element to the wonderful scents of fried beef and gravy, was working.

"You aren't gonna marry Mr. Livingstone, stupid," Tim admonished.

"Don't say that word," Noah told the boy sharply. "He doesn't understand, that's all."

"I do so! I'm smart!" Leo yelled. He smacked the table and flipped his empty plate, flicking about droplets of leftover gravy, for Clare had stopped him moments ago from licking his plate clean. She now grabbed her napkin and quickly mopped up the small mess.

She was glad she'd found the napkins in the drawer. The monogram on them told her they had been left by the previous owners, but they'd brought an air of civility to the rustic charm of the kitchen. Now they were truly needed.

"Leo," Noah began, setting down his knife and fork, "only Clare and I are going to marry. You'll be my brother-in-law. You don't have to marry me to move in here. Just Clare has to." Glancing at Tim for a moment, he added, "And we may as well figure out what we're going to call each other. I think while we're in Proud Bend, especially if you two are in the office, you should then call me Mr. Livingstone, but out here, which will be your home, you can call me Noah."

Clare eyed him as she dabbed the last of the spray of gravy. "Are you sure?"

"We don't have a typical marriage," Noah answered coolly. "But we may as well make the best of it."

She flushed and looked down.

"Why don't you have a typical marriage?" Tim asked.
Clare's cheeks reddened further.

"We have children. You two boys," Noah said without a pause. "Usually, they come after you've been married awhile."

A smile rose unbidden to her lips. She was grateful for Noah's patient words and equally grateful that the boys accepted his explanation. Perhaps, as in the boys' cases, full bellies really had soothed their dispositions. She could only hope the pony outside had found enough grass to fill its belly and smooth *its* disposition.

"Not many newly married couples have two almost-grown-up boys right away." Noah smiled. "We're proud to be different. You two boys make our marriage unique and special."

Leo grinned. Being younger, his moods were more changeable and easier to temper. But Noah's kind words weren't completely fabricated. Their marriage would be different. It would be in name only, with no expectations on either side.

Oddly, though, the thought sank deep into her belly like a cold stone in a still pond.

Why? Wasn't that what she wanted? To be different? And Noah was a reasonable man, wasn't he? He would understand and respect her desire to decide her own fate.

And keep their marriage chaste. Clare recalled how close they'd sat on the bench outside, how his gaze had dropped to her lips before she'd realized how near they'd come to kissing.

How much a part of her wanted it.

Unable to shake off the sudden discontent, Clare began to stack the plates in the sink. "We need to tidy up the kitchen and get you two back home. And we need a plan to bring you both out here with all your belongings." She shot Noah a fast look. "Don't worry. They don't have much. They share nearly everything except a few clothes."

Noah stood. "Boys, there is a box inside the cupboard in the living room that has some toys in it. Why don't you see if there is something you'd like to play with?"

They darted away, happy for the distraction. Clare smiled up at Noah. "Thank you. How did you end up with toys?"

"They were left behind, like these napkins." He held one up. "I think the owners returned East."

"Yes, I remember the family moved back to where they'd come from. And thank you for being so patient with Tim and Leo. I wouldn't know how to explain our marriage to them." She piled up the dishes in the sink and walked to the stove for the full kettle of simmering water there. "You're being so gallant again. I mean, doing so much for us and for no other reason than because it's a good thing to do. It's the Christian thing to do, too. I feel as though I can trust you." She smiled self-consciously, feeling suddenly foolish. "It's as though I can tell you anything."

Noah quirked up an eyebrow, forcing Clare to laugh nervously. "I didn't mean that to sound so silly." Her gaze turned pensive. "But it seems as though I don't have a single secret from you. You've been so patient, while I have run the gamut of emotions, and ended up being resentful that my parents have left us in such a state. Yet, you've been a tower of noble strength." She pulled a comical face and giggled. "Oh, I sound like a woman from those novels my mother used to read!"

Despite her humor, his mouth tightened. "I haven't done anything special."

"That's not true." After pouring some hot water onto the dishes, she set the kettle back on the stove before returning to the fine wooden dry sink. It had a drain hole, too, now plugged with a brand-new wooden-and-rubber stopper.

Removing the wastewater was going to be easy. She remembered, as it was required reading at college, the late Catharine Beecher's rules of the importance of good dishwashing. She shredded some lye soap into the water and set out the tin of wood ashes needed to scrub the fry pan. Then, praying the dish soap wouldn't be harsh on her hands, she plunged them into the full sink.

Only then did she turn back to Noah. "You've done plenty. Look at how much you've helped me and my situation. I've lost my parents and we both know I resented that they were more focused on leaving than what could happen on a dangerous sea voyage. And I'm upset that they've hurt me. It's not right but it's the way I feel." She was trying her best to remain thankful, but it was hard. And she was grateful she could speak what lay on her heart.

"Crossing the Atlantic isn't that dangerous," Noah countered. "Those steamships are the best made. They're strong and sturdy."

Clare began to scrub the dishes vigorously. "Well,

they can't be that sturdy, can they? One of them is lost at sea."

"We don't have all the details yet. They could have just lost an engine."

She forced in a deep breath to calm herself. "I suppose so, but I do appreciate all you're doing for us."

Abruptly, she bit her lip. Noah worked full-time at the Recording Office, and she was sure most of his income was going toward making this ranch viable. Even rescue animals cost money. She'd seen him purchase a big sack of barley in exchange for Turnip. Keeping the ranch afloat until it was viable would take cash.

But now Noah had a family to provide for. Her meager income wouldn't help much. There were clothes and food to buy and lawyer's fees and taxes to pay. There was a late fee attached to the mortgage now, as well. What if the rent she got from the house wasn't enough and her income had to supplement those costs? Would she be forced to get rid of her home? She wasn't ready to sell it yet.

Her heart heavier now, Clare piled the dishes into the rack beside the sink before sprinkling a small amount of wood ash into the fry pan. With more effort than necessary, she began to scrub it.

When the boys' chatter suddenly grew louder, Clare glanced over her shoulder. Noah was already heading into the living room to check on them. She turned back, her attention darting out the small window to the backyard. To the left of her view was the far corner of the paddock. She could see Turnip standing with his back to the house. His ears were pinned back too far to be just listening to the others sharing his paddock. Even from this distance, she could see that he was still skittish, and no doubt resentful himself.

Clare could hear Noah talking to the boys, asking them what they found. She bit her bottom lip. If she resented her parents for abandoning her and destroying all her hopes and dreams, how long would it take Noah to start resenting *her* for getting in the way of *his* hopes and dreams?

*I'm an awful person, Lord. Help me get rid of this terrible feeling.*

She held her breath, but no answer came. No wash of peace, or a hidden word of hope in her heart that could encourage her. Dejected at the reticence, she thrust the pan back into the dishwater to rinse it off.

The evening chores done, Noah helped Clare onto her family's wagon, ignoring the dull throbbing in his shoulder.

"You've been hurt. You don't need to escort me home, Noah," Clare announced as he pulled himself up by his good arm.

"I don't want you on the road with just your brothers."

"It's still light out."

"But not for long. It's a Friday evening and that brings men into town. I don't want you to have to deal with them by yourself."

"And with your sore shoulder, you'll be able to fend them off?" She arched her brows.

"My presence will be enough of a deterrent." He quirked an eyebrow at her as he flicked the reins. "Besides, you're my fiancée now. I'm expected to look after you."

The grim set of her mouth, not to mention her primly folded arms, told him she didn't care for his answer.

Too bad. He was going to escort her home.

It wasn't far into Proud Bend, and having tied his gelding to the back as he'd done when they'd ridden here after work, he would be able to return home before dark. Hopefully, he'd be back in plenty of time to bed down both his horse and Turnip. Keeping his sore shoulder moving was important if he didn't want it to stiffen up.

"I'll bring the boys up tomorrow afternoon," Clare suggested. "That will give them time to pack up their things."

"Don't worry. I'll make sure they're clean for church on Sunday."

"I suggest you clean them up right after supper tomorrow night, and don't let them play the next morning."

"Are they allowed to wash the dishes?"

Clare lifted her brows and glanced behind her at the boys, who had been allowed to bring home a small toy each. "Yes. As soon as any of us was able to reach the sink on a stool we were helping with the dishes." She sighed. "I guess I haven't had the energy to enforce the chores my father laid down. Just don't let them use too much lye soap. It's harsh on their skin."

As they started down the road, he warned, "You can't do everything yourself. What were the chores your father gave them?"

"They had to sweep, help with the laundry and bring in wood."

He looked skeptical. "Can't see them scrubbing clothes."

"They would just hang them up, and then fold them when they were dry. These last few days, I've found it hard to ask anything of them. I guess I was at college for too long. One professor believed children needed stimulation and mischief provided that. I should have stayed home and learned how to discipline them."

She looked resigned. "Instead, I went away and learned I didn't want to be like some of my friends who were quite happy to have family shove them into the role of wife and mother to someone *they* thought was best for them."

He held himself as stiff as possible, trying to keep his face neutral. "What if those friends found a young suitor at school?"

Clare laughed, but it was a short, harsh sound. "Ha! We weren't allowed to talk to men! Not even on a Sunday after church, while the whole congregation stood around chatting. After supper, if there wasn't anything official going on, we were expected to stay in the dormitory and do our assigned duties. After, we could sit on the bench out front, but only with two other women and only until eight in the evening. I used to think the rules the school board had laid down for Miss Thompson were strict until I went to college."

"Three of you on the bench? I imagine that curbed any misbehaviour, not to mention any young man sitting with you."

"It usually did. The rules were to be followed to the letter. Unlike that one professor, Miss Worth felt that discipline helped with our character." She laid her hand over her mouth briefly, and her eyes watered. "But look at me now. Miss Worth would call me a coward."

"You're not." His tone was comforting in the cooling air around them.

"I am. I can't find it in me to force even the simplest chores on my brothers. So they become bored and get into mischief, even if it was supposed to be beneficial." She blinked back tears. "Honestly, I'd make a dreadful mother."

"No, you wouldn't. You're just going through a difficult time right now. I am only helping you." How could she think she wouldn't make a good mother? She cared so much for her brothers and was so patient with them.

Noah thought of his own family. Had he ever been a good son? Would he make a good father figure to Tim and Leo?

His heart squeezed. He wanted nothing more.

Except perhaps a different relationship with Clare.

No. She wouldn't welcome that.

Meanwhile, Clare looked away, off toward the stretch of lowland and foothills. "I shouldn't need you to ride to my rescue like a shining knight from some King Arthur tale."

"Because your mentor, Miss Worth, says you shouldn't?" He attempted to keep the bitter edge out of his tone. "I think she was probably speaking in more general terms, and not to your individual situation. She wouldn't be that unreasonable."

"It was her job to build character. She says we'll need it in due time."

"Why? What's going to happen?"

"We're a new breed of women, she says, and we'll

see great changes in our lifetimes, probably in the next century, but it'll take hard work, so we'd better be trained for it."

"What great changes?"

"Changes like women owning businesses, land, serving in the government."

"You can't even vote," Noah reasoned.

She flared up, turning in the bench seat they shared as the wagon jostled them along. "That will change, as well, and I want to be a part of that, too. I even wrote to my parents about my plans and dreams." She sighed. "Well, you know what happened. Father found the job at the Recording Office for me. He wanted to use my education. Don't get me wrong. I love my job, but a part of me feels as though I'm still being pushed around by men."

"You work for a man. I don't think that will ever change."

Clare went pensive, then deftly changed the subject. "I truly don't mean to sound ungrateful," she muttered. "And I know this is just as overwhelming to you as it is to me."

Noah gritted his teeth. *Overwhelming* wasn't the word he would use. *Exasperating*, maybe.

Yes. His parents had tried to force him to be something he wasn't—like Clare was now being forced to be a wife and mother, something *she* wasn't ready to be—in part because he'd thought of a way to fight back against his parents, who'd expected him to roll over like a submissive dog.

Like Elizabeth had been, allowing her father to arrange every aspect of her future. She wanted all the comforts of the upper class to remain at her disposal and would do anything to ensure that.

Noah felt another pang of conscience. Elizabeth had been his fiancée. He should at least tell Clare about her, but he wasn't sure now was the right time.

He flicked the reins to hurry the horse. So when *would* be the right time?

# Chapter Eight

The next afternoon, as Clare turned the horse and wagon down Noah's short lane, she struggled to throw off the uncertainty she'd felt since he had seen them home last night. Beside her sat Tim and Leo, both silent and still, as if they sensed finality in the whole affair. Behind them were a few boxes, hastily packed with the boys' personal items.

"I want you to do everything Noah asks of you, and not get into mischief," Clare announced. "If it looks like fun, don't do it."

"You've already told us that," Tim pointed out. "Back at home."

"Two times!" Leo held up two fingers.

"Well, it bears repeating."

"I want Ma and Pa to come back," Leo complained softly. "I miss them."

He was sitting closest to her, and she pulled him into a one-armed embrace before kissing his head. He'd pulled off his cap the second he'd climbed into the wagon, and now Clare could smell the soft scent of both little boy and spring sunshine in his hair.

It comforted her, although Leo remained stiff in her arms.

She caught a glimpse of Noah walking around the back of his house, his dog at his side. He was dressed exactly as she'd seen a hundred other cowboys, with pants made from thick denim, wide suspenders and a sturdy cotton shirt with the sleeves rolled up. He had stopped when he'd heard the wagon rattling up his path and now stood tall and strong, with the sun glinting off his dark brown hair. The wind chose that moment to ruffle the wavy locks.

Until now, she hadn't paid the outfit a lick of attention, but today, seeing Noah no longer dressed in his office attire, she found it oddly appealing and felt a curious hitch of her heart.

She looked quickly away, her gaze slamming into the house. The sun beat down on it, one logged side bright, the others dark and cool. As she drew closer, the sun glinted off one window. His home was much smaller than hers was and a thousand times more rustic, yet against the backdrop of Proud Mountain, whose peak was still thick with brilliant white snow, the log house's charm welcomed her. Even now, she could recall the scents of supper and liniment as they mingled with the comforting smell of a warm fire.

Soon, it would be her home. She'd been worried that the boys would hate it here, but it could have easily graced the cover of any of the adventure books Tim and Leo enjoyed. Surely they would end up loving it here.

Would she?

Noah took hold of the horse as she pulled up close to him. It had been an awful week for her, made worse by all the details she'd needed to see to, the appointment with the lawyer Noah had recommended, finding a maid of honor, packing and seeing the haberdasher who also acted as a real estate agent. The list went on and on.

She forced a smile. God had given her this day and this man. She needed to appreciate both. "How is your shoulder?" she asked.

Noah worked it slightly. "Much better. The liniment worked."

"And Turnip?"

He pulled a face. "Not as good. He refused to come into the stable last night."

"Maybe he just needs a bit of time to get hungry or cold, then he'll come in."

Noah said nothing.

"The boys have promised to be good," she offered.

She watched Noah steal a glimpse of Tim and Leo, his expression skeptical as they jumped to the ground. They hadn't really promised anything, but they hadn't announced that they'd planned to act up, either, so she took what she could.

"Clare, I wish things were different," Noah said abruptly.

Her heart plummeted. "What do you mean?"

"Losing your parents."

"I can only take comfort in knowing they're in the arms of Jesus." Clare shifted, turning her attention to Proud Mountain. She didn't feel any comfort, however. Too much anger and resentment lingered. Not very Christian, she knew, and yet, she couldn't seem to shake the torturous emotions. When she looked again at Noah, she couldn't help but wonder how long it would be before they started to resent each other. Noah's noble heart would eventually come to regret all the constant giving.

The desire to end this engagement rose in her, but she suppressed it before blurting out the words. It wasn't the wish for freedom that prompted the thought, nor the fear of more resentment. She looked down at Noah and knew that she didn't want to destroy his giving nature.

Where would that leave her and her brothers? The three of them would be separated. Clare would lose everything important to her.

But to save herself at the risk of turning Noah bitter? She swallowed, and hated that her selfishness was winning.

*Forgive me, Lord.*

"Have you been able to start packing up the rest of your house?" Noah asked, his gruff voice ripping through her thoughts.

She shook her head quickly. "Only the boys' things so far. I have spoken to the haberdasher, as he acts as a rental agent. He said he'll advertise in several prominent newspapers out East that the house is for rent, but he warns it's a slow market right now. People want the land and since they are required to clear it and build on it, anyway, as a condition of acquisition, it's less likely they'll rent in a town." She shrugged, pulling off her gloves. "But I'll try. Some people might think differently."

"You should get your packing done as quickly as possible. You never know. Someone might want it sooner than later."

Nodding, she turned to the boys. "Remember what I said."

They both looked down at the ground. Clare had been away from them before, but it felt too short a time after learning about their parents' disappearance. Her heart hitched. Should she tell Noah that Leo always insisted on a long hug and even longer prayer before climbing into bed? Such a delaying tactic might be viewed with a jaundiced eye by Noah. Should she embarrass both by insisting the routine continue?

Leo looked up. "Will you visit us?"

Her chin quivered, and her vision blurred with tears. Noah stepped forward and took a small bag off the back of the wagon. He handed it to Tim, then another to Leo. "Of course. It's only for a week until we get married. You'll see her tomorrow. Now, go into the house and put these in the spare bedroom. It's the one with the green bedspread. That's going to be your room."

Heads still bowed, the boys trudged into the house. Clare's heart stalled in her throat. "I'm taking them home," she blurted out.

"No, you're not," he answered firmly.

"We'll live in our house. We'll figure something out."

"How? I have a ranch. Remember, this marriage solves your problem, Clare."

"Only the financial aspect. There has to be more to life than that. I need my brothers close and at our home. They're grieving and so am I. Together we can be strong."

"I am already. For all of you."

"That's the problem. Miss Worth said I had character, but look at me. I have no strength. I resent my parents. I want to be noble like you."

"I'm not noble," he muttered.

She waved away his contradiction. "Of course you are. You're self-sacrificing while I still think of the dreams I must give up." She felt her shoulders sag. "I'm going to church tomorrow morning and I feel like such a sinner."

"Then you're in the right place. You're just admitting a feeling, which goes a long way to conquering it, be it anger or jealousy or even resentment," Noah answered, his tone a heavy growl. "You're in the thick of a difficult position."

"I don't want people to think that I'm marrying only because I need you to save me. I should be able to save myself." She sighed heavily. "Don't you think everyone will realize that I'm marrying you to keep my brothers from being taken from me? Will they guess that my father was too short-sighted?"

His jaw tight, Noah asked, "Aren't your brothers enough of a reason?"

Clare wiped her hands across her eyes. "They are. I should be grateful that we can stay together, especially now. But it's not enough for me, and I hate that I think this way! Absolutely hate it! It's more than knowing I'm a sinner. I'm going to church tomorrow feeling like a hypocrite."

"Our church is full of hypocrites."

She snapped her head up at him and gasped. "That's an awful thing to say! They're good people!"

"That's true, but just as hospitals are full of sick people who go to get better, we go to church because we know we're sinners. You've just admitted you are one and you go to church. Does God only want you to go when you're behaving perfectly?"

"He'd never get me in there if that was the case."

"He wants to help you be a better person. Even Jesus said His message wasn't for those who were spiritually healthy, but for those who needed forgiveness. It's the same way now."

"But the Bible talks of how if you have a problem with another person, you are to set your offering aside and go to that person and do your best to fix it."

"Inasmuch as it is possible for you." His expression darkened briefly, and she wondered what was going through his mind. Before he turned away, he said, "Sometimes it's not possible."

Clare felt a wobbly smile come to her lips as she mulled over his words. "I didn't expect a sermon this afternoon, but I definitely needed one. Thank you." She took Noah's hands in hers and was pleased that she'd shed her gloves. His fingers were warm and felt strong as they gripped hers back.

She wanted to draw him into an embrace, too. They were essentially alone up here, not like in town where anyone could watch Noah walk into her home. Oh, they'd start their tongues wagging in malicious whispers.

Only Tim and Leo were in the house. Not even the horse was paying them attention. Clare stepped closer to Noah. He was right about one thing. It didn't matter that she felt unworthy to go to church. In fact, she *should* feel unworthy. She would try all the harder to be a better person.

Like Noah.

"I know I should just work on being grateful for what I have, but it's hard." She tipped her head back and lifted her shoulders in a hapless shrug. "One thing is for sure. I *am* grateful for you."

Then she reached for him.

# Chapter Nine

Guilt stabbed Noah. He didn't want Clare to tell him all her secrets and certainly not tell him he was noble and perfect.

He was neither of those things. He was marrying Clare partly for a reason far removed from her view of him. Yes, mostly, he was saving her from having to surrender her brothers or her home, but a part of him had felt righteous indignation. It had fueled the first flame of this out-of-control fire that had become their engagement.

And yet, to have Clare near him caused his decisions to waver. She was reaching for him and he fought with every fiber of his body the urge to draw her close.

No. He pushed her arms down.

Clare thought *she* was a hypocrite, but he was a worse one. He'd told his parents he would marry only for love, and not because it was convenient for his father and his finances.

Bitterness lingered in his mouth as he stepped away from Clare. She let her hands drop to her sides, hurt flashing over her face for that brief instance.

He pulled a face. He'd hurt her. The urge to plunk her back into the wagon seat raced through him. She should leave, get back to her packing and not let any hurt linger.

It was a good idea. He wouldn't be reminded of all of his mistakes, too, or of Elizabeth back home, the one who'd begged him not to tell anyone who was the real perpetrator of their broken engagement.

He'd told his father the truth, but after having hurt Elizabeth with his rejection, he had allowed her to spread the lie that she'd broken their engagement. She hadn't wanted the embarrassment of being rejected. The lie had been a more acceptable option. Not for the first time did he wonder if his father had talked to Elizabeth. Noah had walked out on both and had never learned if they had even spoken to each other. With the dissolution of their engagement, there would be no reason for the families to talk.

His stubbornness had turned him into a coward.

He looked away, up toward the magnificent vista of Proud Mountain. Clare had just mentioned that the Bible talked of repairing a relationship before worshipping. Since the Bible had added that part, "inasmuch as it is possible" he'd always argued with himself that it was impossible to reconcile with his father. Therefore, Noah had no obligation whatsoever.

But shouldn't he at least tell Clare that he'd once been engaged, but that he didn't want to discuss it? Perhaps not. What would that tell her about him? That he didn't trust her? That he didn't think her worthy of hearing any more of the story?

His stomach ached. He should never have agreed to Elizabeth's lie. He was a far worse sinner than Clare was.

*What am I supposed to do now, Lord? Should I just forget it? Or should I tell Clare and inflict more wounds on a woman I have already hurt? That doesn't feel Christian, either.*

"Go home, Clare. We'll see you tomorrow morning," he announced in a brisk tone. "After church, we'll go back to your house. I can help you pack."

"That's all right. You don't have to."

He frowned. "Don't you want me to help you?"

Clare felt the heat of embarrassment rise within her. "There are a lot of memories, that's all. Some things will need to be given away, too. I'll talk to Mrs. Wyseman and Mrs. Turcot tomorrow before church. They organize the monthly thrift store for charity. Speaking of church, we need to tell Pastor Wyseman to announce our engagement." Her voice hitched. "And my parents' disappearance."

"Are you ready for that?"

She wrung her hands. "I don't want them to think ill of my father. He made a mistake, but he was a good man."

"We'll go in early and meet Pastor Wyseman. He can advise you. Speaking of the house, you can store everything here."

Clare frowned at his house. "You were fortunate to get both land and a house. Yes, I remember when the owners decided this life wasn't right for them. It sat vacant for a long time. I'm surprised that squatters didn't destroy everything."

He followed her gaze as it settled on his house. "The

furniture had been stored in Proud Bend, and yes, there have been squatters, but a bit of elbow grease fixed everything. When I bought the place from the government, I was able to get the furniture back. With the help of my ranch hand, I built the paddock and cleared more land." He paused, gauging her emotions. "I know it's hard to set aside your determination to prove yourself in this world, but let Pastor Wyseman and me help you."

She looked at him with surprise. "Is that how you see me? You must think I'm an awfully stubborn person."

"No. Clare, you don't have to prove anything to anyone."

"I don't?" She swallowed. "I can't help but think that I'll need to prove something after we get married."

"Like what?"

Pain filled her gaze. "My father made a mess of things…and I don't want that to be his legacy. I want to prove that he was also a good man." She studied her hands as if they could solve great mysteries. "I'm still angry at him, and yet, even though it doesn't make sense, I also don't want to share that anger. I don't want others to be mad at him for my sake."

Noah tipped his head to one side. In a strange way, her indignation was all she had left of her father. "If you don't let Pastor Wyseman announce what has happened to your parents, then the rumors will be worse. This way, you can deal with the truth about your father."

"But that's just it. For all his faults, he was a good man."

"He left you in such a disgraceful situation, you have to get married," Noah muttered.

"And that's where I dragged you into my mess." The

set of her mouth and her fast look at him told her she wasn't happy. "And you come out of this all the more noble for your unselfish act."

Noah stepped back. Was she jealous of him? Again, something inside pushed him to tell her the truth. She wouldn't be jealous of him then.

*So, why are you still standing there, saying nothing, Livingstone?*

Before he could speak, Clare let out a long sigh. "Well, I guess it's better than lying to everyone about them. I could never lie. Never."

With that, she walked into the house to help her brothers unpack.

An hour later, after Clare had said her goodbyes, and as they watched her cart disappear, Noah turned to the brothers. "We'll tour the estate, boys," he announced.

"What's that mean?" Tim asked.

Noah laughed, although the sound felt forced. "It means we're going to explore our land. I knew a wealthy gentleman out East who said he did that every evening after supper. Let's go."

The boys trudged along behind him, like reluctant sheep behind a shepherd. At the back of his cleared land, after they'd climbed a trail obviously made by mountain goats, they stopped and turned.

Noah sat on a rock and pointed out Proud Bend in the distance.

"Is that where Clare is?" Tim asked.

"Yes," Noah answered gently. "Can you see the church spire? Your house is just to the left, behind some trees. Clare is inside it."

They all sat on the rock, pondering the view, when

Noah felt a small hand touch his knee. He looked down and found Leo shifting closer to him.

Within a minute, the little boy had climbed up onto his lap. Seconds later, he leaned his head against Noah's chest.

Noah's throat tightened as tears stung his eyes. He could feel little Leo heave a small sob.

"He misses Clare," Tim stated wisely, glancing down at his brother. "And Ma and Pa."

Noah gripped the little boy. "That's a good thing, Leo, really. We'll tell Clare that tomorrow morning. It'll make her happy."

"Clare tucks me in at night, just like Ma used to."

"I will, too, then. I promise. Did you bring a book I can read from?"

Leo nodded. "It's about some boys who go out in the woods at night."

"Then I'll read from it. A whole chapter, if you like."

"But not the scary parts," Leo warned, looking up at him with a fearful expression.

"Never." Noah smiled down at the boy, his heart giving a little flip when he saw a replica of Clare's dark eyes. "You don't want to give me nightmares, do you?"

They all laughed. For a long time, they sat on the rock and watched the land below them, until Noah reluctantly admitted to himself they needed to return.

He didn't want to, though.

The next morning, Noah and her brothers met Clare in front of the church. The boys hugged her as though she'd been gone for weeks, but after glancing at the watch she'd pinned to her coat, Clare knew they didn't have much time. "I spent the evening and half the night packing things. I'm exhausted, so let's get this done with before I drop off to sleep."

Inside, she herded the boys to a back pew and told them to sit there and do absolutely nothing. "Noah and I are going to talk to Pastor Wyseman."

"Are you in trouble?" Tim asked, turning to watch them head into the small vestry.

Noah laughed. With a sharp look toward him, Clare huffed. When they reached the door, she rapped sharply on it.

"Come in."

They walked in to find Pastor Wyseman standing behind his desk. Like his office at home, this one was small and neat and crowded with books. Immediately, Noah said, "We need you to announce the sad news about Clare's parents *and* our engagement."

"Good and bad news at the same time." Wyseman grimaced. "But there's no other option, unless you want to postpone your wedding."

"No!" Clare cringed at the sound of her sharp answer. "There's no other solution. When I was speaking with my lawyer, he felt I had a better chance of keeping my brothers if I was married."

"If need be, I can certainly attest to your characters," Wyseman assured them.

Clare resisted rolling her eyes. She had very little in the way of stellar character, what with all the resentment rolling around inside of her. But only Noah knew of that. She stole a glance at him, but his expression remained inscrutable.

She didn't want the congregation to learn about her

financial woes, either, and therefore sully her father's reputation, especially not before they could even hold a memorial service.

Clare blew out a sigh. To stand here beside Noah and ask for a hurried wedding without explanation, however—what did that suggest about her character? Some would think only of how difficult it was going to be for Clare. Others would drop their gazes to her flat abdomen and wonder if there was another reason.

Heat filled her cheeks. There probably wouldn't be any babies for her. Her and Noah's relationship, not to mention their upcoming marriage, was only one of convenience. As much as the word of the law might allow babies to happen, the spirit of the law whispered to Clare that she couldn't have children with a man she didn't love and who didn't love her.

Yes, it was bad enough she was trapping him in marriage, but to saddle him with more children than her two unruly brothers? That would be cruel.

Clare cleared her throat and tried her best to sound calm and efficient. "We'll worry about getting legal custody of Tim and Leo after the wedding. One step at a time, please. Thank you, Pastor. Like you said, there's no other way around the news. People are going to ask me if my parents are on their way back and I won't lie to anyone."

"Or they'll wonder why we're not waiting," Noah added, "which will raise more questions."

"Hopefully they will see that it's just to help out Tim and Leo," Clare added.

Wyseman nodded. "I will do my best to be as sensitive as possible, but unfortunately I can't control what people think."

\* \* \*

Truer words were never spoken. Half an hour later, Pastor Wyseman made the difficult twofold announcement. People swiveled in their pews, most expressions shocked and sad, but some were not so generous.

Noah drew in a calming breath. He knew Clare would be vilified in some eyes, and he fought the urge to stand up beside her and blurt out that that any of them could find themselves in the same situation that Clare found herself in.

Instead, he gritted his teeth as the protective urge swept through him. He slid his gaze over to his fiancée, just as his hand reached for hers. Her fingers were cold, and he gripped them tightly, pushing her hand down on the hard pew between them so that no one could see the intimate action and jump to even more incorrect conclusions. Yes, they were marrying and yes, it was sudden. However, they didn't owe anyone an explanation.

Abruptly, the service resumed, with Mrs. Turcot starting a hymn on the small organ up front. Everyone rose, offering Clare and him a quiet, all-too-brief moment of peace. The church was warm, the air still and musty, but the pocket of privacy the standing crowd created was welcomed.

Clare clung to his hand, stopping Noah from rising as she shot him a stricken look. "Did you see some of those faces? If you'd handed Mrs. Shrankhof a gavel she'd have passed sentence on me already."

"I'm here," he whispered. "I won't let anything happen to you."

Clare glanced down, but Noah could see her shoulders stiffen and her lips tighten. *She doesn't want to hear that*, he thought with a sinking heart. *It's not a weakness on your part, Clare*, he added silently. *I'm only here to help you stay strong.*

"Thank you." She sighed. Her head dipped farther. "Father wasn't known for his thriftiness, but I, well, I want to tell them all off."

"I know it's difficult. It's confusing to resent him and want to defend him at the same time."

She reached up to furtively swipe her eyes. "Am I being hypocritical? I don't want to be that."

"Perhaps you're afraid this resentment is all you have left of your father. That's why you won't share it. But, Clare, you have good memories, too. You've mentioned that he was also a good man. Remember that and rise above those who want to condemn you."

With a nod and a slightly wobbly smile, Clare stood. Noah followed more slowly. He listened to her slightly off-key singing, and the way she stumbled over some of the words, all betraying her frayed nerves.

And once again, he felt his jaw clench.

*Rise above those who want to condemn you.* The words echoed in his head, convicting him.

No, his situation was different. He was just overly sensitive because he was now intricately involved in Clare's life.

It wasn't until after the service and the strange mix of condolences and congratulations that they were able to thread through the crowd to collect the boys from Sunday school. Clare finally asked her brothers how their first night at the ranch went.

"He made us sit and not do anything all morning," Leo complained.

"For hours," Tim added, his eyes wide.

Noah rolled his eyes. "It took until after nine to get them bathed and cleaned up. Before that we fed the horse then ate breakfast."

"And Turnip?" Clare asked hopefully.

"He still won't come in. With the boys there, I wasn't going to force him."

She looked sad. "I know how he feels. There are days I wish I could refuse to go into my house."

Noah smiled at her as they walked out of the church. Within a minute, they climbed into his wagon. It was already loaded with sturdy boxes ready to be filled and soon they were driving it down the street toward the Walsh house.

Clare looked up at it. "Like now," she whispered, staring up at her two-story home. Noah didn't want to expose Clare to a lifetime of memories while she packed up her parents' effects, but it had to be done. Immediately, she put the boys to work piling wood outside.

"Why don't you start in your parents' bedroom?" Noah suggested gently as she opened the door and he carried some of the boxes upstairs. His shoulder still hurt, but this work could not wait until after he healed. "I'll collect all the photographs and personal items from the living room," he suggested.

She nodded and disappeared up the stairs. He set about taking down the few photographs and one large tintype of people who must have been Clare's grandparents. The afternoon passed slowly. Noah finished his careful packing and as he stowed the boxes into the wagon, he wondered how Clare was making out upstairs.

As soon as he reached her parents' room, he had his answer.

Clare was sitting on a stool in front of her mother's delicate and ornate vanity, weeping quietly.

His heart lurched, the strength of the feeling taking him by surprise. Clare snapped up her head. Hastily brushing aside her tears, she stood. "I'm so sorry. I sat down here and started to sort through my mother's personal things and then, well, I couldn't stop crying."

He stood in the doorway, not sure if he should offer to help. "Take your time."

"No, no, I shouldn't be like this." She held up her hand as she turned away. "There will be plenty of time later for tears, just not now."

While that might be true, if she needed to cry, why shouldn't she?

Elizabeth had cried when he'd told her he wouldn't marry her. Right before she'd turned the tables and demanded he tell the world that she had ended their engagement. She could say anything she liked. He would not marry her simply to line his father's pockets.

But here, Clare's tears touched him in a way that Elizabeth's had not. She demanded nothing from him. She'd merely apologized. She'd lost her parents, not injured her pride. She needed the time to grieve. Time eased all pain, he'd discovered.

He paused. His anger at his father's demands seemed less harsh. The time that had passed since he gave it serious thought had eased the bitterness, but was still short enough for him to be sympathetic toward Clare.

Soon, the lawyer would let her know what was required to declare her parents legally dead. In the meantime, she needed to pack away their things and move out of her home.

Even when she asked him if he was still offering marriage, the tone and attitude was quiet, thankful. *Sad*.

Noah could not tear his eyes from her. This woman would soon be his wife. He gritted his teeth, hating that if he were to offer her comfort, she'd resent him all the more. But how could he stand there and not want to ease her pain? How could he just watch her cry?

He couldn't. She wanted to stand on her own two feet, but right now, she needed to be held. Noah drew her into his arms and held her there, gently, his face brushing against her soft hair and his nostrils filling with some faint, flowery scent that seemed as delicate as her slight frame felt.

The moments passed, and Noah carefully cupped her chin to tilt her head upward. Her eyes were red and swollen and her tears had left pale, whitish tracks down her cheeks. Her nose was red as if she'd been outside in winter too long.

His breath caught in his throat. She was so beautiful.

When she'd started to work at the Recording Office last year, transcribing some damaged ledgers, he'd been the Assistant Recording Officer. She'd been bubbly, always smiling at him, and yet, determination to do her best poured from her with every stroke of her fountain pen.

When he'd been elected Recording Officer, after his predecessor retired, she'd even baked a cake, and everyone at the town hall, including the sheriff even, stopped by for a slice. She'd blushed when she'd offered Noah the first slice.

All through that time and during that celebratory day, he'd been so calm and nothing but polite, trying his best to remain the perfect conservative public official. He'd needed to be. His promotion meant a chance to build his ranch. He'd hired a ranch hand to come in every few days to clear the land and fulfill the requirements of the agreement between him and the state of Colorado, but someday he would hire full-time staff. One day his ranch would run itself.

He shook away the thought. Right now wasn't about him. Clare needed him.

"Noah?" Easing away from him, Clare looked up, her soft, velvety brown eyes glistening. She had eyes like a young fawn.

Noah inwardly grimaced at the foolish description. Sweet-talking was not his strength. What good would it do her anyway? She needed financial assistance, someone to help raise her two brothers, not some sappy man who couldn't even remember his thoughts while holding her.

Outside and below the window, somewhere along the side of the house, her brothers had begun to talk to someone, giving him and Clare a guarantee of privacy. He was alone with her for the moment.

Noah swallowed. Theirs was a marriage of benevolence, offered to give security.

*Offered so he could rail against his parents.*

But in light of Clare's deep grief, his anger suddenly felt shameful and self-indulgent.

Still, for the moment, he could forget everything and stare into Clare's eyes. In his mind, he could easily invent another type of marriage.

The boys' chatter faded away. In fact, all noise faded away as Noah dipped his head down.

Clare blinked up at him, and despite the fact her face was mottled and blotchy, he could think of nothing he'd rather do than take in her beauty. Her lips parted, and a question formed in her expression.

"Would you like me to kiss you, Clare?" He barely breathed out his question.

Her eyes widened briefly, flaring with life in a welcoming way. She pulled in a sharp breath, and her gaze drifted down to his mouth.

Yes, she wanted him to kiss her. His heart pounded fiercely in his chest.

He lowered his head farther, his lips just beginning to brush against hers.

"What on earth is going on here?"

# Chapter Ten

Noah and Clare flew apart, both whirling toward the source of the brusque question. Noah heard Clare gasp.

"Miss Worth!" she cried as she stepped toward the older woman now standing at the threshold to Clare's parents' room. She hastily wiped her face and smoothed her dress. "What are you doing here?"

*And how did you get in?* Noah wanted to add. Then he saw the two boys' heads pop up at the bottom of the railing that skirted the stairs. Ah. They had let her in. Noah had been so focused on Clare, her resplendent beauty and her soft eyes and her desperate need for comfort that he'd willfully pushed aside the world beyond.

He took a step forward to stand slightly in front of Clare. So this was the esteemed Miss Worth, the author of those many sayings on women's conduct that he'd heard repeatedly since Clare began to work at the Recording Office. The older woman stood erect in the doorway, her dark gray bombazine outfit as stiff as her expression. Any buttons or trim that he could see were fashioned from the same material, camouflaging themselves as if to prove that any frivolity or fashion was completely unacceptable.

"I was on my way to the West Coast to visit a niece, and thought I would spend some time with you, Clare. I wanted to know how my star pupil was faring." The last few words were heavy with disappointment.

Clare's mouth hung open for a bit too long, and when she did snap it shut, she forced a smile onto her lovely face. "How nice! I'm just surprised you didn't wire me about it."

"I apologize," Miss Worth answered so briskly that Noah questioned her sincerity. "It was a last-minute decision. I certainly do not want to appear spontaneous. But after I decided, I was unable to telegraph you, as the lineup at the station was unacceptably long and I needed to board my train."

With a back as straight as the lodgepole pines that encircled Noah's ranch, Clare lifted her chin. "Regardless, you're here and I am honored to have you visit."

"Good, then." The woman pulled off her dark gray gloves as her frown deepened. "Now you can tell me why you've been crying and why I have found you in the arms of a man?"

"I'm her fiancé," Noah said. "Noah Livingstone."

"I see. Then you're *not* married yet." Miss Worth's flaring gaze scraped up and down his frame, so harsh he could practically feel the abrasion. He lifted his brows to her but she ignored the action.

"What on earth is going on that you need to forget what I told you about tears?"

"Tears are the weapon of a weak woman," Clare

quoted quietly. "But I must say that my tears aren't a weapon here, Miss Worth."

"Far from it," Noah added. He received a short, scathing look from the older woman for his interjection but kept his expression cool. "Clare has recently lost her parents, ma'am. I was merely comforting her." He refused to be cowed by this domineering woman. He took another step toward her and held out his hand to indicate that they should all leave the room. "It's time for a break. Shall we go downstairs and have some tea? Clare can explain everything to you."

Clare followed behind both Noah and Miss Worth, her heart thudding guiltily. Ahead, Tim and Leo, who'd obviously opened the door to the woman and led her upstairs, scampered down ahead of everyone and, as if sensing something unpleasant was simmering, now thankfully ducked out of sight into the kitchen, an act for which Clare was immensely grateful.

At the bottom of the stairs sat a large portmanteau. For some reason, the sight of the luggage made Clare's heart sink. Of course, Miss Worth would be expecting to stay here. But the house was in such disarray...

"Please make yourself comfortable in the parlor, Miss Worth," she said with brightness she didn't feel. They'd all reached the front hall between the parlor and her father's study. "I'll start some tea."

She cringed as she hurried into the kitchen. She had so little food, having doled it out to the boys in what now felt like thimblefuls. Yes, she had enough tea, she decided as she stoked the fire to reheat the water, but her mentor would want something more substantial after her long train ride.

Then she spotted it. A cake?

Of course. She'd barely registered its existence when they'd come home from church. Now Clare lifted the small card sitting on top. It was from Mrs. Turcot, God bless her. Having learned of Clare's sad news at the beginning of the service, she must have brought it over right after church while Clare and Noah were still dealing with those who offered both congratulations and condolences. Clare never locked her door, so it would be easy enough to slip in and leave it on the table.

She undid the black crepe paper in which the cake had been hastily wrapped. It was a Washington cake. The recipe might be a bit too festive for the occasion, but it didn't matter. Wrapped the way it was, the cake became suitable for a house of mourning.

Clare swallowed. Hadn't Noah told her not to give up hope for her parents' safe return? It felt like she'd given up, and her life was getting more complicated each time she considered what she should or should not feel. Noah had also proposed a solution, quite literally, to the problems Clare now had, all the while telling her not to give up the hope that her parents would make it to Liverpool, England, any day now.

So confusing.

Standing in the center of her kitchen, Clare sagged. What if her parents arrived safely? What would happen to her when they finally returned home? She would be married to a man whose noble act had trapped them both. While hardly illegal, divorce would be considered a smear on both their reputations.

She heard her mentor cough. How on earth was she going to explain all of this to Miss Worth?

*Don't. Simply change the subject.* With that cowardly idea, Clare hurried over to the counter and grabbed the cake. Thankfully, Miss Worth was not a stickler for tradition, despite her austere and conservative appearance. A cake that was traditionally eaten at fine holidays, like Washington's birthday, would not go unnoticed by the older woman, but Clare fully expected her not to be bothered by the less than appropriate timing.

Again, Clare cringed as she thought of what it must have looked like up there in her parents' bedroom. She'd clung to Noah, readying herself for a kiss while her face was a mess from dried tears. And how could she so easily discard her mourning for the shallow comfort of a kiss?

Had she really done that? Clare shut her eyes a moment, trying to answer the question.

No time. Tim and Leo, who'd been sitting quietly at the table as if instinctively knowing the importance of the visitor, watched her intently. While the water was heating, Clare told them to get the good plates and the tea. Within a few minutes, she had sent the boys back outside with orders to stay clean, bribing them with the promise of a piece of cake. Then she threw back her shoulders and carried the tray of refreshments into the parlor.

Miss Worth sat ramrod straight in one of the fine wingback chairs. Noah stood by the mantel, looking as closed off as he had when Clare had come to work the day after his proposal. Both appeared as though they'd just shared a lemon. She set the tray on the low table in front of her mentor before sitting down in the matching chair.

She plastered on her best smile. "How nice of you to visit your niece on the West Coast. I hope she's well."

"Never mind her, Clare!" Miss Worth threw out her hand to indicate Noah. "What's going on? Why is this man here?"

Clare glanced over at Noah, but he offered little help. She swallowed and recounted to Miss Worth what had happened. "My mother's arthritis deteriorated. So my father made arrangements for her to visit a *Kurhaus* in Germany."

Clare pulled in a breath. "Unfortunately, their ship is now feared lost at sea."

She glanced around the parlor, suddenly wondering where she'd placed the telegram. Had she left it at the Recording Office? No, she'd left it on the front hall table. Noah had brought it with him just before he'd first proposed.

Clare's heart hitched at the memory.

"My condolences." Those two words were brief and clipped. Clare knew the woman meant it, but catching a glimpse of her mentor's suspicious glance at Noah, she also knew that Miss Worth expected an explanation for the intimacy she'd witnessed upstairs.

Clare poured tea, spilling only a small amount. "Would you like a piece of Washington cake?"

Miss Worth's cool gaze fell on the cake. "It's a bit late for a Washington cake? Isn't Mr. Washington's birthday in February?"

"Well, yes, one of my church's parishioners had made the cake for her own family, but after she found out about my parents, she brought it over. Surely a raisin cake isn't reserved only for Washington's birthday?"

Miss Worth's mouth a grim line, she made a low, short hum, the tone of it suggesting the idea of cake was simply too frivolous for any occasion. So much for guessing the woman didn't stand on ceremony. "I no longer eat leavened bread or sweetened cakes," she announced. "I have learned that the body's digestion works best with a diet of only boiled vegetables and meat. But I will have a cup of tea. No milk or sugar, thank you. The food I have had to endure on the train trip has left me feeling poorly."

With shaking hands, Clare served tea, and standing, she cast a long look at Noah. When she handed him a piece of cake and a cup of tea, he brushed his hands across hers. The small smile and nod he offered were meant to encourage her. She felt heat rise into her face and hoped her mentor wouldn't notice.

"Thank you, Clare," he said crisply, setting the teacup on the mantel and lifting the fork to take a hearty bite.

"Mrs. Turcot has made this cake with a great deal of love," Clare murmured. "She often has visitors on Sunday, so it was kind of her to sacrifice her dessert. I expect she realized what a difficult time I am dealing with."

"Which is also not the time for tomfoolery," Miss Worth reminded them. "What started that nonsense upstairs?"

Noah set down his plate. "Do you really want to know, Miss Worth?"

The older woman colored slightly. "I want to know why my star student is engaged. When did it happen? Have you set a date?"

Clare felt heat in her cheeks increase. She couldn't lie, but to tell the truth…

"We're going to be married on Friday."

"And your parents left before your wedding?"

Clare cleared her throat. "No. We became engaged after I learned of their ship's disappearance. Let me explain. I have a full-time job at the Recording Office. Mr. Livingstone is the Recording Officer. It was there that I received a telegram about my parents' ship. That day, I realized that there were outstanding bills to pay and that I could lose both my brothers and my house. Since my salary cannot stretch that far, Mr. Livingstone has suggested a solution."

"A compromise." Miss Worth tossed a critical look toward Noah, who, as far as Clare could see, allowed it to deflect off him like rain off a cowboy's long duster.

"A sensible solution that will enable me to care for my brothers as my parents would have wanted. As a married woman, I will be in a better position to gain legal custody of them." Clare kept her words low and calm, although her heart pounded. She fought for the right words that Miss Worth would appreciate. "To do as my parents would have wished. I also plan to rent out this house in order to generate the income I will need to pay my bills."

"A successful woman is a strong woman," Miss Worth quoted. "And a strong woman is one who has enough discipline to manage her finances by herself. Our needs must be simple, Clare. It's our wants that complicate matters. We must make do with the very basics and prove to the world that we are not frivolous."

"Clare has two young brothers to consider. By respecting her parents' wishes, she's proving she isn't in any way frivolous." Noah smiled suddenly, but Clare could see that it didn't reach his eyes. "Miss Worth, do not be harsh with Clare. She has learned self-sacrifice from the best."

Tension crackled through the room, and Clare held her breath. While Noah's words were diplomatic, his tone held an edge as sharp as the filet knife in the kitchen. She dared a glance toward Miss Worth, fully expecting the woman to leap to her feet and be thoroughly insulted.

Instead, the woman colored. Until today, Clare had never seen the older woman's skin anything but white. With a hint of blue from the spider veins.

Of course, she thought belatedly. Miss Worth had been complimented. Who was she to deny his words?

Clare bit her lip. Miss Worth was definitely unused to flattery and yet, if Clare was reading the woman's expression correctly, she was just human enough to appreciate the accolade. Or had the train trip here dulled her usual severity?

Perhaps Clare should better explain her dire situation, for surely the spinster had never experienced anything like this.

However, after careful consideration, she held back. That would leave her father open to criticism. Surely, there were enough tongues wagging this afternoon. Clare didn't need Miss Worth to add to the numbers.

It would be better to let the subject drop. Noah had handled Miss Worth beautifully, defended Clare without putting her mentor on the spot emotionally.

Yet, not once did Noah mention caring for her. They were simply two people sorting out a problem.

Something cold dropped into her stomach.

"What of Clare's job?"

"What of it?" he asked.

"She's to be married. Which means she will be expected to retire from her job." As Miss Worth lifted her chin, there was a note of challenge in her tone.

Slowly, Noah slid his gaze toward Clare. Again, she held her breath. Yes, most women retired from outside work once they married. She'd even brought up the matter, but it had yet to be settled.

"The woman at the general store is married," Noah said.

"Is the man she married the owner of that store?"

"What difference does that make?"

"You know perfectly well the difference it makes, Mr. Livingstone," Miss Worth countered. "They are partners in their business. Yours is a government office."

"Clare is a modern woman," Noah countered. "I have no desire to see her pushed into old-fashioned notions like that."

Miss Worth's expression flared. "Thrice you have called her by her Christian name and once I have caught you in a position where it appeared you were taking advantage of her so-called modernism. A gentleman would never do that. Not even her fiancé."

"In that case," Noah answered tightly. "I should take my leave. Even with as esteemed a chaperone as you, I have no desire to risk sullying my fiancée's reputation."

He nodded to both of them. "Good day, ladies."

With a sinking heart, Clare watched him stride from the room.

## Chapter Eleven

Noah shoved on his Stetson as he slammed the front door closed. From the corner of his eye, he caught a glimpse of Leo peeking at him from behind the tree that marked the boundary between the Walsh house and its neighbor. But he didn't feel like telling the boy he would return for him and his brother. He didn't feel like doing anything but telling off Miss Worth, which was why he left.

The woman didn't even want a piece of the cake given with love and charity. She certainly did live according to the austere guidelines she doled out like penny candy. At least the boys would get a decent-sized piece later.

His steps slowing, Noah felt his jaw tighten. That was probably the only food Clare had in the house. Last night, the boys ate like ravenous wolves and it had been easy for him to coax from them the details of what they'd been eating lately.

Clare had been rationing their food.

Noah paused. He could make a sharp left turn and

head to the parsonage to ask Pastor Wyseman if he could put together a hamper for Clare's immediate needs, but he stopped.

Clare was his fiancée now and his responsibility. Benevolence should be reserved for those with no one to help them. Noah could afford to feed her and her brothers. The general store would help him.

Just as he reached his wagon, he slowed his steps. His own frugality this past year had allowed him to save enough money to hire a ranch hand. It would also allow him to buy some foodstuffs that he could have delivered immediately to Clare, in time for supper with Miss Worth.

A short, humorless smile flickered onto his features as he climbed onto the wagon's seat. Because of his own austerity, he would be able to feed a woman who expected all women to be austere so as not to rely on men. Clare might enjoy the irony, although not today.

When he reached the general store, his heart plummeted. Of course. It was closed on Sundays. His mind had been so focused on the difficulties Miss Worth had caused that he'd completely forgotten what day it was.

Noah grimaced. He appreciated the day of rest, but Clare had no food nor money to take Miss Worth out for a meal, if any decent place existed in Proud Bend. Yes, they had a small pastry shop, one that had been opened earlier this spring by a young couple from out east. They prepared simple meals, but their focus was on baked goods.

They were also closed.

Noah walked down through the nearby alley, between the haberdashery and the saloon. At the end, he turned right and put his back to the saloon until he reached the rear entrance of the general store. A young boy was sitting on the back step, whittling a stick.

"Are your parents home?"

The boy nodded and jumped up. A few moments after disappearing into the back of the general store, which Noah knew housed the living quarters of the family, the boy's father appeared. Knowing the man through church, Noah quickly relayed his problem, and asked if there was anything he could get to tide Clare over.

"I'm not supposed to open on the Lord's Day," the man explained. "But if I give you what you need, you can pay me tomorrow. I won't exchange money on Sundays."

"Fair enough," Noah said, reminding himself to send the money first thing in the morning, with a tip for the man's inconvenience.

Inside the store, Noah ordered half a barrel of beef, a large slab of bacon, which he chose himself for its meatiness, potatoes, even though they didn't look that good this time of year, plus a generous selection of other equally sad-looking vegetables because Miss Worth ate no flour or sugar. Still, thinking of the boys, he did add flour, sugar, oil and tinned fruit to the order. And soap.

On an afterthought, he chose a bundle of stick candy. With a smile, knowing Noah from the church, the owner ordered his son to box everything immediately. Noah was grateful and said as much before taking his leave. Now he needed to get it inside Clare's house before she returned to the kitchen to scout out something for supper.

The temptation to have it delivered grew in him, but he could hear Miss Worth now pointing out that Noah Livingstone wasn't man enough to do it himself.

He was man enough, all right.

Why was he rising to an imagined provocation? For that matter, why was the woman so difficult? As Clare's future husband, wasn't it his responsibility to care for her and her brothers? Wasn't that the Christian thing to do?

Half an hour later, after Noah had retrieved his wagon, loaded it and returned to the Walsh house, he parked on the far side of the parlor.

The boys were playing outside and both stopped to peer at him. "Come help me bring these in, boys," he said to them.

"What do you have?" Leo asked.

"Food. Lots of it. I bet you're hungry, too."

"Oh, yes! But Clare promised us cake."

Tim's eyes widened when walked up to peer in the wagon. "What's in there?"

"Meat, vegetables, oil, tinned food and flour. Everything Clare will need to fill you up." He thought of adding that there was also stick candy and sugar, but guessed that the boys would ask for those items first. Let Clare discover them and dole the treats as needed.

"Will we have food like this when we come to your house?" Leo asked, his face lit with hope.

Noah smothered a laugh. As long as he kept his pantry full, Leo would accept his new home. And with a swallow, Noah admitted to himself that he would like that very much.

Tim eased open the back door that led to the kitchen. Both he and Leo quietly helped Noah unload the food into the pantry. They took away the empty beef barrel for return to the general store. Through the closed door that led into the hall and eventually to the parlor, Noah could hear Miss Worth's booming voice lecturing on something about education and training. Clare's answer was muffled, but the conversation told Noah neither woman had heard the delivery.

Miss Worth was a determined woman, he thought, searching his mind for a word that could describe her in the most Christian way possible. He couldn't find one.

"Stay quiet and let your sister have a nice visit with her friend," he told the boys hastily.

"I don't like her," Leo announced far too loudly. "She told me I shouldn't be climbing trees in my good clothes."

"Shh! She's just thinking like an adult," Noah chided softly. "And you shouldn't be trying to get your good clothes dirty and ripped."

"I wasn't trying. Sometimes, it just happens."

A tattoo of footfalls marching closer drew Noah's attention from the young, precocious boy. He quickly shut the pantry door. The door into the hall swung open and wide-eyed, Clare peered in. "I heard Leo." She gaped at Noah. "I thought you had left." Her mouth shut into a thin line as her brows pressed together. "Or was it just a ploy so you didn't have to talk to Miss Worth?"

"No, it wasn't a ploy, although I had to leave before I did say something unchristian." He grimaced, hating that he even felt that way. "Come to think of it, I need to take the boys home with me. May I take them now?"

* * *

Relief skittered through Clare for the briefest of seconds. Then she cleared her throat. "That's probably a good idea. Boys, go with Mr. Livingstone. If I have the opportunity to come by later, I will."

"There's no need." Noah knew he had the boys' school clothes and tomorrow morning's routine would be much the same as this morning. Besides, Leo and Tim would be hungry and would no doubt announce any second that they wanted some of the food Noah had brought. No need to embarrass Clare any further.

"Let's go, boys," Noah announced crisply. He nodded to Clare but it was brief. "We will see you tomorrow. I'm sure Miss Worth won't insist you take the day off."

Clare smiled. Noah could already predict Miss Worth's words. "She would never deny me an opportunity to work." She felt a bit more relaxed all of a sudden, the first time since she'd received that awful telegram. Noah was taking the boys, though, so she wouldn't be sitting in the parlor wondering what mischief they were getting into. "Thank you. But keep an eye on them, especially around things like lamps."

"I shall. We need to check on Turnip and unhook and brush down my horse. We may even take a walk."

Noah stared at her for a moment, and in that time, Clare felt her heart trip up. Was he going to kiss her? Even on the cheek? His striking blue eyes lingered on her face, and she found herself holding her breath. Mercy, did she want him to kiss her? Like they'd almost done upstairs?

"Come on, then!" It was Leo, ready, as always, for

the next adventure and not in the least bit aware of the awkward attraction. "I want to eat lunch."

Noah's expression flared. "We'll eat as soon as we get to the ranch, I promise." With that, he nodded to Clare. She watched him make a hasty departure. As she shut the back door, she frowned. As much as she might appreciate her brothers not demanding the cake she'd promised them, she couldn't help but wonder why Noah was so anxious to leave. Miss Worth? Her mentor could certainly intimidate even the most stalwart of people, and Clare was sure the woman could stop a battalion of hardened soldiers with just one sharp look.

She hadn't considered Noah a coward, however.

Standing in the center of her kitchen, Clare worked her jaw and could feel herself pulling an unladylike grimace. Noah had slipped in the back door. Why? To retrieve Tim and Leo? What had he said? '*Come to think of it,*' as though the idea had been an afterthought, something that had occurred to him only after he'd completed another task. Such as what?

She glanced around the kitchen in dismay. Miss Worth expected to stay here, but what on earth would she feed the woman?

Then she spied it. A small sack of something sitting on the floor near the pantry door. She didn't recognize it, and she had long since memorized the contents of her pantry. After throwing open the small room's door, she felt her jaw go slack at the sight greeting her. Tins of food, baking needs, even some fresh vegetables, abounded in front of her. The lid on the beef barrel sat slightly askew, a position she would never leave it in. Cured beef could handle a bit of air, just not the flies.

She lifted the sack at her feet to find it filled with coffee beans. The aromatic scent drifted up into her nostrils.

She set it on the shelf beside the tea tin and walked over to lift the barrel lid to peer inside. It was half-full of preserved meat. Sealing it properly, she glanced around. On the shelf above eye level were more tins, a small, glimmering white sugarloaf, one that probably cost a small fortune, for the whiter the sugar, the more expensive it was. There was also an unfamiliar jug of molasses. Even a thick slab of meaty bacon, cured and ready to slice.

All delivered on a Sunday? Noah had enough influence in town to get Mr. Doyle to open his general store, although the man had done so before for emergencies. She would have to pour the molasses into her own jug and return his. She turned her attention back to the barrel and noticed that Noah had swapped the old one for a new one.

She had enough groceries to last weeks. Touched by his generosity, she blinked several times. Noah had filled her pantry! He'd recognized the need and jumped to help. What Clare had thought was impossible, Noah had gone out of his way to resolve.

"Is there a problem? Didn't we hear your brothers?"

Blinking rapidly, Clare spun. Miss Worth stood just beyond the pantry entrance, her expression stern.

"No. And yes," she answered hastily. "I mean, Mr. Livingstone returned to pick up the boys. He's keeping them while I prepare the house for rental."

Miss Worth walked forward and peered into the pantry. Clare held her breath, fully expecting her mentor to somehow guess that he'd also delivered the groceries, and on a Sunday, at that.

"So we have no need to make them supper?" Miss Worth asked primly. "It looks like it's just the two of us. We should get started then. I haven't had a decent meal in days, and frankly, for a while there, Clare, I wondered if all you had to eat was Washington cake."

Still staring at Miss Worth, Clare clamped down on her mouth to stop from confessing that indeed that was all she'd had. She didn't want her mentor to know Noah had saved the day, but she also didn't want to sound as though she was dressing down her mentor by pointing out one of Noah's finer qualities. All she could hope for was that Miss Worth saw the value in this full pantry.

Clare respected Miss Worth. But since the woman was now so careful with her diet, eating only vegetables and plain meat, all thoroughly cooked and washed down with weak tea, she doubted her mentor would see the value in *all* the food. Clare wasn't sure if she herself knew the full cost.

"You don't need to help with supper, Miss Worth. I'm sure you must be exhausted."

"Nonsense. I've been sitting for days. The only bit of exercise I was able to get came when the train stopped. Besides, I don't expect you to wait on me like I'm some high-and-mighty lady." She quickly shed the jacket that matched her skirt, hung it up on the hook behind the back door, and then pushed up the long sleeves of her modest blouse. "I intend to pull my weight. Let's get started, shall we? What kind of vegetables would you like to have tonight?"

Before long, Miss Worth was peeling the carrots Clare had discovered, leaving Clare to prepare the meat and providing ample time for her to mull everything over. Noah had disapproved of Miss Worth's opinions, but still had the generosity to think of the older woman and purchase all these vegetables at the high price they'd be at the end of winter. Had he done this for the sole purpose of showing Miss Worth how good he was?

No. He'd have made sure both women saw the delivery, but Clare was sure he hadn't expected her to catch him. The pantry door was shut tight, but it was rarely so. He must have secured it just before she walked in.

Or was the irony of providing for Miss Worth after they'd shared such terse words too much to resist?

Again, no, she thought. He'd bought it all because the need was there. Still, she hated that she didn't even know her fiancé enough to answer that question.

Clare bit her lip. She would eventually know her husband, but right now, all she could feel was that same warm, heart-wrenching emotion. What he'd done was incredibly touching.

She swallowed. How was she supposed to stay independent while Noah was stepping up and saving her all the time?

She was so ungrateful. Noah was being kind, and she should be thankful she had him to lean on.

It was certainly compelling to have him.

She threw off the unsettling feelings. They would do her no good. Slicing the cured meat thin so that it would cook quicker, Clare knew they'd be able to get a decent meal on the table in less than an hour. Thankfully, Miss Worth cut the root vegetables into fine cubes for faster boiling. She announced that one shouldn't waste wood nor heat a house that was in mourning. Since the older woman avoided flour, Clare had stirred together a small rice pudding, with only a scraping of the new sugar cone to sweeten it, and slipped it into the oven to cook while the meat simmered in a frying pan.

She stepped into the pantry to return the sugarloaf and found a small sack of raisins. She lifted it, but paused. Although her mother had taught her to toss in a handful of dried fruit into rice pudding, Clare decided against it, lest Miss Worth find the dessert too rich. Besides, it would be nice to make a raisin cake for Noah at some point.

Setting the sack down, Clare spied a small roll of brown paper tucked in behind. She pulled it out.

Two candy sticks.

Noah had bought some candy for the boys no doubt, as Clare didn't expect he'd thought that she and her mentor would enjoy sucking on them after supper.

"What's that?"

Clare looked up. Miss Worth had finished her task and was wiping her hands on a towel as she looked down at what Clare held.

"Candy sticks. I just found them."

Miss Worth clicked her tongue. "They're a waste of money and hardly good for anyone."

"They're just a treat," Clare reminded gently.

"Given to children to bribe them to stay quiet." The older woman shook her head. "We need to teach children to sit still and concentrate on behaving."

Staring at the candy sticks, Clare said nothing more. Miss Worth hadn't had to deal with Tim and Leo. Even she had not yet found the special trick that would result in her brothers staying calm and obedient. She doubted it existed. Miss Worth was simply a childless spinster with little experience with small boys.

Had Noah bought these so that Clare would be able to bribe them?

Regardless of the answer, Noah had again thought of everything.

As Clare had noted many times in the past, she could reconcile Miss Worth's ideas on child rearing with her other professor's more liberal advice. Professor Cullen, an older, grandfatherly man, would often say children needed the freedom to speak their minds and be allowed to get into mischief. He believed that the outspoken, curious child would grow to become strong and independent, exactly what the United States needed. Strong, independent children were good for this country. Clare knew he'd fathered ten children who'd then given him over twenty grandchildren so far.

She pushed the treats back in behind the dried goods, with no desire to tell Miss Worth that Noah had bought these. He was already a black sheep just by proposing to Clare.

Oh, dear. Is that how she saw him, too?

"I promise there will be no bribing them," she assured her mentor.

Still, Clare's conscience pricked at her. Who was she trying to fool? She had already tried to bribe Tim and Leo with Mrs. Turcot's Washington cake. She hastily rearranged the tinned goods so that the candy was hidden further.

Her gaze dropped down to the larger sacks of root vegetables. Noah disapproved of Miss Worth's sharp opinions and yet, he had gone out of his way to provide all the food that they so obviously needed. Indeed, he'd purchased extra vegetables as Miss Worth had already announced that she avoided all flour and baked items as she now considered them unhealthy.

What *was* unhealthy was a marriage like the one Clare and Noah were about to have. If it were only loneliness, she would have more readily accepted the reason for marriage. Instead, a financial crisis that left her resenting her own beloved father, then feeling guilty and convicted for it. That had been her reason.

Yes, getting married would help her adopt her brothers, but right that moment, Clare realized with growing sadness, resentment and fear had provided most of the fuel for her decision.

Fear. Selfish fear.

Maybe she should do as Miss Worth always advised. Buckle down, live frugally, work hard and be fearless. Instead, she'd given in to the easiest solution and accepted a proposal from a man who was far too noble and unselfish for her.

How was she going to get through the days, knowing she was the exact opposite?

# Chapter Twelve

*You're selfish*, Noah told himself. *Keeping your secrets, allowing Clare to believe you are noble and honorable. Even your attempts to correct her were feeble and cowardly.*

*You're a liar, too, for allowing a lie to stand was as bad as anything Elizabeth might have said to people after you left.*

He flicked the reins to encourage the horse to a trot, and the wagon jostled over the ruts made a few weeks ago when a long spell of wet weather had turned the roads into muddy soup for days on end. After that, the air cleared and dried and deep ruts remained. Beside him, Leo flopped back and forth and received a push from his brother for his exaggerated antics. Leo shoved him back.

Immediately, Noah remembered the delicate photograph frames and special glass ornaments he'd packed in the boxes that sat behind him.

As soon as they reached the less used trail that led to his house, the ground smoothed. Noah wordlessly took advantage of the opportunity. He stood and deposited himself between the boys. The brothers went still, knowing they'd been caught.

Perhaps it was a good thing that he'd taken the boys with him, leaving Clare to visit with her mentor. Tim and Leo would keep his mind and body busy, as they'd done last night. Keep his mind from constantly reminding him that all those good deeds he'd done for Clare would never negate the fact that he was the least noble person in Proud Bend.

"Why did you buy all that food for Clare and not us?" Leo asked as they closed in on the house.

"She needs it. We don't."

"Aren't you going to feed us?" Tim asked, his tone anxious.

"Of course I am." Noah pulled to a stop between his small ranch house and the stable. He turned to the boys. "But first, give me your jackets."

"What for?" Tim asked.

"I'm going to hang them in the stable. I want Turnip to get used to you. If he smells your scents, and nothing happens, he'll learn to be calmer around you."

The boys peeled off their jackets but stayed out of the stable while Noah hung them up on hooks beside Turnip's stall. The old pony had refused to come in again last night, but Noah could see him through the open door to the large corral. He was watching them cautiously. With the clear sky and cooler weather, the animal would soon want to return to his warm stall. Noah was sure of that.

After unhitching his horse, Noah led the boys, each loaded with a box suitable for their size and strength, into the kitchen. He had enough food left from last night to tide them over until supper. In the cellar storehouse, he had a large, whole chicken hanging there ready to cook. He'd originally planned to cook it tomorrow so he and his ranch hand could have a good meal when the man showed up on Tuesday, but circumstances had changed. Instead, he dressed it and stuffed it into the Dutch oven to cook for supper while the leftovers were heating on the stovetop.

With extra griddle cakes he could cook quickly, he should be able to fill up the boys enough to allow everyone to have something to eat for a few days.

The brothers helped Noah, and he was glad for the distraction. They chattered about all the things boys enjoyed: wild animals and the fast horses they'd seen; the sheriff and his identical twin brother whom everyone thought was him, even the dogs that roamed around town; and that little girl from school who wasn't allowed to get dirty.

As they sat down, Noah reminded them they all needed to pray. Tim shut his eyes lightly, while Leo clasped his hands together and slammed shut his eyes so firmly, a frown appeared.

Suppressing a smile, Noah prayed. It was short, focusing on gratitude for the meal. After he said amen, Tim peered at him. "Are our ma and pa in heaven?"

Noah's hand froze as he leaned over the table to serve the beans. "Yes."

"How is God going to find them if they are in the ocean?"

"God sees everything. You know that."

"Did he see when Leo was pushing me in the cart?"

"Yes."

"I didn't hurt you, Tim!"

"Pa wouldn't have let you do that."

As Leo opened his mouth to refute it, Noah held up his hand. "That's enough. Just don't do it again. One of you could get hurt or fall off the cart."

Tim's eyes narrowed. "So what?"

Noah finished dishing out the food, suspecting the boy was testing him. "Tim, you may not believe this, but I do care what happens to you."

Tim's expression turned skeptical, but he said nothing. Noah drew in a breath, trying to sort out what to say. Finally, after a quick prayer for help, he said, "Your mother and father would do anything for you. As would Clare. Because she loves you. I care for you, too."

"Do you love Clare, too? Matthew MacLeod says you have to love a person to marry them."

Noah swallowed. He could feel both boys staring at him. "I care as much for Clare as I care for you." He smiled and chuckled to himself. Was he adopting Clare's newfangled ideas on raising children?

"Why are you laughing?"

Noah quickly cleared his throat. "I'm thinking of how I can prove to you that I care. Let's see. Food? Got that. Bedtime stories? Got them. What's left? Putting you in your room because you acted up on the cart?"

They both stared with stricken expressions.

Noah burst out laughing. "Eat up, boys. I'll let you go this time."

It was nearly suppertime when the pounding of a horse's hooves caught their attention. Tim and Leo abandoned the small chores he assigned them to race to the window.

"It's Clare!" Tim called out. Both boys tore out of the house.

A few minutes later, and surprised to see her there, Noah helped Clare step down from her family's small wagon. She wore a different outfit than her Sunday best, but the skirt and tailored jacket were simple and modest in design and color.

Her eyes were puffy and her cheeks were stained with whitish tracks of tears. Noah knew she'd been crying on her fifteen-minute ride out there. The boys hugged her as if she'd been gone for years while Noah simply frowned. "You've been crying," he said quietly.

"Just thinking about my parents," Clare whispered back over the tops of the boys' heads. She shook her head as if to ask him to say nothing more about it. "I know it's almost suppertime, but I wanted to come out here before then."

Noah squeezed her arm. Then with a glance into the wagon, he said, "You came alone."

"Miss Worth is sleeping," she explained. "We had a late and rather large lunch and I am sure she didn't sleep on the train. She's exhausted so after she went upstairs I decided to bring over what I'd managed to pack up of my parents' things. I also found some more clean work clothes for the boys. You may need them."

She gave the boys one more hug and set them away from her. "I also want to thank you for all the food," she said to Noah. "You were an absolute answer to prayer, especially buying the extra vegetables."

Noah looked away, answering gruffly, "It was nothing, really."

He glanced back at her. She looked as uncomfortable as he suddenly felt. When their gazes accidentally bumped into each other, she quickly scanned the sky. "The wind is picking up." She peered down at the boys. "Where are your jackets?"

Tim pointed to the stable. "Noah put them in the stable."

She gasped. "You two didn't roll in manure, did you?"

"I want Turnip to get used to their scent," Noah explained. "I figured if he has a chance to smell their jackets overnight, meeting them again won't be so difficult." He looked pointedly at the boys. "But we need to behave around him. Understand?"

They nodded solemnly. Clare rolled her eyes. "Oh, they understand. But do they listen?"

"They will, won't you, boys?" He gave them a knowing look. "Now, let's help your sister." Noah walked to the back of the wagon. He lowered the gate and took the smallest box to give it to Leo. A sack of clothes he gave to Tim. Soon they were all carrying in something from Clare's house.

"Where are you going to put all of this?"

"I have a large wardrobe in the boys' room. We'll get it all in there."

Half an hour later, after Noah had unhooked her family horse and led him into the corral where Turnip and his horse grazed, Clare inspected the careful storage of her family's things. Noah watched her. When she looked up, her glistening eyes wore a hollow look.

He turned to the boys. "Go finish your chores, boys. If you're good, we'll have a treat."

After Tim and Leo left, Clare murmured, "I found the candy sticks you bought, but I didn't bring them. Miss Worth doesn't believe that children should be bribed. They should be taught discipline."

"I agree, but bribery is one thing, rewards are another. That's why I brought two of them home with me."

Clare shut the wardrobe doors and turned the small skeleton key. "Ah, but a little bribery now and again can't hurt. Don't tell Miss Worth I said that. She doesn't know what it's like living with Tim and Leo."

He remembered hearing Miss Worth's booming voice and grimaced. "Don't you want another lecture?"

"No, it actually feels a bit shameful to disagree with her." She looked decidedly resigned. "She's been good to me. When I first arrived at college, I was absolutely lost. I had no idea what to do or where to go, and she took me under her wing."

"You must not have been the only lost soul at college."

"Oh, I wasn't, but I think Miss Worth saw something in me. The same day that I arrived, I stood up to an older student, a woman who liked to throw her weight around a lot. I didn't like the way she was humiliating another young woman for not knowing where to go. I was the same way. When Miss Worth learned of what I did, she must have decided I had what it took to be her prize student."

"You *are* a strong woman."

Clare's expression clouded. "Not strong enough, I expect. Miss Worth doesn't believe I should marry. She thinks I should just work harder, live more frugally and fight to keep the boys." Her eyes glistened. "I have a confession, Noah. I don't think I am *that* strong."

"You are."

Clare's skeptical look suggested a different opinion.

"You're thinking of this morning at church?" he asked.

She seemed to be pondering whether to speak. "Most there are loving and kind. Take Mrs. Turcot for instance. She heard the sad news and did something. She'll rejoice later when I get married because I saw the same thing when Victoria married Mitch. But let's face it. Some of the parishioners can be critical. They will hear that we're having a quick wedding and think it's for a disreputable reason. I know I shouldn't say that, especially about my fellow churchgoers, but it's true."

"Let them think what they like. They'll learn the truth eventually."

"In the meantime, it hurts. I know I should learn to rise above it, as you said in church, but I felt so embarrassed when some people assumed the worst." Clare looked away. "If they knew what my father did, they'd be critical toward him. I don't want that, either."

Again, Noah felt his ire rise. But this time, it was tempered by compassion. Yes, he thought with wonder. Compassion for Clare and all she was going through. Getting mad would do her little good.

He stood still a moment, allowing his anger to cool. When it had done so, he said, "No one has the right to criticize you or your father. Yours is a unique, complicated situation."

"It's not a situation. It's a mess." With sagging shoulders, Clare grabbed his arm. "Miss Worth doesn't seem to understand, and she isn't known for her sympathy anyway. But I can't blame her. She's never had to experience what I'm going through."

Clare's hand lingered on his arm, and the urge to draw her into an embrace rose within him. However, with emotions running like a river in spring, he knew they didn't need to muddy the waters with confusing attraction.

He felt something icy settle in his chest. Regret?

From the kitchen, he could hear the boys finishing their chores. His thoughts went immediately to their misbehaving, of Clare's notion that they were merely missing their parents and acting out their grief. She was trying her best to understand them.

Clare leaned closer and he thought of how lovely her dark, velvety eyes looked. How flawless her skin was. Would it feel soft to the touch? She said, in a hushed tone, "If Miss Worth brings up any of this, please don't say anything. She's been good to me in her own unique way, and I don't want her to think that I don't appreciate all she's done."

He swallowed. Another secret. Elizabeth had asked him to lie about who'd ended their engagement, so that she would not be seen as a spurned woman. He'd agreed not to contradict it because he had been leaving and had felt guilty. It had been wrong, and he'd since asked God for forgiveness, but the request lingered like sour milk in his stomach.

He should do something about the lie he'd allowed Elizabeth to concoct and spread, but he was nearly two thousand miles away and had used the distance as an excuse.

*Lord, how am I to correct this lie?*

Now Clare had asked him to keep another secret, and as understandable as it was, the idea still unsettled him.

"I appreciate all you've done, Noah. All your sacrifices and even the wisdom in handling Miss Worth. I know we'll have a unique marriage, but I don't think sacrifice and honesty will be a problem."

Chilled suddenly, Noah stepped back. To tell Clare the truth would betray his promise to Elizabeth. But if he confided what Elizabeth had requested, *that she had ended their engagement*, he'd be lying to Clare.

He couldn't do that, either.

Clare had no idea how this life together was really starting.

*A life together?* Neither had even told the other if they liked each other, let alone said that they would love and whatever else Pastor Wyseman would have them promise in their vows.

"I'm not noble. Nor am I self-sacrificing," he muttered. "I've told you that before."

"You're being modest," she murmured back.

He cleared his throat. "I'm hardly that. So don't say it." His tone sounded clipped and critical, even to his own ears.

Clare stilled. Noah's tone had chilled, like when the winds descended from the north after a warm day in the middle of winter, and everything around them froze solid.

"Don't start thinking I'm someone who goes around saving people," Noah bit out. "I'm not that kind of person."

Such cool detachment smacked Clare across her face. Why did he say that? What kind of person was she marrying? As a girl, she'd dreamed of her wedding, a never-ending marriage with the love of her life, and all the lace and frothy sweetness that went along with such a childish dream.

But at college, she'd awoken to the desire to remain single and independent. She wanted to be like Miss Worth, preparing herself for a time when women were entitled to do as they pleased.

She was getting neither. Worse, she was dragging a fine man down with her, despite his humble assertions that he wasn't so wonderful a person as she thought.

Regret filled her. Noah had only wanted to help her in her time of need, but now he would never experience any kind of loving marriage, either.

Clearing her throat, Clare swept from the room and headed back into the kitchen. Tim and Leo had just finished off their chore of putting away the dishes.

She'd almost forgotten about them, they were so quiet. Normally she'd have scouted them out to see what mischief they were getting into, but for those few minutes in the boys' new bedroom, she'd forgotten them.

Pulling in a breath, she turned to Noah, who'd followed her. She tried to keep her voice as cool and detached as he'd kept his. "The twenty-first of April is a Friday," she reminded him. "We're getting married on a workday."

"I'll make arrangements with Pooley to see if he can stay by himself for the day. There shouldn't be a problem. Mayor Wilson agreed to oversee the Recording Office in the governor's stead while it's here in Proud

Bend, so I'll talk to him." He paused, watching her with those intense blue eyes. "Friday will work out."

"What are you going to do on Friday?"

Clare looked down. Leo had slipped up beside her and was staring into her face with the wide-eyed innocence that had curried many a favor from her in the past. Like her, he had soft brown eyes, something one should see on a spaniel instead of a child.

She cleared her throat. "Mr. Livingstone and I are getting married. Don't you remember how we discussed this? The wedding will be this Friday."

"You said Noah is noble," Tim said. "Miss Thompson told us noble people are knights. Is Noah a knight?"

Despite the tension in the room, Clare smiled. "In a way he is."

But when she looked up at Noah again, his expression had darkened and her heart sank.

## Chapter Thirteen

Noah scraped a chair across the floor as he stood to set about boiling water for tea. He had some ginger-bread already sliced in the pantry. He'd meant to offer it to the boys at lunch, but had forgotten. They'd stuffed themselves with griddle cakes and potatoes anyway.

He cringed. Was Clare going to tell everyone in town he was so noble, so gallant in taking on the job of raising Proud Bend's most infamous mischief makers?

How was he going to look anyone in the eye?

Never mind. Clare wouldn't be going around regaling townsfolk with stories of his gallantry anyway. That would bring up the whole reason why Noah had proposed to her, and he was starting to understand his fiancée's logic. She didn't want her father to look bad, despite the fact that he really had left them in the lurch. She might be upset with him herself, but she wouldn't want anyone else to be.

"I don't want to stay here tonight," Tim whined as he stared at her. "I want to go home with you."

Disappointment shot through Noah as he moved

to retrieve the gingerbread he'd made. He'd hoped the brothers would see living here as an adventure. Perhaps the season was wrong. After all, the days were still short and the winds could still be raw.

"But you'll need to return here later this week anyway."

"Why?" Tim asked.

"Because we're moving here. I'm marrying Noah and we need to live here. I need to rent out our house."

"To that lady who came?" Leo asked.

Clare hesitated. "No. She's just a friend from college and she'll be leaving soon."

Noah set the plate of gingerbread in front of the boys. He then pulled up a chair and caught their attention. "Boys, everything will work out, but we all need to do our part. You've been good here so far, and you've done your chores admirably. I know you'll try your very best to behave for me until Clare comes. You have each other and that's what's important now. If you try your very best this coming week, we'll do something special."

Leo glanced at the gingerbread. "Like what?"

Noah thought a moment. "Let's see. Today is Sunday. We'll have a picnic. We'll get a cake and hot cocoa and eat them somewhere special."

"Where?"

Noah wasn't sure where. He'd been in Proud Bend for just over two years, but apart from the church picnics that took place on the surrounding grounds, he'd done nothing "special."

"At the bandstand," Clare inserted quickly. "This Wednesday."

Noah's brows shot up. "Wednesday?"

She nodded. "Yes, for a number of reasons. I've learned that their teacher is planning to close the school that afternoon, as she has an appointment somewhere. We can use our lunch hour. And Miss Worth told me over our lunch that she'll be leaving on Thursday. We should do something special while she's here."

"Our lunch is only thirty minutes long," Noah warned.

She thought for a moment. "We'll work through our lunch on Tuesday and give Mr. Pooley a full hour, then. On Wednesday, he can work the full hour. He'll understand once we tell him why." She stood and began to prepare the tea. Before rising to help Clare, Noah watched the boys reach for the gingerbread. Then, following her into his pantry, he reached above her head for the tin of tea.

"It's a wonderful idea," Clare said softly, glancing back at her brothers. "I can see how much better they are just being here for a short time. You know how to handle them."

Noah stalled as he brought down the tea. Was that what he was doing? Handling them, as he would Turnip?

It had been a natural reaction. Turnip needed gentle care, healing after years of abuse. Although Tim and Leo weren't abused, they responded to the same strategy. One of kindness, gentleness and love.

Could he do that with Clare?

Perhaps, but with resentment still lingering in her, it was unlikely they'd ever get past where they were right now.

Which was what? Nothing but a cordial working relationship?

No wonder she resented him *and* her father. That was all her life was going to be.

He stared back into Clare's warm, chestnut eyes. What had she said? Something about how well he handled the boys.

"I know it's difficult right now," he said. "But it will all work out. You're doing right by your brothers."

"Even though you still don't think I should have told them about our parents?"

"I didn't say that."

"You didn't need to," she said as she took the tea tin. "I felt it in the air. You would have preferred I wait."

"There's no way around it. I see that now. You wouldn't have been able to get married without people, Tim and Leo included, asking why you're not waiting for your parents to return." He felt his jaw tighten as he realized what else would happen. "I just dislike how it could cause rumors."

She colored, an attractive flush caused by something he shouldn't have said, but what needed to be said. "Be strong, Clare. You're doing the right thing."

"For my brothers, yes. What about for you?" She flared. "Am I ruining all your plans for your life? Am I asking too much of you?"

Her words were so familiar they stung. He hesitated, and that moment betrayed him. Her eyes welled with tears. She smacked down the tea tin and brushed past him. "Eat up, boys. We're going home."

Leo swung around, his mouth full of gingerbread.

"Are you mad at us, Clare?" Tim asked. "We didn't do anything."

Leo swallowed fast. "Are you still going to get married?"

She shot Noah a fast look. Fresh tears glistened, and her voice was as tight as her new smile. "I'm not mad. Of course, we're getting married. But it's complicated and you don't need to be worrying."

Noah caught her arm. "Clare, there's no need to take the boys."

She set her shoulders back and he knew right then that he would not be able to change her mind. "Please don't tell me what I should do. And let me go. I need to hitch up the wagon."

"I'll do it. Your horse is in the paddock with Turnip and I don't want you in there."

Trying to brush off the disappointment weighing on him, Noah strode outside and set about hitching her horse. As he adjusted the traces, he looked over his shoulder. Clare had marched into the stable to retrieve her brothers' jackets. The pony would have to wait until another time to get used to the boys.

He would also have to wait to try again to convince Clare they were going to be fine.

The next morning, Clare walked Tim and Leo to the Recording Office. They could play outside quietly until the school bell rang. Clare didn't care that some in town might think she should not be working during this time. She had a wage to earn, for surely she was going to pull her weight in her upcoming marriage.

At the thought of being married to Noah, her heart flipped. Nerves, she told herself. Especially after that testy goodbye late yesterday afternoon.

Thanks to Miss Worth, Clare had been far more organized this morning. Even the boys had been either too nervous around the older woman or had actually heard and heeded Noah's warning yesterday. They behaved themselves at breakfast. Of course, Miss Worth had risen earlier than everyone else had and had carved some slices off a nice slab of the bacon Noah had bought. The tantalizing scent had reached the boys and had easily coaxed them from their bed.

Clare had decided the boys should go to school. For now, perhaps staying to a normal routine was the best thing to do.

She'd also reminded them of the planned picnic.

Clare paused. Perhaps the event was too festive considering her recent loss, but again, the idea of a diversion— *a bribe*—might help her brothers. It was only a lunch, eaten at the bandstand. It wasn't as though they would be dancing in the streets.

It would have a cake that Noah planned to buy. With hot cocoa.

Oh, dear. A cake *was* too festive. Miss Worth was right.

For all her opinions and criticisms, the woman wasn't above buckling down and pulling her weight. Over breakfast, she'd assured Clare she would be fine alone for the day. Clare needed to go to work.

Grateful that Miss Worth had reminded her that hard work was the best thing for her right now, Clare had escaped the house early. When they reached the office, the boys stood at the edge of the wooden sidewalk, periodically dipping their shoes down to kick at an errant piece of slag that had been spread along the length of the street. She was about to tell them to keep their shoes clean when she spied Noah round the corner. He often kept his horse at the stable behind the sheriff's office and walked the rest of the way.

"You're early," he commented, pulling out his key.

Clare was thankful he didn't raise the subject of taking back the boys. "Miss Worth is far more organized in the morning than I will ever be."

The corner of his mouth quirked up. "I would guess she was the first up, too."

Clare smiled, thankful that he was willing to forget yesterday's cross words. They should talk about it, but when? They shouldn't use their work hours.

She mentally set the quandary aside, promising herself she'd deal with it later. "Miss Worth even warmed up the house and cooked breakfast."

"Back home, we don't warm a house that's mourning."

"True, but Miss Worth isn't one to stand on ceremony, and it's hard to coax people from their beds if the house is cold." Seeing his doubtful look, Clare shook her head. "She really isn't a terrible woman. She's just tough and uncompromising in her values. But she would never expect me to do something she wasn't willing to do first."

"What does she do for a living anyway? Mentoring doesn't pay the bills."

"She's a professor at my college. She taught Literature and was our matron for several years. At the end of the winter semester, she decided to take a sabbatical."

"What does she plan to do?"

"She wants to return to the classroom to study history." Clare had always enjoyed the sciences and had actually considered remaining at school to earn her master's degree. She'd wanted to be one of Colorado's first women to earn a master's degree.

It hadn't happened. This time last year, she had been preparing to be her class valedictorian. It had been a great honor, and it had taken her weeks to prepare for it, but after graduation, she'd visited her father's family. Before her train had left his town, her uncle had approached Mitch MacLeod and asked him and Victoria to travel with her. That was last year, when Victoria was traveling with Mitch's family to Proud Bend.

Her uncle had then slipped Clare some extra cash in case she'd needed it. For a moment, Clare reminded herself that she would need to telegraph him with the sad news.

It could wait. She didn't want her father's older brother to descend on her, making decisions, telling all in earshot what a mess his younger brother had made of things.

Yes, she'd wait on that telegram.

Clare had returned home to discover she'd needed to stay. Her mother had been too sick and her father had found her work in the Recording Office.

Her mother's condition had kept her from returning to college.

Feeling her face warm, she turned to her brothers. "You may play out here, but come in to say goodbye when you hear the school bell. And don't get dirty."

Inside, Clare began her routine tasks. The small building was already warm, thanks to the caretaker, and Clare quickly shed her jacket.

"I'm glad Miss Worth didn't think it necessary for you to stay home and entertain her," Noah said.

"She wouldn't be much of a mentor if she needed constant entertaining, would she?" Clare asked wryly. "Besides, if we're going to have a picnic on Wednesday, I need to put in as many hours here as I can."

"I'll ask Mr. Pooley today if he will stay through his lunch."

As if on cue, Pooley walked in. He offered his usual reserved hello and nod. Clare knew him to be a pleasant, albeit serious young man, married with a small child. He went straight to his desk.

She glanced at Noah, who asked him to stay on Wednesday, explaining where they would be doing. He shot Clare a surprised look before answering, "A picnic together?"

Clare cleared her throat. Stiffening, Noah explained, "I asked Miss Walsh to be my wife and she has agreed."

"Congratulations, sir." Pooley looked at Clare, his expression a little confused, as if he should have seen an office romance, but had somehow missed it. He was probably remembering how she'd recently lost her parents, too. "And congratulations, Miss Walsh."

"Thank you. Our engagement will be short, but it's only part of the reason for the outing," Clare explained. "My mentor from college is here visiting, and there is no school that afternoon. We'd like to enjoy a slightly longer lunch. A picnic at the bandstand. A quiet one, considering the circumstances."

"You're going to picnic at the bandstand?" Pooley echoed.

Again, Clare colored. It was her father who had lobbied to have the bandstand built, hoping that the town would someday have its own citizens' band. That had not materialized. After it was built, the structure then became a long-running and much-suffered joke around town.

"Yes," Noah answered briskly. "It may as well be used for something."

"Miss Templeton and I have eaten our lunch there," Clare added hastily. Victoria Templeton, now Victoria MacLeod, had accepted an invitation from Clare last year to eat lunch at the bandstand. Clare had enjoyed getting to know her and had been a stalwart friend to her, even when Victoria and her cousin, Rachel, had struggled through attacks on their lives and the death of Rachel's father.

"I don't mind working through my lunch," Pooley said. "I hope the weather cooperates. April is a contrary month."

"Thank you. In return, Miss Walsh and I will work through tomorrow's lunch. You may take a full hour off that day."

Pooley's face broke out into an uncharacteristically broad smile. "Thank you, sir!"

In the distance, the school bell rang. Clare glanced out the window just as Tim threw open the Recording Office door. "We're going!"

Before she could wish him and his brother a good day, the door banged shut. At least they'd obeyed her. She stole a fast glance at Noah. Had his influence kindled this spate of good behavior?

Her mother would be so proud of them.

Clare's heart clenched. *Mother will never know.*

After Noah settled back into his work, she rose and walked into his office in need of his signature on a stationery order form. As she handed it to him, she said, stiffly, "I wonder if a cake on Wednesday is a bit too festive for the occasion."

"The occasion of our upcoming nuptials?"

"No," she snapped. "I mean about the loss of my parents. I don't want the town thinking we're callous."

"Do you think we are?"

She shrugged aimlessly. "I don't know." She then paused. "I'm going to see Miss Thompson at lunch today," she said, wondering if he could follow her thoughts. "To tell her about my parents."

"She wasn't at church yesterday?"

"She often travels up to Denver on the weekends because her mother lives there and is in poor health." Noah nodded. As he did, Clare also thought about the boys during their free afternoon. "And I didn't want Miss Worth to have to deal with my brothers."

Noah's eyes twinkled. "Or the other way around?"

"No!" She couldn't stop a tiny smile from appearing. "I mean after having cake."

Noah set down his pen and looked thoughtful. "Instead of a cake, how about I order a few small pastries from that new pastry shop? They make special ones and they'll deliver them if we give them enough time. But remember that this picnic is a reward for the boys' good behavior. It's not a celebratory event."

"True." Clare rubbed her forehead. At some point, a celebration would be in order, for a wedding should be a joyous occasion, surely.

But there was still the loss of her parents. "It's hard

to decide what to do. We're getting married, yet it's overshadowed by my parents' disappearance."

"We'll make our wedding a quiet affair. We'll keep the guests to a minimum."

Clare hadn't even considered a guest list yet. "Have you telegraphed your parents? Will they be coming?"

His congenial expression dropped. "No," he retorted. "I am no longer in communication with them."

Not in communication? What did that mean? Another question, *why*, rose to her lips, but she hesitated.

Noah suddenly softened. "I'll ask Alex Robinson to stand up with me."

Clare nodded vaguely. Alex Robinson was Proud Bend's sheriff, and for a short time last fall, he'd gone missing. A few days later, he'd been replaced, in a secret move, by his twin brother, Zane, who'd wanted to find him and a young woman who had also disappeared. The secret switch had been designed to oust a kidnapper, it was rumored. After the sheriff had been found, Zane had returned to his hometown with his new wife, Rachel. Although Rachel had returned briefly for her cousin's wedding, Zane had stayed out East. Clare had heard they planned to return someday.

She paused. Rachel and Zane's wedding had been a quick, quiet affair, as it had been shortly after Rachel's father had died. Such a thing was possible and acceptable.

"I'll ask Victoria to be my maid of honor," Clare finally said. "She's busy with her new family, but since we're having a modest ceremony, she'll be able to stand up for me, I'm sure."

Noah nodded. "It will all work out. I'll finish the

paperwork and ask Mrs. Turcot to help organize the refreshments afterward. She enjoys that sort of thing."

"Thank you," she said before clearing her throat. "Your influence with the boys is commendable. I didn't expect they'd obey me when I told them to stay until the bell rang."

Noah accepted the paperwork Clare still held, all the while keeping his attention on her. "Does that bother you?"

Did it? She could feel her mouth tighten. It really shouldn't, except that one day with those pint-sized hooligans and Noah had calmed them down. He'd been a wonderful influence on them, where she'd had little success. Her mother had done her best, and her father had organized the chores Tim and Leo did, but still, her brothers managed to find trouble as easily as a cat found a mouse.

"I was surprised, that's all," she answered, folding her arms. "My parents had not been that successful at disciplining them."

"I'm a new person in their lives. I'm sure the obedience will wear off. Don't forget that they've only been acting on their feelings."

Clare sniffed and looked away. Was he using her words against her? He hadn't believed her before but he didn't sound like he was scoffing at her. She looked down at him, for he was still seated, while she'd remained standing. She'd walked in here to give him the stationery requisition, and to ask that their upcoming picnic be less festive. Resentment had followed her in.

*Lord, please rid me of it.*

Noah stood and walked around the desk. Clare shot

a nervous look through the glass to where Mr. Pooley was busy with a man who'd just entered.

Noah took her hand. His tone was gentle. "You're jealous."

She yanked it back. "I am not!"

He didn't answer, but from the way his lips quirked she knew he disagreed with her.

She swallowed. Yes, she *was* jealous. Noah had been kind and noble and had even managed to control Tim and Leo in ways that no one in her family had been able to do. And in a far shorter time.

Hers was a natural reaction, she told herself, nothing to be ashamed of.

Yet it *was* something to be very ashamed of. She called herself a Christian, but look at her. She resented her fiancé, a man she didn't even love, and just mere days before their wedding. She resented him and was jealous of him and if that wasn't enough, she appreciated how he wasn't rubbing her nose in it.

And a part of her didn't mind any of it. That part of her wanted to change.

Honestly, this whole affair was getting more confusing. How were they ever going to make their marriage work when her emotions toward him were changing with every minute?

Clare picked up his fountain pen and handed it to him. "Please sign that requisition, Mr. Livingstone. We need the supplies." Then she walked out of his office.

## Chapter Fourteen

It was Wednesday already, Clare marveled as they approached the bandstand. Where had the time gone?

At lunch on Monday, while the children played outside—including Mary Pemberton, whose dress and pinafore could be in danger of soiling—Clare told the boys' teacher about her parents.

Miss Thompson had hugged her and offered her help in any way she could. Clare had thanked her and, in case she started to cry, she had beaten a hasty exit a short time later.

Tuesday swept by Clare with the speed of a steam locomotive across the prairies. She'd worked in silence all through her lunch, saying little to Noah.

She didn't want to be jealous, and afraid she was, she'd kept her head down and toiled away all the harder. At home, she'd whirled around the kitchen like a windup toy, declining Miss Worth's offer of assistance. Leaving her to it, Miss Worth must have surely felt that Clare was taking her advice on hard work to heart.

Now, Wednesday, falling into step beside Noah,

Clare peeked up at the sun and grimaced. She had left her parasol in her office, and now in the brilliant sunshine, she regretted her negligence.

*I'll be as freckled as a farm boy.*

Over at the bandstand, holding the picnic basket, stood Miss Worth. The boys were kicking a rock back and forth in front of her. Clare straightened. This day was for her brothers, a way to reward them and take their minds off their grief for a short time.

Guilt nibbled at her. Shouldn't she be in mourning? Shouldn't she be hiding in her home and planning a memorial service? Something worthy of the family's standing in Proud Bend. Theirs had been one of the first families to settle here.

Clare swallowed. Would people see her wedding as a way for her to keep out of the poorhouse?

It wasn't. Nor did she care that Noah's ranch house was more rustic than her comfortable, two-story home. Her marriage was only a way to keep her family together.

*Except that you have already told half the town you were never planning to marry. How does that make you feel?*

*Shamed.*

Clare shut her eyes a moment. *Be that as it may, you knew you were going to face adversity, thinking that women deserved more rights than they had. You'd told yourself you were strong enough to face the life God had planned for you.*

Resolute, she threw back her shoulders and marched across the street in front of a wagon rumbling past.

"I'm glad the town built seats in this," Noah said as

they crossed the street. "We wouldn't be able to use it otherwise."

Clare looked at him. She'd made some sandwiches with thin slices of cooked chicken. She'd also boiled eggs and made a dozen or so fig macaroons.

"I mentioned to my father after I first invited Victoria to have lunch with me, that the bandstand needed seats. Father asked the mayor, and lo and behold, there were seats before winter. I think my father could spin a good reason for anything."

"All we need is a band, then."

She snickered at the town's long-running joke. "You've heard me sing in church. I won't be a part of anything musical."

Right then, Clare noticed the pastry shop's door open. She could see the owner's wife carrying a tall steel pot with a covered tray atop it. The much-coveted pastries and hot cocoa were on their way. She glanced hastily around, but the street was empty.

Inside the bandstand, Noah nodded to Miss Worth. "Thank you for coming," he said politely. "I hope your visit with Clare has been good."

"It has." Miss Worth studied him only briefly before setting out the food.

The boys sat cross-legged on the floor. While everyone was eating quietly, Clare lingered with her thoughts. Noah had ordered just the right desserts, the boys had behaved, and Miss Worth had even allowed herself to eat half of a sandwich, although, to the boys' delight, she'd split her pastry into two parts for them.

Noah had done himself proud. She stole a glance at him and she felt her heart leap without reason.

"I wish I could stay for your nuptials, Clare," Miss Worth announced as she dabbed her mouth. "But I'm expected in San Francisco on Saturday."

"I'm sorry, too," Clare said, packing away the remaining food. "I wish I'd been able to spend more time with you. But I do need to finish preparing my house. A man from out East is interested in renting it for his family. I got the telegram yesterday and asked the lawyer to draft a lease."

"I wish I could stay and help, too. Now, as a thank-you for all your hospitality, allow me to care for the boys for the rest of the afternoon." She consulted the watch she'd pinned to her basic jacket and nodded briskly. "There are twenty-five minutes left in your lunch hour. The boys and I will take the basket home. I noticed a few games in the parlor yesterday that you have not yet packed away. Perhaps we can play one of them."

"Leo loves Chutes and Ladders," Clare advised. At the name of his favorite game, her smallest brother perked up.

"Thank you, Miss Worth." Noah loaded up Tim with the basket. He and Clare watched the older woman herd the brothers back to their house.

Clare stole a look at Noah. Would he suggest they forfeit the remaining free time and simply return to work? She found herself holding her breath.

Noah had no intention of wasting what was left of their extralong lunch. Nor did he wish to return to work. Last year, they'd always closed for the lunch hour, but in January, Governor Pitkin had ordered all state offices to stay open then, forcing the staff to rotate their breaks.

He'd hoped to increase commerce, and Proud Bend's mayor had heartily agreed. To have this time off and not worry about work was a treat. Noah did take his lunch break, but often stayed in the office during that time.

More importantly, he and Clare needed some time to talk. And not about planning their wedding, or deciding on a routine at his home afterward, either. Instead, he just wanted them to enjoy the extended lunch—and one another's company.

He felt brightened by the thought.

He dared a glance at Clare, finding her closer, her expression indecipherable. What was she thinking?

Was she quiet because she was still dealing with her grief, or was she still thinking of how she didn't want to be married?

It was the only way they could solve her problem, regardless of Miss Worth's unreasonable suggestions that harder work could fix everything.

"I'm sorry," he said softly, watching her profile and wondering how he could erase the small creases forming between her brows.

She turned to him. "About what?"

"About the compromises you have to make. About hating how you can't solve your situation by yourself and now must rely on me. We both know Miss Worth's answer isn't the solution here. You could work harder, but you'll just work yourself sick and where would that leave your brothers?" He rubbed his forehead. "But remember, Clare, I didn't suggest marriage to prove to you that you're weak."

"Why did you suggest it, then? You don't need a family to keep your job or your ranch. Was it just to help me out? You keep saying that you're not that noble, and yet, you don't explain why I shouldn't think that."

Noah hesitated. He couldn't answer her question, for no matter which way he answered, he would be hurting someone. He'd blurted out his proposal to Clare without thinking. He'd already insulted her with the look of dismay he wore after realizing what he'd offered.

Still, he didn't want to tell her about his parents and all that had happened, either. He didn't want to bring up Elizabeth at all. She should never have demanded he go along with her suggestion that she'd ended their engagement. She'd caught him at a moment when he'd felt so awful for hurting her that he'd agreed to it. But to tell Clare the truth, that he'd ended his engagement to Elizabeth, would break a foolish promise to her.

"My reasons for marrying aren't important," he finally said slowly. "Your situation was dire and I couldn't allow your father, even if he might be dead, to tear apart your family."

Clare looked down at her hands. Noah noticed that she had yet to slip on her gloves again. She furtively picked at her nails. Then, as if realizing the bad habit, she shoved on her gloves. "Thank you. When Mr. Burrows came to register his new land and boasted about getting some boys to help him, I was terrified that I would lose Tim and Leo. As for my parents, I'm supposed to honor them, not get mad at them. I ask for forgiveness one minute and the next, I start resenting them all over again."

"God will forgive everything that comes from a contrite heart."

"I'm not sure I have that yet." It was a simple statement, but the tone revealed that Clare wasn't ready to try. Their gazes met, her eyes peering deeply into his. "You said you're not in contact with your parents. Whatever they have done, *you* can't forgive *them*?"

Noah knew that someday, Clare would ask this, but had not counted on it happening so soon. He stared off beyond the bandstand, in the direction of Clare's home. That was one question he didn't ever want to answer. Yet, he'd like nothing better than to show Clare that forgiveness was not only possible, but essential. And achievable. So why wasn't he forgiving his father?

Noah felt his back stiffen. His father had ended the relationship, not him, by telling him to leave if he wouldn't do as demanded.

He felt her hand slip into his. "Noah, forget I asked." She gripped his hand all the tighter. "I want you to know how good today has been. Ever since you said I was jealous of you, I've been short with you. It was wrong of me."

"Clare, you don't need to apologize—"

"Yes, I do." She gave him an imploring look. "Please, Noah, let me finish."

He nodded silently, prompting her to continue.

"You were right. I *am* jealous of you. You've managed to tame Tim and Leo, and you've been kind to Miss Worth, who isn't the most likable woman sometimes. You have so much integrity and honor. I know it can't be easy for you to take on my family." She sighed. "I'll eventually forgive my father, and get over this jealousy. I know that, but it'll take time. Thank you for being patient."

Then today *had* been good, Noah decided, hearing a

wheezy whistle in the distance. A train was approaching the depot, but he had already stood to study the mountains so he did not turn.

Instead, he thought about what Clare said. She would eventually forgive her parents and even let go of her jealousy of him. It wouldn't happen right away, but Clare's loving nature would win out.

He'd been patient with Tim and Leo, too. A gentle breeze, warm with the hints and hopes of the summer that would soon arrive, brushed his face, and he looked away from Clare to the mountains that practically glowed with sunshine. God had once said He was in the smallest of breezes. Was He here, now? Had He put Noah in Proud Bend to help Clare? He'd always assumed God wanted him out West to rescue horses, but was he also here to tame Tim and Leo?

To tame even Clare?

A rush of wanting swelled through him. Yes, he *did* want to be here for Clare. To show her how to get past her resentment and jealousy and keep her family together. She had a loving, vivacious personality, and deep down, he wanted to be the sole focus of it. To have someone in his life who cared for him. *Truly cared.*

In that moment, that was the only reason he needed to marry her.

Yes, the day was proving to be very good, even if they would soon need to end their lunch hour and return to work.

Idly, he watched a pair of magpies swoop down and peck at the gravelly road beyond the bandstand. The bold birds wouldn't move for anyone save a wagon, choosing instead to hop away from people, like their cousins, the crows, out East. They were determined to eat the bits of stones that winter had scattered. Soon, they would hop close in search of discarded crumbs. In a way, Clare was like a magpie determined to get what *she* needed.

He smiled. Not a flattering comparison, for magpies were nuisances, but Clare could be bold and striking, refusing to give way to the despair around her and adjusting her life as the situation demanded.

"Miss Walsh?"

His thoughts and gaze still on the birds, Noah idly listened to a male voice address Clare. It sounded familiar. Whoever it was had come from the opposite direction, but no doubt someone who'd heard of either her upcoming nuptials or the sad news of her parents. He continued to stare at the birds. He should give her some privacy in which to answer.

"Yes?" Clare answered as Noah shifted away.

"I'm Mr. Townsend. I sent you a telegram saying I wish to rent your house. I know it's only for a short time, but my daughter Elizabeth and I would prefer to be together rather than stay in a boardinghouse—"

Cold washed through Noah as he snapped over his head and stared in horror at the couple standing in front of Clare.

How could this be?

# Chapter Fifteen

Noah stood slowly, cautiously. What were his ex-fiancée and her father doing here? He glanced around. Where was her mother? "Rupert? Elizabeth?"

He could feel three shocked gazes riveted on him. Then Clare moved her attention from Elizabeth and her father to him and back again. Several times.

"Noah!" Being a short woman with a delicate stature, Elizabeth easily slipped past her father. "I didn't expect to see you so soon. I mean, I wasn't sure where you…"

Her words faded to nothing as her gaze darted between him and Clare. Her expression turning canny, she narrowed her eyes ever so slightly, but enough for Noah to guess that she knew that she and her father had interrupted something intimate.

Noah shut his mouth. Why did she say she didn't expect to see him so soon? Their visit here was no co-incidence, then. Two years ago, he'd walked out on his family and their demands. He'd told his parents that he had accepted the position of Assistant Recording Offi-cer here in Proud Bend, so probably his father had told

Rupert Townsend where to find him. Still, he hadn't expected to see anyone from his hometown again.

Had Elizabeth spread that lie about who ended their engagement? If she had, there would be no reason why his parents would tell her or her family where he'd gone, for they knew the truth, that he'd ended the relationship. He'd told them, *and only them*, knowing that pride would keep his father's mouth tightly shut.

Noah's father had groomed him from an early age to carry on the family business, but for Noah, as the teen years rolled into his twenties, he'd realized that it wasn't what he'd wanted. Each time he'd broached the subject, his father had brushed him off.

Then, suddenly, two years and four months ago, Noah's father told him that he'd arranged a marriage to Elizabeth, thus implementing a business merger. There was never any option, never a choice of dates, even, nor a warning. A few months later, a mere week before the nuptials, it all fell apart and Noah walked out, saying only that he was going to Proud Bend to work at the Recording Office and save enough to start a ranch.

Now on the bandstand, Rupert Townsend stepped closer, his expression far more serious. "Noah, I hadn't planned to see you yet. We were looking for Miss Walsh, and one of the men at the train depot pointed her out."

Noah glanced behind him. The town center was small enough that one could see the bandstand from the depot. With the telegraph office within the depot, and Clare having lived here all her life and having received her sad news just days ago, she would be easy to point out. Hadn't they just had a picnic lunch right here, where everyone could see?

Oblivious of his thoughts, Clare shoved out her hand. "Welcome to Proud Bend, Mr. Townsend. How was your trip?"

"Very well, thank you." Rupert shook her hand. "This is my daughter, Elizabeth. We telegraphed you about renting your home."

"Yes, I received it." She shook Elizabeth's hand, pumping it far more vigorously than Elizabeth would have preferred, Noah noted briefly. "I wasn't expecting you two until the weekend."

"I apologize for that, but we couldn't wait." He looked over Clare's shoulder to Noah.

Clare frowned, unsure what he meant by that comment. "This is Noah Livingstone, but I guess you already know him." She shot Noah a confused look.

"We do," Elizabeth answered. "He's my ex-fiancé."

The words, weighted like a large stone, fell between them. From his position, Noah could not see Clare's expression, but she'd gone still. Dead still.

"What a coincidence." Clare found the voice she'd briefly lost. "Noah is my...current fiancé."

She cringed inwardly. Her words made her sound as though she'd had a bevy of fiancés. She instantly regretted her forced answer, but frankly, what else could she say after this young woman's shocking revelation? She'd had no idea that Noah had once been engaged.

Why had it ended? Why was the woman here?

She straightened. Noah was her fiancé. Didn't she deserve to know about his past?

*No*, a voice inside admonished her. Their engagement was a merely a convenient arrangement made by a compassionate man who didn't want to see her family separated. Clare looked again at Elizabeth, finally noticing how petite the woman was. What a twist of events to have this very woman be the one who was renting her house. Clare had been so grateful to find a respectable family willing to move in that she hadn't even asked why they were coming to Proud Bend.

Judging from the furtive, cautious looks Elizabeth was firing at Noah, Clare might dare say it was to mend a relationship.

*No, it can't be.*

That thought, and its immediate denial, squeezed her throat closed and stilled her body. She couldn't find the strength within her to steal a look up at Noah to attempt to guess *his* reaction. He'd stiffened all right; that was all she could tell, but was that just from shock? She didn't know.

She was too scared to check.

She shut her eyes. When did she become such a coward?

Her stomach tightened and with nothing left to do, Clare forced out a smile. "It's nice to finally meet you."

"Thank you," Mr. Townsend murmured.

"So, how long have you been engaged?" Elizabeth asked with a crisp edge to her words.

Clare swallowed. "Only a few days."

"It's just happened?" The news seemed to brighten the woman up. "How long have you been courting?"

Although it wasn't a rude question, the tone was accusatory. Clare wasn't sure how to answer, but she knew one thing. She couldn't lie. "We haven't done any courting until just a few minutes ago."

Brows raised, both father and daughter gaped at her and Noah. Clare felt her heart plummet. What on earth did they think of her? Did they assume she was in the family way and needed a husband? Did they assume Noah was the father of the fictitious babe?

For all her cutting tone, did this Elizabeth even deserve an answer? From her expectant look, she believed she did, and Clare couldn't allow the woman to believe the worst of her.

She threw back her shoulders. "It's a financial arrangement designed to assist me. My parents were recently lost at sea and I have two small brothers."

Then silence, a still, dreadful, awkward silence. One that wasn't even punctuated by polite condolences, Clare thought testily.

No longer able to stand the quiet another second, she blurted out, "The house is not quite ready. As I mentioned, I wasn't expecting you until the weekend."

"Yes. Sorry about that." Mr. Townsend didn't sound sorry. "We should have telegraphed you with our change of plans." He cleared his throat. "I suppose we could stay at a boardinghouse for a few days." He glanced around. "There doesn't appear to be an inn here."

"There's nothing you'd find suitable." Clare flicked her gaze up and down his frame. Townsend was a well-dressed man, his suit a fine cut and his boots highly polished.

They were obviously wealthy and could afford to rent a large home. But where would they stay until hers was ready?

For all of the woman's rudeness, she couldn't send them away, but she had to be honest with them.

Clare shut her eyes, half-expecting Noah to offer his home. They knew him. They had nearly become family.

But he said nothing. Finally, she dared to look at him. He seemed to be in shock.

Catching his eye, she flicked her brows up slightly, pointedly staring at him.

Noah continued to stare back blankly, forcing her to frown even more intently at him. Why on earth was he so quiet? Clare turned to the Townsends, offering a smile she didn't really feel. "Would you excuse us for a moment, please?"

Right then, she grabbed Noah by the forearm and steered him down the bandstand steps between the father and daughter and out around the huge sagebrush that grew wild nearby.

At the far side of it, hidden from view and hopefully from sound, she stopped and captured Noah's attention. "You need to offer your home to them!"

He stiffened. "No, I don't."

Clare gaped at him. Words formed in her mouth. Indeed, she opened it to speak, but she felt as though she'd been struck dumb. Where was that man who'd offered her his name and security mere days ago?

"Why not?" she finally blurted out.

Noah folded his arms. "My reason doesn't concern you, Clare."

She pointed into the center of the sagebrush in the direction of the bandstand. "We're getting married and your previous fiancée has arrived for an extended visit. It *does* concern me. Especially considering I didn't even know she existed fifteen minutes ago!"

When Noah refused to answer, Clare pushed on further. "The only place in town available is Mrs. Shrankhof's boarding house, but her only tenants are men. That's hardly suitable for Miss Townsend."

"She'll be with her father."

"Will she be sharing a room with him or have a separate one? Neither of those options is acceptable. She's a young, single woman. She won't want to sully everyone's first impression of her."

As he looked away, Noah made a noise that Clare didn't want to interpret. It didn't sound flattering. With few options, she touched his folded arm lightly to draw his attention back to her. "Why are you so adamant not to help them? Did she hurt you? Did she break off your engagement?"

"You should stay out of this, Clare. It's for the best." His jaw hardened. "Don't get involved. Least of all with them."

Clare stepped back at his harsh tone. "Are you saying I shouldn't rent to them? I have to. Noah, I *need* to rent my house. Besides, if I refuse, where will they go?"

His brows shot up with a surprisingly callous expression as he turned back to her. "They can go back home."

"That could leave me open to a lawsuit. I can't afford that! And above all that, it feels dishonest. I won't do it." She felt her ire rising. "I can't believe you expect me to!"

Noah blinked and looked away, but his mouth remained firm, a thin line of stubbornness.

This was ridiculous. She had absolutely no idea what was going on. Did he really expect her to leave herself open to losing everything, stranding a family in the process and simply trust in him to sort it all out?

She was already vulnerable enough, relying on him

for support. She wasn't going to make another family vulnerable.

Clare spun. Just as quickly, Noah grabbed her arm and caught her attention. "Where are you going?"

"I'm going to do the only decent thing." She yanked back her arm. "It's what any Christian would do."

"Only because you're a Christian? A few minutes ago, you were admitting you weren't a very good one." He waited for her answer. When it didn't come, he added, "Or are you just saving your home?"

She stiffened. "Why can't I do both?" When he said nothing more, she tugged down her jacket and stomped around the big bush. She would talk to Noah about this later. Right now, she had concerns that were more pressing.

Clare could hardly expect this family to wait on the streets until she finished cleaning out her house. She had enough room. Miss Worth was staying in the spare bedroom, and Clare could move into her parents' bedroom. The boys could stay at the ranch and she'd put Mr. Townsend in their room. She'd offer her own to Elizabeth.

She approached Mr. Townsend, a smile practically hurting her face. "You must stay with me. I'm almost finished preparing the house, anyway, and Noah and I are getting married on Friday."

Elizabeth paled and let out a gasp. She tossed a hasty glance at her father. "You are?"

"Yes. Just a small ceremony." Clare stopped short of inviting them. Something about Elizabeth's stricken look, and the narrow-eyed frown now forming on Mr. Townsend's face, warned her against it.

"I know this is all very awkward," Clare stated briskly, "with you being Noah's ex-fiancée and all, but I'm sure everyone will be civil."

Mr. Townsend puffed up like a rooster. "My daughter ended the engagement. Immediately after that, Noah stormed out here to Colorado. Nothing has been civil, but I'm here to change that."

Clare tried her best not to recoil at the harsh words. She glanced at Elizabeth to find the woman looking away and oddly dropping her gaze. Those tiny hairs at her nape rose inexplicably. She heard a noise behind her and turned. By now, Noah had stepped out from the bushes where she'd dragged him in the hopes that she could talk some sense into him.

Her heart lurched at the pained look on his face. Did he catch Mr. Townsend's sharp retort? Was that why he wanted nothing to do with this pair? Had Elizabeth broken his heart?

Clare caught another glimpse of the young woman as she swallowed. What on earth was going on? Her heart lurched. Did she dare ask?

No, but she wasn't a coward. She would get the truth from Noah. Something unspoken told her that he was the one she should trust, and not these two.

"It's all right, Clare," Noah ground out as he approached. "They can stay with me."

Really? Clare held back a snort. The concession sounded more like Noah was offering to clean a pigsty when no one else volunteered.

She might not know what was going on, and right now, Clare decided she didn't want to know. Her only concern had to be for her brothers and the home she was at risk of losing.

No, she would rent her house to the Townsends, and if they wanted to continue the relationship with Noah, it would have to be after her wedding to him. In fact, keeping them close was probably for the best. She could keep an eye on the pair.

A thought lurched around inside of her. Was she suddenly protective of Noah? Or was she doing this in defiance of him?

Clare swallowed. She wasn't sure.

Regardless, she held up her hand. "No! I've already offered my home, and they are going to take possession of it at the end of the week anyway, so there's no point for them to go to your ranch, Noah. My mind is made up."

He stepped up and turned his body slightly away from the Townsends. "You wanted me to offer my home," he whispered to her. "Why the sudden change of heart?"

Clare arched her brows at him. *Why your sudden change of heart?* she wanted to counter. Instead, she dredged up a smile and brushed past him. She wasn't going to tell him that she didn't trust the Townsends.

She faced the twosome. They watched the sly conversation she'd just had with Noah with far too much interest to be considered polite. The hairs on her nape rose farther.

Yes, Clare felt the overwhelming desire to protect Noah.

From these two in front of her?

She pulled back her shoulders. Never mind. She'd figure it all out later. This pair, no matter how suspicious they appeared, needed a place to stay and she wasn't going to ignore her Christian duty and turn them away.

"We're just surprised to see you so early," she said as smoothly as she could manage, all the while reaching forward to touch Elizabeth's forearm. She smiled so brightly, it hurt as much as it had a moment ago. "And, of course, I am surprised to learn that you already know Noah."

She waved her hand lightly. "But never mind. Noah can take my brothers to his ranch, and that will free up another bedroom." Her smile broadened, although she had no idea how that was possible. Honestly, it hurt enough as it was. "Their room is big enough. You would not believe how much space two small boys can take up! Now, where is your luggage?"

Ten minutes later, Noah held open Clare's front door to allow the women to enter. Then, he stalked back to the train depot's wagon in order to assist the young porter Rupert Townsend had paid to deliver their bags.

How long were they planning to stay? he wondered, staring at the plentiful number of suitcases and the one large trunk.

Dread then filled him. More importantly, why were they here?

No way had they come all this way to tour the mountains. Yes, Proud Bend was a quaint town with magnificent vistas and a welcome dry air, not to mention a pleasant summer climate, but not for a moment did Noah believe those were the reasons for this visit. It was April and still cool out. Rupert had mentioned, albeit briefly, that he'd planned to meet with Noah. Why?

His heart squeezed. If Rupert was delivering bad news, a telegram would have sufficed. But it couldn't be that. Rupert and Elizabeth didn't look as though they had misfortune or heartache.

Or delivering a demand from his father. A demand to return. His father's birthday was approaching. Could that be it?

Noah had spent *his* birthdays alone. His every holiday, every special occasion, in fact, had been spent alone, trying not to grieve that he'd cut all ties with his family because they'd demanded the impossible from him.

Had *he* been selfish, too?

He hauled the trunk off the wagon with far more force than he'd wanted. His thoughts were just running amuck.

When he'd left, everything had been set in place to work out for the best. Noah had a younger brother who was better suited to run the family business. Jacob had a head for figures and the ability to appreciate their father's greed.

He turned, finding with surprise Clare staring at him from just outside the front door.

"What's wrong?" he asked testily.

She blinked as she walked up to him. "I…I didn't think you were that strong." She indicated the large trunk he stood there holding as if he was some feeble-minded imbecile whose only gift was his strength.

"I run a ranch. I'm not a small man. We should get your brothers to help."

"They may think they're strong enough for all of this luggage, but they're not. I just talked to Miss Worth. I think she senses something isn't right, because she asked them to show her around Proud Bend. They're leaving out the back door."

Clare then glanced over her shoulder at the open doorway. "I'm going to be busy for a while, but I'll bring the boys over later. Mr. Townsend can take their room. Miss Worth is—" She peered at Noah, trying to capture his wandering attention. "Are you listening? We need to talk."

He lifted the trunk again. "About what?"

Clare hurriedly overtook him, stopping at the front door and trying to block it with her slim frame. Her expression tried to be forceful but with those soft brown eyes of hers, she wasn't successful. Reluctantly, he set down the trunk as she spoke again. "Don't be obtuse, Noah. You know perfectly well what we need to discuss. Don't think you're going to avoid it, either, because I'm going to take the boys to the ranch just as soon as everyone is settled. And don't bother riding off into the sunset to look for wild horses to adopt. I *will* find you."

He had no doubt she would. *You owe her something*, a part of him reminded himself. With a sigh, he nodded brusquely. "All right, but don't think you can talk this thing to death, Clare. Now, allow me to deliver this trunk. And remember, we still need to return to work. We're late as it is."

Surprise flared on her face. Had she forgotten about work? "Yes, of course," she said quickly. She spun, pushed open the door as far as it would go and held it open until he and the young porter from the train depot had delivered the entire set of luggage.

Wordlessly, Noah took the trunk upstairs, finding, to his chagrin, Elizabeth alone in Clare's bedroom. He knew that Rupert, fatigued from the journey, had already chosen to lie down. From the bedroom Noah knew to belong to Clare's brothers, he could hear the deep snores that indicated the older man was already fast asleep.

Another thing bothered Noah. Rupert usually traveled with a manservant. Elizabeth had a personal maid. Where were they?

He glanced around. This was far too big a house for just her and her father. With four spacious bedrooms, it was better suited to a large, boisterous family, a family that Clare's parents had probably planned to have, but had been prevented because of Mrs. Walsh's poor condition.

Suspicion rose within him. Was Rupert Townsend planning to bring others out here?

*Stop it*, he ordered himself. Clare's home was probably the only one available for rent, and no doubt had been advertised out East by the owner of the haberdashery. He dabbled in real estate and would have assisted Clare for a small commission. Things could have fallen into place very quickly.

"Noah?"

He turned after setting the trunk down in the center of the room. Elizabeth hastily closed the door just enough to leave it ajar a few inches.

She turned. "You're upset with me."

"You have developed a knack for stating the obvious, I see. I'm also upset with your father for bringing you here."

"Let me explain, then."

"No, thank you." Noah was also upset with himself. He had been selfish and rude and was still fighting the uncharacteristic desire to go home and brood about their arrival. He brushed past her. Better to leave now before he said something he would later regret.

"Noah!" Elizabeth spun as he strode past her and threw open the bedroom door. "Listen to me!"

"No. It's inappropriate for us to talk here. Or anywhere alone. We're no longer engaged."

"It's not inappropriate."

He turned at the door. "It is, and you know it. What's more, it's wrong for you to lie to your father."

She looked away guiltily.

"So you did. I didn't catch everything your father said back at the bandstand—"

"When you were hiding behind that bush."

He sighed, ignoring the biting accusation. "I wasn't sure if you *had* lied to him, but now I see that you really did tell him *you* ended our engagement." He shook his head.

"You agreed to that lie, Noah, so don't be self-righteous."

Noah bristled, and suddenly, his conscience pricked him.

*Lord, forgive me.*

Noah rubbed his forehead. Elizabeth wasn't above reminding him of his own faults in order to divert attention from hers. "I felt badly that I was hurting you," he muttered. "That's why I agreed to allow the lie to stand. But it was wrong and I see now I was only hurting your pride."

"So why didn't you tell the truth to Miss Walsh? Don't tell me you have. It's as plain as the nose on your face that she didn't even know I existed."

Noah flinched. "I said nothing because I didn't want to lie to her, nor did I want to break my promise to you, although I'm not sure why."

"An omission is as bad as a lie."

He worked his jaw. She was right. But another important question was why Elizabeth was trying to drag him into her sin. She knew how wrong it was.

"Noah, what exactly did you tell your parents?"

Why did she want to know that? Surely, she would have realized by now that he would have told them the truth. It had happened before he'd spoken to her. "Elizabeth, I told them that I couldn't do what they demanded of me. My father called me a fool, among other things, and I called him equally awful names. I've destroyed my relationship with my parents. After you and I spoke, I wasn't going to return to my parents and tell them I was wrong and that you had broken off the engagement instead. I figured you could deal with whatever happens, and I left."

"You told your parents you could only marry for love. Are you doing that now? Because from what Clare said, it sounds like a financial arrangement."

He felt his shoulders tense. This was none of Elizabeth's business and he refused to confirm or deny her accusation. She would use it against him. Besides, he knew Elizabeth. She was working up to some declaration. Noah narrowed his eyes. "Has your father spoken to my father?"

"Not for a long time," Elizabeth answered crisply before clearing her throat. "After I told my father that I had ended our betrothal, he went to yours to see what could be done. Your father said it was *you* who'd ended the engagement and that I was lying."

"You had lied." Understanding dawned on Noah. So that was the point of her needing to speak with him. "What happened?"

Elizabeth looked away again. "They had a terrible argument and they haven't spoken since."

Noah took a step forward. "They were the best of friends, Elizabeth! Look what your lie has done! You didn't correct it?"

She spun around, her eyes glistening as they blazed. "No! I couldn't! I didn't want the shame. I knew your parents wouldn't say anything because the fact that you left was humiliating enough for them. I knew they wouldn't say a thing!" She blew out a frustrated sigh. "Yes, it was my pride that hurt! It still does! Who cares about love! I want to be comfortable, and my father wants to make sure of that."

"You need to tell the truth." Abruptly, he realized she *was* telling the truth right now. She was showing who she really was. She only wanted Noah to provide her with a comfortable life, one that she could manage as easily as she'd expected to manage Noah.

"I can't tell the truth now! Mother got sick just a few weeks after the fight. She died within two days. Father was devastated." Tears started their tracks down her cheeks and she laid her palm on her chest. "*I was devastated!*"

Noah shut his eyes. "I'm sorry to hear that. My condolences. But the fact remains that you allowed your mother to go to her grave believing a lie."

"Yes." Elizabeth hung her head. "To add to it, father's suddenly estranged relationship with your father really hurt him. Your parents didn't even come to Mother's funeral. And that hurt has festered for two years. Now Father has started to realize that he can't leave this world without knowing that I'm being cared for."

"There are plenty of fine gentlemen out East. You live only two hours' train ride from New York City."

"Father always admired you. He wants you as his son-in-law, partly to mend his friendship with your father."

"He can't fix it without me?" Anger swelled in Noah as he added, "You'd be willing to marry me even after I ended the engagement?"

"If it pleases my father."

Which would work to her advantage, Noah realized.

Elizabeth continued. "So what if we don't love each other? It's about business and keeping the family purses where they should be."

*Money.* For Elizabeth, it was only about that. Like his father. Noah sighed. He knew firsthand his father's stubbornness. Unless there had been a substantial change in the man's attitude, he doubted his father would open his home or his heart to Rupert Townsend.

*Or him.*

That thought cut him sharply. Elizabeth only wanted

to be comfortable. In comparison, Clare had said nothing about the basic home she'd be moving into on Friday.

Elizabeth tossed her head. "My father has brought me here because he thinks he can mend this relationship. He thinks that if I tell you that I want to marry you, you'll welcome me back with open arms."

"How did he convince you to accept me back?"

She swallowed. "I…I said I might have been a bit premature in breaking off the engagement."

"You lied to him again?" He shook his head in disbelief. For all of Clare's faults, he had to give her one shining quality. She did not lie.

"No!" Elizabeth argued back. "Not exactly. I just, well, allowed him to make certain assumptions while we talked."

"You never told him the truth at all."

Elizabeth stepped up closer to him. "I couldn't. Noah, I know it's wrong, but you have to understand something. Father isn't a young man anymore. He is afraid he'll die and leave me alone. Think about what he's gone through! He's lost his wife and his best friend. Planning this trip, hoping for reconciliation and a secure future for me—that gave him something to live for again."

"But it's all based on yet another lie."

"I know, but what was I to do? I couldn't tell him I'd deceived him! It would have destroyed him. He'd defended me to your father. Then he'd lost Mother, who'd asked him before she died to fix everything between us. To tell him I'd lied to Mother and to him would break his heart and his hope." She looked down at the floor. "You may think that I've made a terrible error in judgment because of my pride, but I don't see it that way. I've saved my father's life, Noah Livingstone. So I can't allow you to tell him the truth!"

Noah folded his arms. She couldn't *allow* the truth? She was being bold, indeed, but her boldness was backed by a lie.

Clare was bold, too, but only in trying to be the best for her family. She wasn't perfect, but compared to the wily Elizabeth here, her flaws seemed incredibly benign.

Elizabeth took another step closer to him and grabbed his jacket by the lapels. "Noah, I can't let my father down again. The promise of our engagement is the only reason he gets up in the morning. That's why I came here with him. That's why I felt that we needed to speak in private as soon as we met. Please don't destroy the one thing that keeps my father going."

She was only now saying please? "I'm engaged. He knows it's too late."

"It's only a marriage of convenience. We could… compensate Miss Walsh for her inconvenience, enough to make it beneficial financially. Not enough that she wouldn't need to rent her home, but enough to entice her."

Noah felt heat rise to his face. He was sure if he didn't do something right now, his blood would boil.

Even as he simmered, he thought again of the resentment Clare would surely show toward him eventually. She didn't want to be married.

No. It was wrong for Elizabeth to think she could purchase her own way. And Clare would never agree to such a settlement. As much as she knew she needed money, she knew life wasn't solely about that. Her brothers needed a stable home, and although they hadn't spoken of it, those boys needed a father figure.

"No. It's a commitment I made to Clare. I plan to honor it."

Elizabeth pushed herself away from him. "Like you honored your commitment to me?" She raised her voice and pleaded. "Noah, do what's right here! Think of our families! Your father is miserable, and our families have been tied to each other for decades!"

"It would have been a marriage of convenience, but only to our fathers."

Her voice turned shrill. "Our marriage would have been more than convenience! We would have been wealthy together, not to mention improved our social standing! Now you must do what's right for our fathers!"

She was in tears when she collapsed against him. Noah hauled her up and guided her to the bed.

He had absolutely no idea what to say to her, so he left.

And that was when he saw her. Clare stood at the top of the stairs, gaping at him.

## Chapter Sixteen

Standing outside of Noah's stable Wednesday evening, Clare glanced over to the west. The sun was just brushing the top of Proud Mountain, threatening to plunge the town into deep twilight, as it did each day. April saw lengthening days and pleasant evenings, but tonight, a cool breeze rolled down from the still snow-covered mountains, chilling Clare.

Or was it the thought of approaching Noah?

He was talking quietly to Turnip, having been successful in coaxing the pony back into his stall. All he needed now was to hang up Tim's and Leo's coats to allow the pony to smell them in relative safety.

Turnip snorted in disgust as he caught a whiff of either her or her gelding. Or perhaps he'd heard her stealthy footfalls?

Stealthy? She stiffened her spine. She was not going to skulk around like a thief. Thanks to the lamp hanging up in the center of the stable, Clare could see Turnip clearly, his ears back, the white of one eye practically glowing.

Noah glanced up at his pony's reaction, and then turned. He stilled.

Clare fought the urge to run. *No!* She was made of sterner stuff than this. She hadn't run away before. She'd climbed the stairs to the bedrooms and had seen Noah and Elizabeth embracing in the doorway to the spare bedroom. The small woman barely reached the center of Noah's chest, but her arms had been wrapped tightly around him.

Then Noah had broken the embrace and walked out. He'd stalled for a moment before brushing past her and down the stairs.

At the bottom, he'd turned to face her and had said, "I'll see you at the Recording Office, and after work, I'll collect the boys."

At that moment, Clare had forgotten about work, but remembering Miss Worth and her brothers had been touring the town, she knew she should return to the office.

So she did. Clare did not speak to either Elizabeth or her father. Yes, they were guests, but they could look after themselves. Mr. Townsend had said those exact words as he'd walked upstairs before his nap.

It had felt so strange after lunch, returning to work while strangers stayed in her home, with Noah an integral link to all and yet, saying nothing to her for the entire afternoon. Not until he'd retrieved Tim and Leo. Even then, his words had been short and terse, only telling the boys to say goodbye.

They needed to talk, Clare decided again as she stared into the stable. That was why she was here. After work, she'd said her goodbyes to her brothers and Noah had taken them to the ranch. As if sensing something wasn't quite right, they'd been quiet and obedient.

Now she was here. Supper done with, Miss Worth offered to tidy up while the impromptu guests retired early. Clare now took the opportunity to slip out and visit with her fiancé.

Even after the short ride out here, she had no idea what she wanted to say. It was all she could do just to deal with the wild beating of her heart.

Was she afraid to ask the obvious questions? She'd heard Elizabeth beg Noah to do what was right to re-align their families.

Noah was honorable. Hadn't he come to *her* aid?

Her heart continued to pound. The knot forming in her throat warned her that she'd better be prepared for bad news.

But that didn't mean she wasn't strong. She could handle this, no matter what the outcome. She could deal with her parents being gone and she could deal with this.

Her chin up, she walked into the stable to stand under the kerosene lamp. The scents of horseflesh and fuel filled the air. "We need to talk. Now."

Noah looked like a deer caught in a coach light when it stepped in front of an approaching wagon. "Now?"

"Yes, now. Do you have someplace you need to be?"

"Like checking on your brothers?"

"I just did. They're fine." As soon as she'd arrived, she'd hurried into his ranch house and found the boys, still a bit nervous at the tension in the air, obediently tidying the kitchen. It was a welcome shock to Clare. Yes, they'd done chores before, but only with firm supervision, and never with the attention to detail that they were giving this task now.

Clare took another step toward Noah. "I think that I deserve an explanation."

"About what?"

"Stop it, Noah. You know perfectly well why we need to talk."

He strode out of the stable and sank down on the narrow roughly hewn bench that lined the wall facing the house. Pulling in a restoring breath, and hoping the bench would not snag her skirt, Clare followed him and plunked herself down beside him.

After a moment of waiting, Clare realized Noah was not planning to start the conversation. "Elizabeth was your fiancée," she finally stated crisply. "First up, I think that I should have known that small fact before now, but that's a moot point, so we may as well put that aside."

He slid a sideways glance toward her. "Then what else do we need to discuss?"

His reticence annoying her, she straightened even more. "Noah, what's going on? Why is Elizabeth here? I can't believe for a moment it's because they want a holiday here, or have come to consider moving here. They've come because of you. Why?"

"What did you hear?"

"I'm sorry for eavesdropping. I came upstairs to let them know I needed to return to work and that Miss Worth had volunteered to see to their needs, if necessary."

Noah's brows lifted briefly. "Miss Worth is full of surprises. I see she even ate half a sandwich today."

"She's not the subject of this conversation. You are."
Yes, Miss Worth was a difficult woman and Clare had disagreed with some of her beliefs, but even with the aside that Miss Worth was invaluable right now, Clare refused to be diverted from the reason she had come this evening.

When Noah said nothing, Clare pushed on. "I heard only something about Elizabeth asking for help. And I saw you two embracing." Daringly, she placed her hand on his arm. "Noah, I know I have no right to demand you tell me anything and no right to be hurt or betrayed, but—"

"Are you?"

She frowned. "Am I what?"

"Hurt? Betrayed?"

She withdrew her hand. Was she? Her heart hadn't stopped hammering since she spotted him in his stable. *Oh, dear.* Yes, she *was* hurt, but she didn't dare admit it. She had no right to his heart, only his name, and only because he'd agreed to help her out by marrying her. In two days' time, they would exchange vows, pledge to keep themselves only for each other and be joined as man and wife.

Two days? Panic flared in her. She was going to marry a man who was deeply embroiled in something she didn't understand.

He had two days to back out. Would he? While fear clutched at her, she recognized another emotion.

Sadness.

Clare pulled in a long, deep breath. She needed to stay strong, because she knew she could never lie. "Yes, it hurts. I won't lie to you. I know it shouldn't, but regardless, it does." She gripped his arm tightly. "But whatever happens, Noah, please let me help you with it. You've done... I mean, you're *doing* so much for me. Let me help you in return."

Noah laid his hand over Clare's. A scant few hours ago, another woman had been this close to him, even closer, but she'd been begging him for help because she'd forced them both into a difficult situation, one built on a lie, and she had expected Noah to save her and her pride.

*You caused the situation in the first place.*

Hating the accusation, he stared at Clare. She had refused his help initially. Noah knew she'd want to help him regardless of whether or not they were engaged. She was that kind of person.

But help him how? By releasing him from the burden that was this marriage of convenience, so he could heal two families? To preserve one woman's pride?

Carefully, painfully, he peeled her hand free of his arm. "It's all my fault, Clare. First, by what I refused to do, and second, by allowing a lie to stand as the truth."

"Start from the beginning," she answered softly.

"My father and Elizabeth's father own companies that complement each other. They manufacture various steam engine components. A merger would benefit them, and they'd be stronger and bigger than just the sum of the two." He cleared his throat, then went on. "They'd been friends for years, too. I think they were old school buddies, playing together even, although, back then, boys were expected to work hard with no time to play. Each would have had to learn the family business, unlike now. Boys get just a few chores and get to go to school, even though here in Colorado there is no compulsory law."

"I read in the newspaper that it will come within the decade."

"I'm sure it will. Suffice it to say, my father and Rupert had known each other a long time. Then, almost four years ago, they decided that I should marry Elizabeth and take over a merged version of both their companies. I don't believe that they'd considered the idea until their businesses were mature enough to benefit from a merger."

"Why was that so bad?"

Noah pursed his lips, probably too tightly. "They told no one until only a few months before the wedding date, just over two years ago. They'd set that date based on what was best for their businesses and no other reason." He blew out a frustrated breath. "But I wanted to decide my own life. I still do. I was twenty, and frankly not very mature. I just thought I was. I want to be successful at what I do, not be successful at something that was already doing well. I also didn't want to be managed as though I was a business acquisition. Long story short? I didn't want to have my life completely dictated before it even started."

"But surely your father would retire eventually?"

"Back then, it seemed too long a time for that to happen. Besides, I wanted to go West, to be my own person. I like working with horses, and hated that animals were often mistreated. They are an integral part of our country. They have helped to shape it as much as any of us. They are God's creation, too."

"What did you tell your father?" Clare looked rapt, as if holding her breath and afraid for his answer.

"Nothing. At first, my father didn't tell *me* about the arrangement, I think in part because he just assumed I would do his bidding. He was that arrogant. He just kept me employed at our business. Just over two years ago, our family started to see more of the Townsends when Rupert and my father began to talk openly about a merger. Then my father told me what he expected of me. I told him I wanted to marry only for love, that I want a wife who could share my vision and my dreams."

Beyond them, Turnip neighed with great disapproval. For the briefest second, Clare almost flinched. From that pony's disgust, or what he had said, Noah wasn't sure.

"My father demanded I do as he said," he continued, "but I am as stubborn as he is. I told him no, and that I was coming out here to start my own life."

"How did Elizabeth take that? Or did she even know about the engagement yet?"

Noah thought a moment. He actually felt better just discussing it. "She'd found out around the same time. But her father would have played to her pride. It's her downfall. When I told her I wasn't going to marry her, she did not take the news well, as you can imagine." He scowled darkly. "She couldn't stand the thought that she had been passed over for the West. I was so stubborn in my defiance, that she said it made her look like an ugly sow whose fiancé would rather roam the West like a vagrant than settle down to a fine career with her as his wife."

Clare cringed. "Did she really say that?"

"Yes, and more. All of her friends were married, and

she felt it was a slight against her. More than a slight, I guess. She was humiliated and demanded that I tell everyone that she broke off the engagement because she'd wanted something better."

"But your parents knew the truth."

"Yes, but that wasn't the worst part. I left the next day, so angry with my parents, I vowed never to speak to them again. I was…" He paused, and then hung his head. "I was a lot of awful things. Worse, there was the lie Elizabeth had told her parents—that she had ended the engagement. Letting it stand was the least I could do for her after humiliating her. But as time went on, the lie festered in me."

And now? He looked down at Clare. For the last week, the festering had eased, although hadn't left completely.

"And your father?" Clare asked. "Surely he and Mr. Townsend talked, or were they too mad at each other?"

"They talked, but when Rupert told my father that Elizabeth ended our engagement, because she had told him that, my father denied it. They fought. So much so, there is a rift between the families now."

"'Oh, what a tangled web we weave,'" Clare quoted softly.

Noah stared off into the distance. Should he tell Elizabeth's father the truth? Would it crush the man to learn his daughter had lied to him and he'd been perpetuating that lie ever since? And to have Noah be the one to tell him? Mortifying.

"This is the first time I've ever talked about it. You can see my dilemma. If I tell Rupert the truth, I will be breaking a promise I made to Elizabeth. If I lie to him, or even allow the lie to stand, how can I call myself a Christian?"

"You've told me the truth. Was it hard? I think the truth is always best. You don't have to remember a lie. You simply have to remember what happened."

Noah nodded slowly. "I wanted to tell you before now. But I believed I couldn't break my promise to Elizabeth."

Their gazes collided and both looked away just as quickly. "And me?" Clare asked quietly. "What about the promise you are supposed to make to me on Friday?"

"I'm sorry, Clare."

She gasped softly but he pushed on. "I should have told you about Elizabeth as soon as we were engaged. It wasn't fair for you to learn about her this way. I promise I won't keep anything from you again."

A small frown creased her brow briefly. "What's wrong?" he asked.

She seemed to pull herself together. "Nothing." She smiled abruptly but it looked a bit forced. When she reached out, she squeezed his arm. "It was a lie you made because you never expected to deal with them again." She cleared her throat. "But it was serious nonetheless."

"Yes. I believed it was okay because I thought I wasn't lying to anyone, and I thought it wasn't hurting anyone. My engagement to you changed that."

"Now that Elizabeth is here, what's going to happen?"

He looked into her anxious expression. She shifted her attention away. "I'm sorry. I'm concerned about the house. If you tell Mr. Townsend, he'll pack up and leave. I just got used to the idea of renting it. I'll be back at square one, like that silly board game Leo loves."

She looked back up at him again, looking contrite. "But I'm being selfish. I shouldn't be so concerned about the house. Please forgive me. Your dilemma is far more vexing than my situation."

She believed she was being selfish? Hardly. Her situation was far worse. She still didn't know the truth about her parents. She had to think about her brothers and sacrifice so much for them.

While here he was, unsure of what to do, and worse, unburdening himself on her as if she could solve his problems. They were problems he'd created himself.

"What exactly does Mr. Townsend expect to get out of coming here?"

Noah sank back against the rough slabs of wood that were the stable's outer walls. He shut his eyes. He didn't want Clare to see anything in his expression that he hadn't carefully thought through.

Because he hadn't thought through anything yet.

"I think you've already figured that out." With his eyes still closed, he murmured, "Rupert wants Elizabeth to reconcile with me. He thinks if he puts us together, she will acquiesce and I will take her back. He may even think that having lived in the wilds of Colorado for several years I would be pining for civilization."

He heard Clare's soft gasp and opened his eyes. The urge to wrap his arms around her swelled in him, but theirs wasn't that kind of engagement. She didn't love him. Her gasp was one of surprise and worry.

Her eyes, wide as saucers, focused on him. "And since he doesn't know that you ended the engagement?"

"He knows Elizabeth only wants to remain comfortable and keep her standard of living. At least she hasn't lied about that."

"But in that whole time from his first suggestion of this trip, right up until now, she has never told him the truth?"

"She said she couldn't. When her mother died shortly after I arrived here, her father was bereft. He'd not only lost his wife, but shortly before that, he'd lost a good friend in my father."

Clare's expression clouded. "That poor man! I'll pray for him."

Again, Noah looked in awe at her. She'd lost her parents; even though he'd told her not to give up hope, he'd no more believed they were coming home than she did. They were lost at sea, and all he'd wanted was for her to wait for the right time to tell her brothers, after she'd accepted the sad news in her heart.

Nevertheless, there she was empathizing with another person whose loss was just as great. She was setting aside her pain to help Rupert, who wanted to send her life off the rails again.

Noah's thoughts wandered to Miss Worth. The critical woman would have taught those values of prayer and selflessness. She'd also been no-nonsense about doing her share to help Clare after arriving so unexpectedly. While Elizabeth and her father had simply arrived and hoped they would get into the house sooner rather than later, no doubt treating everyone around them as little more than servants.

"What are you thinking?" Clare asked gently.

He flicked up his eyebrows. "I was thinking about Miss Worth."

A small, confused smile flickered over her lips. "Miss Worth? I got the distinct impression that you don't like her."

"I don't approve of what she generally believes, such as the strictness and frugality she would like to see us all practice, but today, for instance, she took your brothers so we could spend a few minutes together. She's done her share of the regular chores. She's taught *you* to help to carry others' burdens by doing so herself. You've done that by praying for Rupert."

"Maybe my parents taught me before I went to college."

He said nothing, but in doing so, he knew he was conveying to Clare that he didn't agree. She leaned forward to capture his wavering look. "Noah? I know you don't really think my father did the right thing taking all the money." Her gaze turned pensive as she flicked it around the slowly darkening yard. He couldn't see any tears in her eyes, but there was a catch in her throat as she continued, "I am still angry at him, too, for how he's left us in this bind. But I don't want anyone else to think that way. Maybe it's like you say, that I think it's the only part of my father I have left." She suddenly drew in a sharp breath. "It's time I dealt with it."

"I would say she's taught you more than your parents, then."

Wonderment danced across her features and even in the dim light, he could see dimples forming. "So you like her now?"

He folded his arms. "I wouldn't say that." He cleared his throat. "We're getting off topic, Clare. You practically accused me of doing that same thing a few minutes ago."

"I'm sorry. I couldn't resist. It's as though a naughty part inside of me wants to come out." She bit her lip. "Oh, dear, I'm just like my brothers."

"You're getting off topic again, probably because you want to avoid something that could be said. Look, I want to tell you what's going on. My father and I haven't talked since I told him I didn't want to marry Elizabeth or take over his business. My brother has a much better head and heart for it, anyway. Except that my father is a stubborn man, and I suspect that it's that stubbornness that led to the rift between him and Rupert."

"I would say that Elizabeth led to the rift." Serious once more, Clare watched him closely. He prided himself on being able to read her delightfully candid expressions, but suddenly, he couldn't. What was wrong with him?

Clare drew in a breath before speaking. "Meanwhile, Elizabeth can't bring herself to tell her father the truth. And nor can you."

"She thinks it will devastate her father and that he's been devastated enough."

"I disagree," she began slowly. "Not that he's been devastated enough. I think it's her pride that's stopping her from admitting she'd lied."

*Most likely*, Noah thought. But at the same time, it was more complicated. "She's willing to take me back. She says that if it would please her father, she'd do it."

"So magnanimous of her," Clare murmured. "Now

she can live in the style she's always lived in. Wait! Why doesn't she marry your brother?"

"My brother's already married to a woman of his own choosing. That added to my anger. How could my father allow my brother one thing, but me, his eldest, wasn't allowed to choose one thing about my life, all because I was born first?"

"Pride's a funny thing. We can be too proud to do one thing, but unashamedly do something else. Elizabeth is a perfect example. Too proud to admit she'd been spurned, but willing to allow her father to choose her husband for her. And to take you back."

"And as the first child, a son, I represented more than any other children."

Clare looked resigned. "I guess if Elizabeth told everyone she'd ended the relationship, then taking you her back would make it seem as though you had begged her to reconsider and as such, she was deigning to give you a second chance. I wonder if she thinks it would make her look better in her friends' eyes."

Noah rubbed his forehead. Just when he thought he had women figured out, more confusion arose. But perhaps in Elizabeth's mind, she was still maintaining her dignity.

"Like I said before," Clare continued, "'*Oh, what a tangled web we weave, when first we practice to deceive.*' On the outside, Elizabeth seems like a wonderful, obedient daughter, but we all have sins inside of us."

He shot her a fast look. When he realized that the night had plunged itself completely upon them, he rose and brought a lantern from inside the stable. He could feel Clare's gaze upon him as he walked quietly over to the house. He found the boys staring out the dim kitchen window at them. He lit a lamp and hung it up beside the stove, then told the boys to dress warmly for they needed to escort their sister home.

"What are the boys doing?"

"Staring at us. So we'd better be good role models."

Despite the tension, Clare laughed. "Oh, they can find trouble regardless, believe me."

Noah sat and both remained quiet for some time. The silence was comfortable, something he liked. Finally, he rose. "It's time we escorted you home."

She didn't move. "I can ride by myself."

"Yes, you can, but it's not safe. Your brothers don't need to lose you, too."

Nodding slowly, she accepted his hand to help her rise. But, still gripping it, she stepped in close to him to capture and hold his attention as she peered intently up at his face.

Clare's heart tumbled in her chest. She and her brothers had crushed Noah's dreams, those he'd wanted more than anything, forcing him to divert precious money, time and attention to them instead of his ranch.

What about her dreams? She'd wanted to decide her own life and though it might never come true, it had been her dream and could never be taken away. Noah had his own aspirations, that much was obvious. Did he really want to share them with a loving wife, as he'd suggested to his father?

Of course. Those words may have been said in the heat of his argument with his father, but they must have carried some truth. As a result, they'd caused such a terrible rift between him and his family.

It had to stop. She'd realized that a few minutes ago, when he'd told her about his brother.

"Noah," she said, gripping him tighter. "We all have gone astray."

"Yes. I know that."

She tightened her grip. "I'm not talking about Elizabeth and her pride. I'm talking about *you*."

Clare surprised herself with her words. Yes, she would be determined and liberal enough to know that she had the right to her own opinion, but to dare to tell the man she was going to marry in two days' time that he was wrong, well, that realization suddenly curtailed her nerve.

She squared her shoulders. No, she needed to say what was settling inside of her. Not her anger at her father, or her new tenants' pride and mistakes, none of that was weighing on her like this one realization was.

"Noah, Elizabeth was wrong to lie, and so were you to allow that lie to stand. But that isn't the big issue here. Not the one that affects you the most."

His shoulders stiffened and drew back. "What do you mean?"

She weighed her words carefully. "Noah, your relationship with your father is ruined."

"Yes, because of his pride."

"No. Because both of you are too proud." She tightened her grip. "Noah, you need to mend your relationship with him. *Now*."

A muscle ticked in his jaw. "He's the one who started it." He tried to pull out of her grip.

She held fast to him. "That gives you the best reason to end it."

"I did… I left," he gritted out. "There was no talking to him."

"You're as stubborn as he is. But you have to be the bigger man."

"I am. I'm taller."

She glared at him. "That's not funny. Noah, one day, your parents are going to be gone, and you won't ever again have the chance to fix things. I know."

"Did you and your parents argue before they left?"

"No, but I was upset that I'd lost them. I was so confused. The worst of it is that I'm never going to be able to ask their forgiveness or tell them how I feel."

"Don't say that."

"I can't help it! You know, my mother is—was— very understanding. She understood me, all my woes and anguish." Sadness washed over her and her voice cracked. "I know that she would have understood my anger. She was wise that way."

She released him and made an inane action with her hands, like she was rolling up a ball of wool. "All my feelings are jumbled together and I can't sort them out. It just hurts. And frankly, it's going to take a long time to get over it and let go of that hurt. I won't ever be able to tell them how I feel and maybe somehow hear from my father how sorry he was for leaving me in a bind.

"The regret is awful, Noah," she finished. "I know my anger is wrong, and I want to apologize to him."

"He never knew you were angry at him."

Clare swallowed. This was the first time Noah had openly admitted that her father was gone. Did he truly believe that? Had his words of not knowing for sure what happened to their ship been only to give her false hope?

She steeled herself. "Noah, you still have your father while I have to live with the regret that I was angry with him and will never hear him forgive me. That's an awful feeling. I don't want you to feel that way. You must repair your relationship with your father. It's the right thing to do."

She reached for him, her palm grazing his cheek. He needed to shave, and the short bristles scrubbed her palm. He looked down at her, those light eyes turning soft and wary in the lamplight.

Noah swallowed, and the urge to comfort him bubbled up. Just as she was about to tell him she would be there beside him when he spoke to his father, supporting him, he stiffened. What was he realizing?

He cleared his throat. "Right thing or not, it's impossible with my father. Now, get your brothers. I'll hitch the wagon to take you home."

She waited for him to say something more, but after a moment, walked slowly into the house.

# Chapter Seventeen

Clare perched stiffly on the edge of the wagon's bench seat beside Noah, fighting the rocking and jostling as she stared dead straight at her fiancé's horse. Tied to the back tailgate was her horse, obediently trotting behind. In the box behind them, wrapped up in blankets against the chill of the April evening, her brothers huddled together silently. Thankfully, both were too tired for mischief.

She was going home to spend her second-to-last night in her home. As a single woman. Tomorrow, Miss Worth was leaving, and Clare would be stuck with the Townsends.

She wondered how long they would stay here, if Noah were to tell them they were wasting their time. There certainly wouldn't be any reason to stay once she and Noah were married.

Clare bit her lip. She needed them, though.

Because she could no longer afford to live in her own home.

And she'd soon be married to Noah.

Who'd proposed to her to solve a problem. Who'd had a relationship with the people now renting her home. Who might be considering canceling the wedding to solve another dilemma. Who she wasn't sure should marry anyone right now.

Clare fought a sudden headache that had begun to pound her forehead. How was everything going to work out and how was she going to make her marriage, if it was to go ahead, a success when her husband refused to work on his own relationship with his father? What if he started to resent her as he obviously resented his own father?

Noah was so stubborn in his refusal to forgive his father. What if, someday, she did something wrong? Would he forgive her? Where was that integrity she'd seen before?

Clare stole a look over her shoulder at her brothers. The light from the lantern attached to the wagon wobbled over their faces, telling her both had fallen asleep, each propped against the other.

Next, she stole a furtive glance at Noah. His steely attention remained nailed to the dark road. She could hear a yip of some small animal, a fox or a coyote, far to their left. But the sound didn't even cause Noah's horse to break its stride.

It was as determined as Noah was.

"Why did you propose to me?" The question blurted from her so suddenly, it shocked even her. She shut her eyes. Why was she so impulsive?

As if knocked from some reverie, he glanced at her, his expression confused. "Pardon me?"

She repeated her question, despite not knowing why she'd asked.

He looked straight ahead. "It was the most honorable thing to do."

"Honorable? Yes, I thought you were that, but now, I've learned that you ended what could have been an honorable engagement and a good life."

"Don't be so sure of that."

Clare frowned. "I've also learned you refuse to mend your relationship with your father, too."

"Yes, I was there for that conversation."

"It's biblical to do all that you can to keep peace. I don't know where in the Bible it says that, but I know it's in there."

"Are you saying I'm not honorable?"

She didn't answer.

"Come on, Clare," he said quietly. "You're not that reserved. You just asked me why I proposed to you."

"I guess I'm really just wondering if you're honorable at all."

His brows shot up. Turning away from him, she huffed to herself. *Why was he surprised?* "In fact," she continued, raising her voice somewhat, "I think you only asked me to marry you to get back at your father. You told him you would only marry for love. But you're not. Ours is not going to be that kind of marriage."

Her heart squeezed at her admission. She'd known that from the beginning, so why should it hurt now to hear herself say it aloud?

"As I mentioned before, I didn't want my father dictating my life. I wanted—and still want—to make my own life, and to succeed on my own terms, or fail on my own terms, if that's what happens. I don't want my father behind the curtain, controlling me like a puppet."

"Then why did you tell your father you would only marry for love? You proposed to me easily enough. If you truly believed what you told your father, you wouldn't have done that. But you wouldn't have said it unless a part of you meant it."

He frowned as if not following her logic. "I guess I just said it because he was pushing me to marry Elizabeth and take over a merged business. There were no secret longings."

"Would a life with Elizabeth have been so bad?" She cringed. Did she have to ask that?

"Yes. My father might have said I was to take over the business, but he would still run it."

"So your defiance was solely because of your father's control. You want to control your own destiny."

"Is that so wrong?"

"No, but proposing to me to defy your father is, don't you think?"

She could see his lips tighten. "Really, Clare, tell me what's on your mind."

Clare folded her arms. "Your sarcasm is inappropriate."

He fell silent.

She sighed, then pursed her lips. Was she disappointed in Noah? Had she held him in such high regard that upon the discovery that he was not perfect, she blamed him for her own disappointment?

Was she doing that to her father, too?

Tears sprang into her eyes, and she blinked them away. Noah was not as honorable she'd believed him to be. He refused to repair his severed relationship with his family. This didn't bode well for their marriage, which was already dangling on tenterhooks, stretched like a muslin rag trying to dry.

She wanted to cry. She would have if she hadn't remembered that Miss Worth was waiting for her. So, instead, she blinked and held herself so tight it hurt.

As the town center grew closer, Noah could feel Clare's disappointment like a cold fog. Finally, he reined in the horse and brought it to a halt. Behind them, Clare's mount let out a snort of disgust for the interruption.

"What's wrong?" Clare asked.

"We need to talk."

"Are you being sarcastic again? Or did you really want to talk?"

"Clare, my resentment toward my father is my own business. It doesn't concern you."

"I think it does. We're supposed to be married on Friday."

"Then we also need to discuss your resentment toward your father."

"If I had the chance, I would jump at mending that relationship."

"You can say that because—" he glanced down at her sleeping brothers and his voice dropped "—your parents aren't coming home. But let's face something here, Clare. Knowing you resent someone is very different from forgiving them. That's another big step."

"One that you're not willing to take."

He worked his jaw as if mulling over her comment.

"No, I'm not. I don't believe my father is ready to forgive me, either."

"You don't know that for sure. Losing his best friend might have made him reconsider his own mistakes."

There was a short, brusque shake of his head. "It wouldn't. There's no talking to a man like that."

Clare held back the urge to throw up her hands in disgust. Couldn't he see how important it was not to waste time?

"Fine," she snapped with sudden, dogged determination as she flared at Noah. "You believe you're the better man? Prove that your proposal *to me* was better than what your father tried to arrange."

"It was."

"How so?"

"It wasn't to make a business better. Or to line either of our pockets."

"It was to make your life easier. I work for you. If my private life was destroyed, I wouldn't be an effective worker."

He rolled his eyes and shook his head. "That wasn't the reason and you know it. My father wanted his business to be more successful. It was his only concern."

"And your only concern was to ensure I didn't end up in the poorhouse. It's a slightly different slant on the same economics."

"I proposed to help you and your brothers."

"You proposed for revenge." Her voice dropped and caught. "I thought you had integrity."

"And I don't?"

"You've only proposed because in some odd way,

it is getting even with your father. You weren't honest with yourself about that."

"Clare, it may seem that way, but I didn't propose to you just to get revenge against my father. Yes, a part of me thought of that reason, but I asked you to marry me because you were at risk of losing your brothers. That was the main reason."

Her eyes watered. "You weren't even honest with me about a previous engagement."

Noah glared at her. "Are you suggesting we end this engagement?"

Her heart seized for a moment. She had to make him see that he needed to talk to his father. But how? Anger flared in her at how frustrated he made her. "Wouldn't it be ironic that you're not the one ending the relationship? Would you insist we perpetrate a lie so that you can tell Elizabeth it happened again?"

Clare slapped a hand over her impulsive mouth. What was she saying? Did she want to break off her engagement?

*Lord, stop my angry words. Help me!*

Noah's expression turned blank. His words were as frosty as the evening air. "Is that what you want, Clare?"

She looked away, hating that she'd even brought up the subject. "No. I'm sorry. I'm upset because it's all so confusing. You aren't who I thought you were, and you haven't been truthful." *And I'm scared.*

"About my previous engagement? Or the lie Elizabeth wants me to continue?"

"Both." She turned back to him and plowed on before she lost her nerve. "You must tell her father the truth. I know it's not my business, and I know it will hurt him, but unless there is some real and valid chance that you will marry Elizabeth instead of me, it's wrong to allow Mr. Townsend to continue to hope for reconciliation."

She leaned closer to him, her heart pounding as she waited for him to answer. This conversation had taken a terrible turn. But if he was honest with Mr. Townsend, he might realize he needed to go home, also. Perhaps talking to Mr. Townsend would show Noah how much he missed his family.

Noah said nothing. Clare shut her eyes. Why was she even doing this? She must be insane to push him toward a solution that could see her lose her home.

She couldn't allow that to happen. Was it selfish to want to keep her family together and do everything in her power to ensure that?

And what about her growing feelings for him? A short time ago, she was thinking that starting to care deeply for him was going to be disastrous, but at the same time, she liked the way it warmed her and made her feel all gooey.

Now, that same feeling was also prompting her to help him mend his relationship with his father, regardless of what it would do to her life.

She waited for Noah to speak, to offer assurance that her life wouldn't fall apart, that her brothers weren't going to be shipped off somewhere.

Noah said nothing. The silence continued until Clare quickly shimmied to the far side of the wagon, where she dropped to the dirt road with all the grace of a lame calf. She straightened, brushed herself off and began to walk swiftly away from the wagon.

## Chapter Eighteen

Dumbfounded, Noah watched her melt into the night, out of the circle of thin light from the lantern.

One of the boys shifted and Noah glanced back at them. He hadn't wanted them to suffer. He'd offered marriage to help them all out.

*And to hurt your father.*

He hated the condemnation, but it was true. A part, much smaller than the other reason, proved he'd wanted to hurt his father, albeit in absentia only. He was also letting Elizabeth suffer and her father believe there was a chance at reconciliation.

*Lord, forgive me. Help me. I don't know how to solve this situation. If I tell the truth, it will destroy Elizabeth's relationship with her father.*

*I know how that feels.*

And he didn't want to hurt Clare, he realized with a jolt of his heart.

With a flick of the reins, Noah urged the horse forward, afraid that Clare had made significant enough progress that he would not find her in the moonless evening. Regardless of how safe Proud Bend appeared, there were still plenty of wild animals about. Several months back, Noah had heard that there had been a cougar prowling around the general store late one night.

"Clare!" He shot a fast look over his shoulders to find Tim rousing and looking worriedly up at him. Noah turned back, ready to kick himself for letting her slip away.

Clare appeared in front of the horse. She stood stiffly within an arm's length of the animal. Noah quickly reined it in before leaping down from the bench seat. "You shouldn't have run off."

In the darkness, he sagged, hoping that Clare couldn't see that action. He'd stupidly started his apology with a condemnation. It wasn't the smartest thing to do.

Clare was facing the dim light and he could make out a stiff and unyielding expression. "I didn't run off. The night is cool and I want to get home."

"We're still a good quarter mile from your house. I can take you there."

"We're not that far and it's not that late, so don't make it sound like I'm prowling the streets like a stray cat. You need to get my brothers home, or they will be bears in the morning. I can walk. Or as you put it, run."

"It's not safe."

"I shall be running. I'm sure I can outrun any robber if I hike up my skirt."

He wanted to argue that point further, but knew better. She was only avoiding the real reason why she jumped down and dashed off. "No. You're going to stand right here and listen while I apologize."

"Apologize?" The sound of surprise in her voice was

a welcome relief to the clipped tones of her disapproval a moment ago.

"Yes, apologize. I should have told you about Elizabeth as soon as we became engaged. It was wrong." He took her hands and drew them up to his chest.

"And the lies you two fabricated?"

"I didn't—" When she began to protest, he added, relief pouring through him at the confession, "You're right. I'm in no way faultless. I allowed a lie to stand and told myself I owed her that much. I thought that if I never actually heard her lie, I was in the clear. I wasn't. It was wrong of me."

She tore her hands free and for a swift, scared moment, Noah thought she was going to shove him away and march off again. Instead, she grabbed hold of his shoulders and pulled herself close to him. Her stare was intense. "*I* forgive you, Noah. You know that I am not guilt-free, either. Why, I still feel so much resentment against my father, it sits on my chest like a sack of flour. But I can never ask him for his forgiveness."

"He'll know."

"Yes, perhaps. But am I ready to ask for that forgiveness? Or forgive *him*? That's much more than just knowing I've sinned." She sighed. "I can see why they say that forgiving someone really frees you. The pain inside of me feels almost—" she paused "—like the way my mother couldn't even walk some days. But that's me. I didn't mean our conversation to turn into an argument. I was trying to get you to see why you need to fix your relationship with your father."

Her words felt as though someone had punched him in the gut. He looked away, but she touched his cheek with her gloved hand and drew it back to face her. Noah shifted and he could barely see Clare's face in the thin lantern light. Why couldn't there be a moon, even a sliver of one, instead of them relying on that weak little lantern that seemed to be inexplicably dancing several yards away?

Clare continued, quietly, but with firmness. "And you must do something about Elizabeth. Now. You can't ignore this any longer. You've hidden behind the idea of building a ranch long enough."

He stiffened. Had he been using that as an excuse?

Her next words were soft, anxious. "And you need to decide who you want to marry."

"What do you mean?"

"Are you delaying talking to Mr. Townsend because you wonder if you should marry Elizabeth?"

Noah felt his mouth fall open.

"Noah?" She seemed to be desperately trying to recapture his attention. "The day after tomorrow is our wedding day. You need to decide what to do. *Now.* It can't wait. It's not fair to me or the boys or even you." Her mouth thinned. "Noah, I've seen you at work. I know how you saved Tim and Leo from Turnip. I know you're not afraid to do the really difficult things."

Noah shut his eyes. He didn't want to condemn Clare to an unhappy marriage, but knew she would marry him only to keep her family together. She deserved an answer, and his reticence wasn't fair to her. She'd deal with this head-on, like a bighorn ram would take on a rival.

Clare continued to search his face. Her lips had parted and her frown had deepened. It was getting cool, for he caught a glimpse of her sigh, a frosty stream, and he noticed that she was shivering. He wanted to pull her close and warm her up and suddenly that desire rose up to capture his full attention.

What had they been arguing about? Reconciliation? Marriage? Her proximity fogged his mind. Inundated his senses. Did she think he wanted Elizabeth?

Somehow, one of them had slipped nearer to the other. Which one, he didn't know. The faint remnants of her perfume lingered in the air. He watched her, trying to discern her thoughts.

All he could think was that she was so beautiful, so vibrant and impulsive and honest. A scant few days ago, she'd turned his proposal down, determined to be the person she'd vowed to herself she would be.

Except that she was also sensible and self-sacrificing, not wanting her brothers to suffer, so she'd accepted his offer of marriage.

She'd set her dreams aside, albeit with tears. A small concession, a mourning of sorts to say goodbye to that person.

She was a far better person than he could ever be.

"Noah?" Her soft voice pierced his thoughts. "Are you wondering who you should marry?"

He gaped at her. Marrying Elizabeth would go far to mending his relationship with his father, something Clare had told him was the most important thing right now.

But if he married Clare, he'd be destroying the woman she desperately wanted to be. Wasn't that important, too?

If he *didn't* marry her, would that force her to seek another man's hand to keep her family together?

Clare to marry someone else? Covetous jealousy flared in him, surprising him with its strength. And what about Tim and Leo? Those little ruffians were worming their way into his heart. He hated the thought of never seeing them again.

Was this really happening? He'd never thought that he would ever have such strong feelings, but here he was, fearful that he would lose everything with just one wrong decision.

How did his life get this way?

How could he fix it, and yet, at the same time, not condemn Clare to a life she didn't want?

Clare held her breath. Why was he not answering her? Fear gripped her and in that sudden icy moment of dread, she did the absolute unthinkable.

She caught Noah's face and yanked it close. His lips met hers with an almost painful slam. This was a hard, desperate kiss, and Clare knew she was trying to sway the vote in her favor, but she couldn't help herself.

She'd never kissed a man before. In college, they were watched so closely by various chaperones that one could barely manage a moment of privacy.

Here in Proud Bend she wasn't much freer. Convention and conservative values kept Clare from being alone with any man save her father. Look at her now, though. She was out and about after dark, kissing a man who, although he was to be her husband, might actually be considering reneging on his offer of marriage.

So Clare continued to kiss him, desperately, fighting the pounding of her heart that was bound to come with such an intimate act. And all Noah had done was grip her upper arms. Was he going to push her away?

He didn't. Instead, he yanked her close and returned the kiss with matching ferocity. She loved it. Her world swam as his passion rose.

"When you're done kissing, can we go home?"

Clare leaped back in horror, peering around Noah toward the juvenile voice.

Tim stood mere feet away. Behind him, Leo stood on the bench of the wagon, close to the lantern still on its hook, peering toward them with a concerned frown on his small, freckled face.

Her hand flew to her mouth. What had she become?

A woman in such a desperate situation that she would do anything to solve it, that was what.

Tears sprang into her eyes, and she couldn't stop the sob from escaping as she turned and fled.

She reached her home in record time, knowing all too well that Noah had followed her at a discreet distance and with a great deal of shushing toward the boys.

At her front door, she glanced once over her shoulder, catching Noah's expression in the lamplight. Deep, desperate concern marred his handsome features. And as she stopped, he jerked forward slightly, but she dropped her gaze and hurried into the house before she did something incredibly foolish, like return to him and beg a man who didn't love her to kiss her again.

The next morning, early, Clare and Miss Worth walked silently toward the train depot. Her mentor had told Clare she wasn't to take time away from her work just to see her off. She was fine just sitting at the depot for a few hours until the train to Denver arrived. She had her Bible and a puzzle book "to keep the mind sharp."

Clare consulted the watch pinned to her coat. She had half an hour before she needed to be at work.

"Don't worry about me, Clare. I'll be fine. Your work is more important than sitting with me."

Clare still felt as though she owed Miss Worth more than obedience. Her visit had hardly been a quiet and peaceful affair, with the exception of this morning. Without Tim and Leo, and with the Townsends sleeping in, breakfast had been one of the few enjoyable, quiet moments. "I just wish we'd had more time," she told her mentor.

"There will be other times. I'm not moving out to the coast, just visiting. Before my trip home, I'll telegraph you with the details, so we can plan a decent visit." She smiled almost sadly at Clare. "I know I've always challenged you more than the other women, Clare, but I knew you were up to the task."

"What task?" As they walked, Clare smoothed down her long skirt as if the action would remove the wrinkles. It wasn't her work skirt, but a traveling one of fine quality, dark in color and suitable for somber occasions.

"The task of life as a modern woman. And it will be a task. This century will be ending sooner than you think and we will do more than ever before."

"It's not going to end for seventeen more years. Don't you think we have a bit of time?"

"Time goes by faster than you realize. You will need to be prepared for what lies ahead. I predict great things for women in the twentieth century."

Thinking of her foolish behavior last night, Clare was just hoping to get through this week. There wasn't a lot of room in her head for the next two decades. "Miss Worth, I'm sure I'll be ready for it when the time comes, but my life is quite full as it is. I keep feeling as though I should apologize for disappointing you."

That shocked the older woman. "When have you done that?"

"I'm getting married."

Miss Worth shook her head. Her small, conservative hat stayed snug on her head. "Not every woman should stay single, my dear. If that happened, a lot fewer children would be born. It's those children who will grow up to change the laws and minds of the people. They will recognize that women have rights, especially if we do our due diligence on the matter."

By now, they'd reached the train depot. Peering down the rail line toward Castle Rock, Clare said pensively, "I'm glad you're not disappointed. It's just that marrying Noah feels a bit…"

"Like a compromise?"

Clare cringed inwardly. It had felt that way at first, but as Noah had begun to make the legal arrangements for her wedding, and after Clare slowly got used to her situation, and after the tears of grief assailed her less and less, she'd realized that the marriage was for the best.

Her throat suddenly hurting, she swallowed to relieve it. Noah had hesitated after she'd asked him if he wanted to marry her or Elizabeth. Had he not wanted to hurt her?

And what about the kiss they'd shared? Noah had kissed her back. Even his look when she'd reached her house was confusing. She had no idea what it all meant, and she was too afraid to sort it out.

There was also his fractured relationship with his father. And the lie Elizabeth was still perpetuating. Obviously, he didn't want to tell her father the truth and risk a split between father and daughter.

Clare bit her lip. Even she could see that marrying Elizabeth would hurt fewer people. But deep in her heart, it felt wrong. But if Noah chose her, he'd send Elizabeth and her father back. The lie might never be settled and his relationship with his father would remain unresolved.

"It's more complicated than just a compromise, Miss Worth."

"I see." The older woman drew her to a short bench under the eaves. "Let me tell you a story. I was in love once."

Clare straightened. "You were? What happened?"

Miss Worth looked out at the platform. "I fell in love. I was loved. We wanted to marry. There wasn't any disapproval in either family. He was from good, hardworking stock. My family didn't have much money, either, but our families liked each other. I had a benefactress, a wealthy elderly woman who wanted young women like me to succeed." She looked down at her hands, pressing them around her books. "But my beau died of yellow jack when he went down to New Orleans to help with the outbreak. He was training to become a doctor and couldn't sit by while there was so much suffering. Next month, it will be thirty years ago."

"I'm sorry."

"I didn't want to marry anyone else." She slid a sideways glance at Clare. "I don't discuss him because I don't want people to think I have turned harsh because of his death."

"I'm sure that's not true." Clare's thoughts turned to Noah, who disapproved of Miss Worth's critical attitude. Would he agree with that assessment? "You're firm, not harsh, and there are many incidents in our lives that mold us."

"You're being kind, Clare." Miss Worth patted her hand. "My point is this. I was in love and I lost that love. I only had that one chance. In the blink of an eye, and by something insignificant, your life can change."

"Death is hardly insignificant." Clare studied her mentor. "And it's unlike you to talk around a subject. What exactly are you warning me about?"

Lips closed a moment, Miss Worth looked to be considering her words. "At the time, they didn't know what caused yellow jack. We know so much more now. It's the bite of a mosquito. That's the tiny thing I'm talking about. Clare, don't lose your opportunity for happiness because of a small thing. So decide what the small things are and don't let them ruin the important things."

"I won't." Clare wasn't sure what she was really saying.

"I know your life is complicated," her mentor went on, "and I am saddened that I didn't get a chance to meet your parents. They've hurt you—that much I can see. We both know our loved ones didn't mean to die and abandon us."

All of a sudden, she stood and set down her books on the bench. "Now, you need to go to work, and I am perfectly fine waiting here until the train comes." She gave Clare a brief hug, as cool as it would always be. "I'll telegraph you with my return plans."

With that, she picked up her books and walked into the depot's small, ladies-only waiting room.

Clare had no choice but to go to work. To face Noah, from whom she had dashed away last night without even giving her brothers the hugs and kisses they deserved.

Never in her life had she been so unwilling to face the day.

# Chapter Nineteen

Noah had one task to do before going to work. It was still early, and with the boys in tow, he went straight to Clare's house.

He was thankful to discover she wasn't there. Having answered the door wearing a fine brocade dressing gown trimmed in thick, forest-green velvet, Rupert reported that Clare had walked Miss Worth to the train depot thirty minutes ago. Leaving the boys outside with a warning not to get dirty and knowing such a warning was probably said in vain, Noah stepped into the front hall.

"Where's Elizabeth?" he asked.

"She's still asleep. You know women."

Noah also knew Rupert. He'd dropped off to sleep so quickly yesterday afternoon that he hadn't even heard Elizabeth's shrill demands.

"Come into the kitchen," Rupert said, as if he owned the house. "It's been a long time since I cooked a meal, but I'm managing quite well, I think. My manservant, Angus, became ill on the trip out here. Elizabeth's maid stayed with him in Kansas City." Rupert looked up at him. "You wouldn't happen to know where I might hire some servants? I want only the best-trained ones. I saw a very fine home on the way to the bandstand, so I should be able to borrow theirs, don't you think?"

"I doubt that the Smith Family lends out their servants," Noah muttered.

"Too bad. Elizabeth won't like preparing her own toilet. But if I can handle cooking a meal, she can manage without Marie."

With growing irritation, Noah followed him into the kitchen. The scents of coffee and bacon filled the air. He gritted his teeth. The bacon he'd purchased to help Clare was sizzling away in a deep fry pan on the stove.

Enough was enough. This family might have been longtime acquaintances, and at one time, this man was supposed to have been his father-in-law, but that time was long gone and they should be, too.

"Coffee?" Rupert asked, pouring himself a cup.

"No, thank you. Rupert, what *are* you doing in Proud Bend?" Noah had heard Elizabeth's answer but wanted to hear it from the man's own mouth.

Rupert stirred cream into his own coffee, further setting Noah's nerves on edge. Clare would have allowed the milk he'd purchased to rest, and then skimmed off the cream to store separately until she had enough to churn.

Rupert took a sip of the coffee before pouring more cream into it. "Now, what did you ask me?"

Noah sighed. "Why are you here?"

"It was time to fix your relationship."

Noah folded his arms. "With whom?"

"With Elizabeth. I know she didn't treat you properly, but you have to understand my reasons."

"I've already heard about it. My condolences on Martha's death. It was untimely." Noah had actually liked Martha Townsend. She was a quiet woman who'd only ever wanted harmony in her life.

A shadow passed over Rupert's expression. "When Martha died, I knew I couldn't leave my daughter alone in the world. She needed to start her own family."

"There are plenty of men in New York State."

"But none I trust more than you."

"Trust to do what?"

"To see my business merged with your father's. And to see to it that my daughter is comfortable for the rest of her life."

"Rupert, you and my father aren't speaking anymore."

Rupert's mouth tightened. "This is a business transaction. Nothing more. Nothing personal, but your father is mistaken about some things, and once they're settled, we'll all be able to get back to the merger of our companies."

Noah resisted shaking his head. Rupert was so much like his own father it was almost laughable. Barreling through life and expecting all and sundry to do his bidding. No wonder they'd fought.

"Rupert, my father was mistaken about some things, but not about who ended the engagement. I ended it, not the other way around."

Rupert rose and flipped the bacon. "Elizabeth wouldn't lie to me."

"She would and she did. She felt so humiliated that

she asked me to say she'd ended the engagement so she wouldn't appear to have been spurned. I didn't want to perpetuate the lie, but I was leaving anyway, so I let it stand. My father was telling you the truth."

Rupert's face mottled with anger. "I don't believe it! You and Elizabeth only need to talk this out."

Noah tightened his lips. "There's nothing to discuss! I didn't want to marry Elizabeth and I didn't want to run your or my father's business."

Rupert smacked the spatula down. "Why not? You would have done far better than what you have here in this forsaken town! Your only dream is to run a stupid ranch for abandoned mules!"

"All equine."

"How many do you have?"

Noah gritted his teeth. When he didn't answer, Rupert flared up. "I met a man on the train who said you only have one stupid mule!"

"It's a pony and it's none of your business."

"So because your dream has failed, you want to destroy Elizabeth's, too? That whole ranch idea is a fool one that you need to forget. It's time to settle down and make my daughter happy. And stop accusing her of lying!"

"Elizabeth wants to maintain her standard of living. She doesn't care who's providing it. But she did see how despondent you were when your wife passed away. She allowed you this idea of reconciliation because it added purpose to your life. She also thought a merger of your and my father's companies would give her a higher social status, too."

"No! Elizabeth isn't that shallow."

Noah leveled him with a hard stare. "The new company would have earned more money, giving Elizabeth a higher social standing. It's not just pride. There's greed also fueling her actions."

Rupert's face went bright red. "How dare you say that about my daughter!"

Noah hadn't wanted to say any of this, but it had reached the point where it was due diligence for justice. "She lied because she was embarrassed that I refused to marry her. But that doesn't matter. I'm not coming back with you. I have my own life here. You may not think it's successful, but it's my dream."

"And that silly thing you plan to marry?"

Noah drew in a sharp breath. "Clare is not a silly thing."

"She's latching on to you because she doesn't want to end up in the poorhouse. This is a fine home, and she's afraid she'll lose it. You condemn Elizabeth, but Clare Walsh is no better."

Noah fought to be patient. Rupert was merely upset that Elizabeth had lied to him and was lashing out.

"You're marrying to get even with your father," Rupert accused. "You can't even do that right. How do you expect him to learn about it? You two aren't even talking." Rupert's tone was triumphant.

Noah worked his jaw. "Go home, Rupert," Noah finally ground out.

"Do you love Clare? I know you told your father you'd only marry for love. So let me ask you. Do you really want to marry her?"

The questions came out unexpectedly. Noah paused. Being with Clare was becoming increasingly important to him, but was it love? Did he even know what love was? What if he couldn't make her happy?

He didn't want to condemn her to a life of unhappiness, not after all she was enduring now.

He wanted her happy.

As he hesitated, Rupert let out a mocking noise. "See, you don't! Don't expect her to love you, either. It's going to be a difficult life for both of you, especially if she has to move into some shack in the mountains. She may not mind it now, but women are fickle and fussy."

"I don't love Elizabeth, Rupert."

"But you two will have the money to make your lives comfortable. If you marry Clare, all you'll have are her family's debts."

Noah frowned. "What debts?"

"I was poking around in the desk in the parlor and found several unpaid bills stuck in the back. Her father has left her not only penniless, but in deep debt."

Fury simmered in Noah. Clare's privacy had been shattered. "You need to leave, Rupert. *Today.* There is a train to Denver leaving in a few hours, and I want you two on it."

"Only Miss Walsh can evict us."

"Clare is going to be my wife tomorrow."

"A wife you don't even you want."

Noah stiffened.

"I've rented this house for several months," Rupert continued, his chest puffed out. "I figured it would take that long to get it through your thick head that you should come home."

"Clare will return your deposit. I'll see to it."

Rupert's laugh was short. "I haven't handed over any

money yet, but I have a lease. And that's even better. I'll sue if I don't get this place." As if to mock him, Rupert picked up a slice of bacon and took a hearty bite.

"You've already moved in while not paying one cent? That's going to change." Noah drew in a restorative breath. "There's no reason to stay. Remember, you just said I'm as stubborn as my father." He folded his arms. "It's also too bad that you can't see that your daughter has lied to you. It's too bad that you can't see that I don't want the life you think I will gratefully accept."

He stalked over to the back door. "You have a choice. Pay a month's deposit and a month in advance, immediately. Or leave." He pointed to the food. "And you'll be billed for the meal you're eating."

Noah might not want to run a big company, but he'd learned from his father's shrewd dealings. Men like Rupert didn't carry cash. He would arrange for the money only after checking out the house. He'd hang on to his money as long as possible. Clare, however, was gracious enough to wait, not realizing that she could wait weeks.

"I know you don't have any cash, or any reason to stay here, so I expect you to be on this morning's train."

"You're a fool, Noah!"

He didn't answer. He simply walked out. But as he did, all he could do was remember how he'd walked out on his father the same way two years ago.

Noah carried his foul mood into the Recording Office a few minutes later. Clare noticed it immediately. After mumbling out a greeting, he caught Clare eyeing him furtively. He stayed in there, leaving only once for that one important task. The MacLeods came by in the early afternoon with an offer to take Tim and Leo for the night.

He could hear Clare gratefully accept Victoria's promise to deliver the boys to the church Friday morning, clean and fed and ready to behave for their sister's wedding. "I'll be praying for you. You'll need it," he could hear her say.

Both ladies laughed. It had been the only levity of the day, and such humor seemed to pluck at the tightly strung air.

Staring at his paperwork, Noah swallowed. He was getting married tomorrow, and he'd barely acknowledged his bride-to-be's presence today.

She'd kept her head down herself, most likely because of his foul mood.

He needed to tell her what had happened. He was going to promise to love and cherish her for the rest of his life, but he'd sent her only tenants packing, essentially forcing her to surrender her home to pay those debts Rupert had found when he disrespectfully rummaged through her personal belongings.

At the end of the day, after Pooley left, Clare gathered her courage and walked to Noah's office door. It had been closed all day, with Noah leaving the glassed-in room only once. He'd left the building completely, in fact, and had been gone for half an hour. A few minutes later, the train whistle blew. Shortly after, Noah returned.

Whatever errand he'd attended to had left him cool and distant.

Now he sat there, glaring at his desk. Clare was sure he would burn a hole straight through it, like her brothers had tried to do one day using a dry leaf and their father's magnifying glass. Until she caught them and hid the glass.

Her heart pounded. What should she say? She'd rushed away from him last night like a silly schoolgirl, afraid to hear that he didn't want to marry her. Afraid she'd misinterpret his compelling expression.

*Lord, guide my thoughts and words.*

Silence lingered around her, reminding her that Tim and Leo were at the Smith home, in the care of Victoria, who'd cannily realized that Clare would need the night to prepare herself.

She straightened. Victoria had thought of the boys, and so must she. Hadn't she promised she would always take care of them? She wasn't sure what it meant in terms of Noah, but it gave her sudden courage. With pursed lips, Clare tapped lightly on the door before pushing it open.

Noah looked up warily.

Clare swallowed. What if he had decided not to marry her after all? Her heart sank at the thought. And another strange emotion coursed through her. For a brief moment, she wanted to blurt out that he should reconsider, but reining in her wild thoughts, she reminded herself that he had yet to explain his reticent mood. Maybe that should come first.

"I'm done for the day," she found herself saying.

His wary look continued, and for one ridiculous moment, Clare was sure if she made a sudden move, the cornered Noah would jump out of his skin.

She cleared her throat. Oh, her mischievous mind! "I should get home, then. I expect Mr. Townsend will have some money for me, and I want to—"

"The Townsends are gone."

She shook her head slightly. "What do you mean, gone?"

Noah stood and drew in a long breath before speaking. "I stopped by your house this morning, but you'd already left to walk Miss Worth to the train depot. I told Rupert the truth about who ended the engagement."

Confused, she could only gape, openmouthed, at him. "H-how did he take it?"

"Poorly. He doesn't believe me."

"Then you've done all you can," she slowly answered. "You can't control what other people think. You can only tell the truth."

"He called me a fool." Noah's words held no petty edge. He may as well have been predicting tomorrow's weather, if such a thing was possible.

"I'm sorry."

His chin lifting, he added, "After that, I told them to leave."

"Leave?" she echoed. Her heart stalled. "As in leave Proud Bend?"

"I saw them get on the train. That's where I went when I left for the short time this morning. By the way, I helped Miss Worth into the ladies' car. The Townsends had enough help getting into first class."

"Oh," she answered vaguely. "Thank you. I think."

Still confused, Clare stepped farther into the office and sank down into the chair across from him. She stared up at him, feeling the tears well up in her eyes. Didn't he realize what this meant?

Besides leaving her without tenants, of course.

Her heart tripped up. Did this mean…?

Noah tipped his head, looking even more cautious. "The last time you sat there, you burst into tears."

She tossed up her hands. "Of course I did! I was accepting your proposal!"

He quirked an eyebrow with skepticism. "Yes. They always cause a woman to cry."

"I'm sorry." Clare shook her head. "I—I didn't mean it the way it sounded. What are you trying to tell me?"

"I'm telling you that I sent Rupert and Elizabeth packing. Rupert wants to ensure his daughter is cared for and his business is thriving. He doesn't care about her or anyone's personal happiness. To him, it's only about the money."

That wasn't what she meant. All she wanted to know was that he wasn't considering marrying Elizabeth. Did that mean he was ready to marry her even after her demand that he mend his relationship with his father? Was he going to do that?

"Why did you hesitate last night when I asked you if you wanted to marry Elizabeth?"

"I didn't know how to answer you. Our argument was going in all directions."

She swallowed. Did that mean he was willing to reconcile with his father? How could she marry him if he had no intentions of that? And, having sent her renters packing, how did Noah propose to solve her financial woes?

No. One problem at a time, she told herself firmly.

"What did Elizabeth say?" Clare rubbed her forehead.

"This morning, I spoke to her father only. At the depot, she gave me the cold shoulder. She's still willing to marry me, I believe, but only because it means her social standing will be guaranteed. Of course, pleasing her father will—how shall I put it?—increase his generosity?"

"I see." She didn't see a thing. Never in her life had she been so confused. What was it about being around Noah that confused her so much?

Noah cleared his throat, his gaze scattering about the office. Was he nervous? He stood. "Shall I pick you up at your house tomorrow morning? Or will you meet me at the church?"

So he was still planning to marry her? Her heart leaped.

Then plummeted. She was marrying Noah tomorrow and yet, he had said nothing of reconciling with his father.

She should remind him. But they were getting married tomorrow! There was too much to do, even for a ceremony as small as she was going to have, to sit down with Noah and have a deep, important conversation about his father.

Clare's heart lurched. She would never see *her* father again and tell him about *her* anger toward him. Despite his flaws, her father was a good man and had often listened to her bemoan childish things. She ached to pour out her feelings to him one more time.

She'd never be able to hear him defend his decision to abandon her and her brothers, either.

Noah must never face this guilt, this grief. He'd never forgive himself. But what could she do?

Clare stood, tried desperately to pull herself together and say something.

But nothing came except one terrible idea, and she dared not suggest it here.

## Chapter Twenty

This was starting to get annoyingly repetitive. Clare pulled her family's wagon up close to the stable and with care, she alighted. The evening was cloudy and cool, but thankfully, she'd slipped into a warm, older skirt after work, an outdated style that allowed far more movement than this year's snug fashions. She'd planned to cook herself a small supper. She had also planned to spend the evening figuring out what to wear for her wedding. But not now.

Hers had been the most atypical engagement ever.

Just as well, considering what she was going to do.

She was going to end this engagement. Noah needed to do something more important. It hurt far more than expected, but she couldn't allow her wedding to go forward.

He needed the impetus to return home and fix his relationship with his father before he moved on with his life. Then he could marry for love, when he finally met the right woman.

Icy cold plunged into her stomach at that thought. So much so that it stalled her steps. Would she someday see Noah in town, wife and children in tow, happy and in love?

She hated that thought. But there was nothing she could do.

A small sob caught in her throat and she forced it back down.

"Noah?" she called out, hoping he was in the stable caring for Turnip. She wanted to get this difficult conversation over with. If done quickly, she could ride out to the MacLeod ranch, retrieve her brothers and still be home in time for them to get a good night's sleep. After all they'd been through, they certainly needed it.

*Think of them. Think of doing the right thing for Noah, too.*

"Noah, are you here?" Her question bounced around the small yard, against the rough boards of the stable and back at her.

With a pat on her horse's neck, she stepped toward the stable. "We need to talk."

She hesitated. Behind her, her horse let out a sharp whinny, startling her. The hairs on Clare's neck rose inexplicably, fueling sudden doubt.

Why was she doing this? Why was she destroying her only chance at keeping her and her brothers together? Hadn't she promised them she'd keep them safe? And why was the memory of Noah holding her, kissing her, suddenly invading her mind? She didn't need this confusion.

Forget it. She couldn't secure her family's unity at Noah's expense. Shouldn't they both be pure in heart and soul when they were wedded? It didn't feel right to have Noah's ill feelings toward his father hanging over their heads after they were married. Would Noah use the excuse of a new family to avoid mending his relationship with his father?

A marriage should not be used in this way, or to solve her problems. Marriage was too sacred for that.

But to lose Noah? She tried to force her feet to move, but found they refused. The mere idea cut her so deeply, it nearly made her cry out.

This was ridiculous. The more she thought about her decision, the harder it was becoming to implement. Nevertheless, she must not let her own fears stop her from doing what was best for Noah.

If he needed a nudge in the right direction, she needed to give it to him.

Forcing her feet to move, she pushed aside the door into the stable a few inches and slipped inside. The relative dark engulfed her, for the far door to the paddock beyond was tightly closed.

Clare blinked, barely seeing the large dark mass jerk around in front of her. It reared up, let out a resentful scream and only then did Clare realize how very dangerous it was.

From the far end of the paddock, Noah heard Turnip's scream of anger. Galvanized into action, he bolted immediately, and by the time he reached the fence beside the stable, Noah was at a full gallop. Smacking his hand down on the top rail, he easily vaulted over the horizontal logs. He landed on the free side and continued his race around to the front of the stable.

Clare's wagon and horse stood there. In fear, her

horse was trying to back up, but the wagon was hindering him. Noah gasped and roared into the stable.

The interior was dark, a blinding and heavy blackness. Noah shoved hard on the sliding door to let in light. His blood ran cold at what he saw.

Clare lay before him on the dirt. Having unhitched his door with his mouth, as Noah had seen him do before, Turnip was prancing around, his screams and snorts proving his anger.

Noah gasped and dived toward Clare, sweeping over to shield her from the pony's attacks. A large canvas tarpaulin hung nearby. Noah grabbed it and swung it outward. It sailed over to land on the pony's head and neck. Startled, Turnip backed up, and Noah knew he had only seconds to get Clare to safety.

He hauled her into his arms and rushed outside. After setting her as gently as he could against the stable's wall, he shoved hard on the sliding door, trapping the furious Turnip inside.

His heart still pounding, Noah lifted Clare once more and charged into his house. The room he'd given to the boys was the closest and he gently laid her down on the bed.

She stirred, her eyes fluttering and a groan slipping from her throat.

"Don't move," he warned. He did a quick check of her bones, and thankfully, nothing felt broken. She winced once as he skimmed past her elbow, but after easing up her sleeve, he discovered just a graze.

She would be bruised and sore tomorrow, but nothing else.

*Thank You, Lord.*

Another sharp, equine cry rent the air and reached them, even through the thick log walls of his home. Turnip, still angry. A series of hard cracks followed. He was trying to kick his way to freedom.

Noah hurried outside, afraid that Clare's horse would try to bolt while still attached to her wagon. He quickly unharnessed the big animal and led it around the stable to the paddock gate, all the while soothing it. Once Noah opened the gate, the horse hurried into the paddock, as if understanding the safety it offered.

Another series of bangs echoed from inside the stable. Turnip's tantrum rose.

Noah eased around the stable's corner. The sliding door was bearing the brunt of Turnip's fit.

With each kick, the door's lower half rattled and sent shards of wood outward. The realization hit him hard.

The pony could not be tamed.

His first rescue was a failure. Noah swallowed. Bitter disappointment caught in his throat and he fought back the urge to argue with himself.

For months now, he'd tried to convince himself that he could tame Turnip. He'd even thought he'd had some success.

No, he told himself. He'd just been able to anticipate the pony's moods, read the language the animal was displaying and act accordingly.

This morning, he'd noticed the animal had been agitated and had kept it in its stall and in the dark in an attempt to calm it. With water and some feed, the pony had been fine for the day. Or so he thought. The animal had undone the bolt and freed itself from its stall.

Another series of harsh bangs began. Clare must have really surprised Turnip for him to act this foul.

Clare. She could have died because of Noah's prideful refusal to admit a failure.

Time to let the pony go. He wouldn't risk lives for the sake of pride.

He slipped along the wall until he reached the far side of the sliding door. He carefully pulled on it, allowing it to glide toward him.

Turnip spilled out, an angry, bucking and stomping mass that seemed larger than the pony actually was. Noah stayed dead still, knowing as long as he pressed against the wall with the unhitched wagon in front of him, the pony would not see him as a threat.

At one point, the beast stopped, his ears pinned back so deeply, they lay flat against his neck. He turned, lifted his head and sniffed the air. The whites of his eyes glowed as he spotted Noah.

Then, with a snort and a spray of dust, he raced off toward the mountains. A sad smile hovered on Noah's lips. At least Turnip was heading away from danger. Yes, he was taking with him Noah's dreams, but he would be safe in the mountains, away from angry ranchers. Turnip would never go near people again. He'd be safe.

Having hurried achingly into the kitchen, Clare sagged at the window, never so thankful in all her life. That pony had barely given Noah a glance before dashing away and leaving him unhurt.

Then her heart dropped along with her shoulders. Noah stood behind her wagon, watching the pony run off.

His only attempt at rescuing an animal had failed.

He'd saved that creature from death with the hope of breaking it and selling it and starting his ranch on a positive note, but now, that dream seemed as distant as the pony was.

Noah had deliberately released the animal even though it was the last thing he wanted.

Her heart lurched. She had to do the same thing with Noah. Release him from his promise to marry her.

It was the last thing she wanted, she suddenly realized. But it was for the best.

Yes, she needed to let Noah go. It was the only way to force him to fix the things that should matter in a person's life. Family. The chance to marry someone he truly cared for. To love.

Love? Like she loved him right now?

Yes, she loved Noah and ached with him at his failure. She ached to rush out and pull him into a loving, comforting embrace.

Her breath caught in her throat as she remembered Miss Worth's words about love. Had her mentor recognized that Clare loved Noah, even before she did? One small insignificant thing like a mosquito had stolen Miss Worth's love away from her. She had been warning Clare that small things could ruin her life.

What small thing had Miss Worth seen?

Elizabeth? The tiny woman had wrecked several lives and was on her way to ruining her own. A petite woman with an enormous pride, like the mosquito Miss Worth discussed. A small creature with a terrible germ.

Heat rose into Clare's neck and cheeks. Yes, she loved Noah. A strange feeling gripped around her heart, and she instantly recalled last fall when she had first started to work at the Recording Office. She'd excitedly told Victoria all about her new job. But her mind had been on Noah.

She'd been starting to fall in love then. All these months, and she hadn't even realized it.

Yes. She did love him. And a part of her knew that before she'd even kissed Noah. It didn't take a sage to see that she'd kissed him in a desperate attempt to convince him to stay and marry her.

It was because she loved him that she knew what she now needed to do.

Clare watched Noah walk slowly across the yard toward the house, his face a mask of deep pain. She swallowed, remembering a time this past winter, when a mild day had hinted at spring, and her father had been approaching the house, in his hand various pamphlets. His expression had been the same.

It hit her then. Truly loving her mother, her father had been willing to take all the risks for her well-being. Clare remembered turning around in time to spy her mother wincing. Father had risked everything for Mother, and as wrong as it had been for her father to ignore his children, it had been wrong for Clare to resent him.

*Lord, forgive me for my sinful attitude.*

The memory dissolved as Noah stepped into the kitchen.

He stopped when he spied Clare standing in front of the window. Her heart lurched anew at his pained expression. Oh, how she wanted to take away his hurt, to help him carry his burden.

To love him fully. Except that her love came with

the responsibility of two boys and the truth that she would be destroying Noah's chances to be happy, not to mention the possibility of mending his relationship with his father.

"You're hurt. You should be lying down," he told her quietly.

Her hands went immediately to her wayward hair, confirming how much of a sight she must look. "I was just shaken up, that's all. My elbow hurts, but nothing's broken."

"Why did you come here, anyway? I thought we weren't supposed to see each other before the wedding."

"Superstitions. I don't believe in them." She drew in a breath to rally her courage. "Noah, we need to talk."

Noah's heart was still pounding as he shut the back door. Just a moment ago, he'd watched Turnip gallop away. He'd watched the animal kick the air and shake his head, allowing his mane to dance about in the wind. Noah watched him until he disappeared over the rise that led deep into the mountains that held the source of the Pride River.

How selfish he'd been. He'd wanted so badly for his ranch to be a success that he'd tried to force a wild animal to bend to his will.

Similar to what his father had tried to do.

Now, as he looked with caution at Clare, he knew he hadn't treated her right, either. He hadn't been honest with her.

Looking pale, Clare indicated the kitchen chairs. "Let's sit down. I need to get off my feet for a moment."

Noah sprang into action, hurrying over to pull out

one of the kitchen chairs for her. With a sigh, she sank heavily into it. But he remained standing.

"Thank you for dragging me out of there. I don't know what got into Turnip, or who let him out of his stall, but if you hadn't come along, I'm sure I would have been injured far worse than I am now."

"As wild as he is, Turnip's still smart. Remember how I told you and the boys that he has managed to unlock his stall door with just his lips? I've seen it with my own eyes. It doesn't help that those door bolts are old and worn. What happened today was my own fault. I kept putting off replacing them." He stopped and swallowed. "Let's not talk about that. I don't want to even think about what could have happened."

"You let him go."

"I couldn't keep him." Noah started to pace. "I've been telling myself I could break him and train him, but I've just been fooling myself. I've been too proud to admit failure."

She frowned suddenly, and her mouth thinned. "Noah, pride has brought many people down. So it's good to see you can overcome it, because you need to do it again."

"What do you mean?"

"You need to swallow your pride and go home."

"I am home."

"No, I mean home to New York State."

"Why?"

She sat straight. "Pride has destroyed your relationship with your family. You shouldn't start another important relationship until the first one is mended. You told your father you would only marry for love. It may have been just words to get out of a situation, but I think that a part of you really meant it. Your deep concern for horses and for Turnip, especially in letting him go, shows that love is important to you."

"I don't need to go home."

"You do. Marriage is too sacred a relationship to come to it with all that hurt and pain and resentment. Even though you are willing to marry me to help keep my family together, you still have a lot of hurt. It's wrong to marry with that lingering."

Panic flared in him. "What about your brothers? Your home? How are you going to keep them?"

"I don't know, but I know I can trust God to help me." Clare rose and walked over to him. She touched his cheek and shook her head. "Noah, I have forgiven my father and you need to forgive yours."

What she was daring to do made her vulnerable.

Clare continued, her words a little faster, as if she wanted to get them all out before her courage flagged. "I love you and I can't let you marry me for all the wrong reasons. I would be burdening you with more than what your father had planned."

He stilled, his heart pounding so fast he could feel it in his chest and throat. Did he just hear...?

She loved him? She was letting him go?

Yes. Because she loved him, she was letting him go. Just as he'd done with Turnip.

"You love me?" he whispered. He could hardly believe what she'd said to him.

"Yes. I know you don't love me and I know I can't drag you into my life and all the problems it has." She laughed softly, sadly. "At first, I thought you had so much integrity. Then when I found out that part of your reasons to marry me were your feelings for your father, I thought that you had *no* integrity. Perhaps the reason is right in the middle. You do have integrity, but you are as human as I am."

She cleared her throat. "I resented my father for what he'd done to my brothers and me. But by realizing I love you, I understand how much my father loved my mother and how much her condition worried him. He made a difficult decision, and I shouldn't resent him for giving in to love."

Clare blinked several times as she sighed. She looked up into Noah's face and he could see love there. She really did love him.

Wonder struck him. "And I was wrong to allow Elizabeth's lie to stand, and walking in here a moment ago, I asked for God's forgiveness, but I didn't know how to fix it. But God has a plan. With Elizabeth, Rupert, and with the second chances I've been given."

She shifted closer to him, laying a hand on his chest. "Take the next step. Go back and reconcile with your father. You may not get that chance again. I didn't."

"Clare, listen—"

"No! I wish I could see my father one more time. He wasn't perfect, but he cared for my mother. That was true love and I was wrong to resent him for it. He's left me in a bind, but God is in total control. He'll help me sort it out."

"You'll let me help, too, I hope."

"Noah, I'm releasing you from that responsibility."

He grabbed her hand and held it tight to his chest as

he stared hard at her. "Loving you is hardly a responsibility."

She opened her mouth, but nothing came out. A frown marred her forehead. Finally, she spoke, her words soft. "You love me?"

"I do, very much so. More than anything on this earth. Clare, it was disappointing to let Turnip go, but that dream, whether or not it ever comes to fruition, will never come close to the love I feel for you and your brothers. Until this moment, I had pushed it to one side, time and again denied it, but the thought of losing you made me fully realize it."

She laughed softly, her eyes glistening.

"Clare, just as you realized that marrying for love was important to me, I can see something that is important to you."

"What is it?"

"Your independence. That's why you initially turned down my proposal. So if it's important to you, it's important to me. I know you've seen many friends lose their freedom to their husbands. I will be head of our household, but God says we are to cleave together and unite."

She giggled nervously. "It's silly that cleave also has an opposite meaning."

"I prefer the uniting meaning. The one mentioned in the Bible. I want to love you, protect you and give myself only unto you."

"But you cannot marry me while your relationship with your family is so estranged. It hurts you, and you need to start a new life free from that hurt."

He felt his own tears unexpectedly cloud his eyes, but he knew she was right.

*Lord, forgive me. Help me fix this.*

"I'll do my best to mend my relationship with my father first. But that means we won't be getting married tomorrow."

She gripped him tightly. "We will marry, though, and hopefully with your family in attendance."

Noah wrapped his arms around Clare and lowered his mouth to hers.

A banging on the back door jolted both of them out of the embrace. Shooting a concerned look to Clare, Noah hurried to the door and opened it.

In spilled the young errand boy from the telegraph office. "I knew I'd find you here!" He held up a narrow sheet of paper. "It's from New York!"

Immediately, Noah felt the blood drain from his face. It wouldn't be bad news about Rupert and Elizabeth. They would barely be in Kansas City by now. His father? He grabbed the telegram, ignoring the boy's stumbling protest as he read.

"No, sir, Mr. Livingstone. I've been looking for Miss Walsh. The telegram is for her."

But Noah had already finished scanning the scant words, and with a growing smile, he handed it to Clare. Confused, she cautiously accepted the telegram and read it.

Dearest Clare,
We are safe on Tenerife. Blown off course. Letter to follow. Mother is well. We will return soonest.
Love Father.

Noah caught Clare as she sagged with relief. She smiled up at him eyes glistening. "All the more reason to postpone our wedding, then. Don't you agree?"

He laughed and kissed her soundly. At that moment, the sun, having dipped down to touch the mountains, broke free of a cloud and beamed through the small kitchen window.

In the warm rays, Noah lifted his head. "Let's go get Tim and Leo. They need to be a part of this, too."

# Epilogue

The wedding was lovely, albeit several months later than planned. Mrs. Turcot had decorated the sanctuary with late roses and wildflowers. The air smelled fresh with their scents. Clare wore a beautiful white gown, borrowed from Victoria. Noah looked dashing in a fine gentleman's suit.

Clare turned with Noah to allow Pastor Wyseman to introduce them as Mr. and Mrs. Livingstone, taking the opportunity to look around Proud Bend's small church with excitement.

Mother and Father beamed from their pew. Clare had never been more grateful to God than at that moment. He'd brought her parents back, safe and healthy. Between them sat Tim and Leo, scrubbed clean and behaving for a change. They were thrilled to get their parents back.

She'd learned all the details of her parents' adventure, being lost at sea for weeks, engine gone, no way to check where they were, save a sexton, and even then, the days and nights were cloudy. They'd drifted on sea currents that led the ship to the Canary Islands, whose dry, hot climate proved a better *Kurhaus* than anything in Baden-Baden, Germany. Mother was healthy, and Father was relieved and revitalized and ready to return to work to take care of the family and the bills. They were beginning their lives again.

And in the time it took for them to return, Noah had acquired two mares from an old rancher, one ready to foal. Both were responding well to his care, and he'd already met with a businessman in town who wanted to purchase the pair once they were trained.

Across the aisle sat Noah's parents. Noah and she had traveled to his hometown. With much prayer and the time of loneliness for both Noah and his father tempering their emotions, they'd talked and rebuilt their relationship. Clare had cried along with Noah's mother when his father had asked for forgiveness for his arrogance. She'd cried further when Noah had done the same.

That was real courage, Clare had told Noah later that evening. She knew he had it in him.

Now, in the front pew, his mother was dabbing her eyes. His father beamed and Clare could see love in both their eyes. She felt Noah squeeze her hand and she turned to face the love of her life, tears filling her eyes. When she blinked, some slid down her cheeks.

Noah leaned close, his blue eyes glistening tenderly. "I remember when you promised me you wouldn't cry at our wedding."

"That was before I realized how much I love you!" She glanced once more out at the congregation. All imperfect people loved by God.

*Thank You, Lord.*

* * * * *

*Don't miss Barbara Phinney's other stories*
*set in Proud Bend, Colorado,*

**THE NANNY SOLUTION**
**UNDERCOVER SHERIFF**

*Find more great reads at www.LoveInspired.com.*

Dear Reader,

Thank you for reading this book. I must admit, it wasn't easy to write. There isn't any of the suspenseful danger that often fills my stories, but rather, I focused on emotion.

Clare resented being abandoned by her parents, and yet she knew it was wrong to feel that way. It wasn't until she understood love that she could forgive her parents.

Noah struggled against his father when he'd tried to bend him to his will. He also participated in a lie, but didn't know how to fix either problem.

Asking God for forgiveness and help is the best way to start to fix any problem. But you need to trust Him. All in His perfect timing.

Love isn't always easy, but its rewards are worth it when we set aside selfishness. Carry one another's burdens. Love as God loves you.

Happy reading and God bless!

Barbara Phinney

"'Widower with four-year-old son seeking a marriage of convenience. Prefer someone older with no expectations of romance. I'm kind and trustworthy. My son needs lots of patience and affection. Interested parties please see Preacher Arness at the church.' I'm applying," Annie said with conviction and challenge.

"You're too young and…" He couldn't think how to voice his objections without sounding unkind, and having just stated the opposite in his little ad, he chose to say nothing.

"Are you saying I'm unsuitable?" She spoke with all the authority one might expect from a Marshall…but not from a woman trying to convince him to let her take care of his son.

He met her challenging look with calm indifference. Unless she meant to call on her three brothers and her father and grandfather to support her cause, he had nothing to fear from her. He needed someone less likely to chase after excitement and adventure. She'd certainly find none here as the preacher's wife.

"I would never say such a thing, but like the ad says, Evan needs a mature woman." And he'd settle for a plain one, and especially a docile one.

"From what I hear, he needs someone who understands his fears." She leaned back as if that settled it.

*Don't miss*
*MONTANA BRIDE BY CHRISTMAS by Linda Ford,*
*available October 2017 wherever*
*Love Inspired® Historical books and ebooks are sold.*

www.LoveInspired.com

SPECIAL EXCERPT FROM

*Love Inspired* HISTORICAL

*When Annie Marshall answers single father
Hugh Arness's ad for a marriage in name only, the
preacher refuses—she's too young and pretty to be
happy in a loveless union. But after he agrees to Annie's
suggestion of a four-week trial period, Hugh might just
realize they're the perfect match.*

*Read on for a sneak preview of*
**MONTANA BRIDE BY CHRISTMAS by** Linda Ford,
*available October 2017 from Love Inspired Historical!*

"Mr. Arness—I'm sorry, Preacher Arness—I'm here to
apply for this position."

"How old are you, Miss Marshall?"

"I'm nineteen, but I've been looking after my brothers,
my father, my grandfather and, until recently, my niece
since I was fourteen. I think I can manage to look after
one four-year-old boy."

That might be so, and he would have agreed in any
other case but this four-year-old was his son, Evan, and
Annie Marshall simply did not suit. She was too young.
Too idealistic. Too fond of fun.

She flipped the paper back and forth, her eyes narrowed
as if she meant to call him to task.

"Are you going back on your word?" she insisted,
edging closer.

"I've not given my word to anything."

# Get 2 Free Books,
## Plus 2 Free Gifts—
### just for trying the Reader Service!

*Love Inspired.* HISTORICAL

## MONTANA BRIDE BY CHRISTMAS
*Big Sky Country* • by Linda Ford

When Annie Marshall answers single father Hugh Arness's ad for a marriage in name only, the preacher refuses—she's too young and pretty to be happy in a loveless union. But after he agrees to Annie's suggestion of a four-week trial period, Hugh might just realize they're the perfect match.

## COWBOY LAWMAN'S CHRISTMAS REUNION
*Four Stones Ranch* • by Louise M. Gouge

After fleeing from her late husband's cousin, who hopes to extort money from her and take her children away, Evangeline Benoit relocates to Colorado at Christmas. But will local sheriff Justice Gareau—the man whose heart she once broke—help her?

## MISTLETOE MOMMY
by Danica Favorite

Unable to afford a nanny, widowed single father Luke Jeffries seeks a wife to care for his children. But even as a secret from mail-order bride Nellie McClain's past puts their future together in jeopardy, can Luke and Nellie find true love in their marriage of convenience?

## A MISTAKEN MATCH
by Whitney Bailey

When his mail-order bride arrives, James McCann believes there's been a mistake—Ann Cromwell is beautiful, despite his request for a plain bride. As they wait for the matchmaking agency's mix-up to be fixed, Ann struggles to prove she can be a good farmer's wife after all.

---

LIHCNM0917